"What can I do, Elizabeth?" Corey inquired softly.
"What can I do to get that frightened look off
your face?"

But he knew it as well as she did, and he slowly bent
to kiss her on the lips. Beth caught a trembling
breath as his lips left hers, but he only moved his
head to kiss the shoulder his hand uncovered. His
hand rested upon the curve of her bare waist and
the springs of the sofa rustled faintly as he shifted
his weight closer to her. "Don't let me frighten you,
Elizabeth. Tell me when I frighten you."

Corey's face rested against her neck, his hand upon
her waist, no other parts of their bodies touching.
She knew he would stop if she asked him...she knew
she was not going to ask him....

ABOUT THE AUTHOR

Rebecca Flanders is a native of Georgia who began her writing career at age nine. She completed her first novel by the time she was nineteen and sold her first book in 1979. Rebecca's hobbies are oil and waterpainting and both composing and listening to music.

Books by Rebecca Flanders

Suddenly Love

REBECCA FLANDERS

Harlequin Books

TORONTO • NEW YORK • LONDON
AMSTERDAM • PARIS • SYDNEY • HAMBURG
STOCKHOLM • ATHENS • TOKYO • MILAN

Published February 1984

First printing December 1983

ISBN 0-373-16041-0

Chapter One

Beth Greene was getting a cold, and that was the least of her problems. She had had approximately four hours sleep and the airport traffic had done nothing to improve her disposition. The inside of her head felt like one of those television clips of the tail of a storm in which debris and flotsam were being whipped violently about on a churning black sea—which was only appropriate, she reflected dryly, as no one short of the brink of derangement would be up and about at seven o'clock on a Sunday morning—tourists excluded, of course.

The source of her cold was an early morning dip in the chilly Atlantic waters with Steve yesterday. It had seemed like the thing to do at the time, the way so many stupid things do, and if she was to spend the next two weeks wrapped in flannel and inhaling eucalyptus steam it was no more than she deserved. The source of her sleeplessness had been a very disturbing phone call from her sister at one o'clock in the morning—whether Linda had simply forgotten about the time difference between Phoenix and Virginia Beach or merely did not care, Beth didn't know, but her much-needed night's sleep had been effectively ruined just the same. The reason for her tumultuous state of mind was both of the above, with the added pressure of a hectic weekend with too many things to do and say and not enough time for any of them, leftover tensions and unfulfilled expectations, a hurried airport good-bye, and the general feeling that, after years of a routine, satisfying, and basically sedentary life, everything was happening to her at once. She was definitely, she reflected behind a yawn as she pulled up to a stop sign at the bottom of the hill that led to her street, in no condition to be on the road. And in even less condition to join her father for church and Sunday dinner in less than three hours. All she wanted to do was go home and crawl into bed with a bottle of aspirin.

Beth signaled her left turn and checked carefully both ways for traffic. At this time of year on a Sunday morning the streets were deserted, and nothing approached the intersection except one lone jogger. She eased her foot off the brake and began her turn. And then she sneezed.

It all happened in that split-second length of time it takes to sneeze. She heard a sound—later she thought it might have only been the sound of her own scream—felt a definite thump, and when she looked up a man was slumped over the hood of her car.

Even as she was in the grip of hysteria, her reflexes were quick. The ignition was off, the brake applied, the gear in Park, and then she only sat there, shaking violently and gasping for breath and thinking, *Oh, my God, my God, I've hit him. I've killed him. I've actually killed a man....*

But then he moved. Beth was out of the car like a shot, and when she reached the front of the car he was turning to face her, looking dazed, disheveled, but very much alive. A high voice was screaming at him—in horror she realized it was her own—"Why didn't you stop when you saw me coming? You ran right in front of me! Are you blind? Didn't you see—"

Her jaw shut with an audible snap as a pair of murky hazel eyes focused on her and raked her coolly. A heavy midwestern voice drawled the only possible reply, "Pedestrians have the right of way."

Weakness swept her. Her limbs turned to chilled, shuddering gelatin and she groped for the hood of the car to keep from falling. She swallowed hard, staring at him without seeing him, and managed in a tiny voice, "I—I'm sorry." She didn't know what had come over her; she couldn't believe she had screeched at him that way, but he was alive, he was alive and on his feet and talking to her after she had hit him with her car.... Beth swallowed again on a whirling nausea of pure terror as she thought how easily it might have come different, and she demanded urgently, "Are you—are you all right?"

He politely returned the question. "Are you?"

She closed her eyes against a sudden blurring of the blue-green day. Her voice was thin. "I think I'm going to throw up."

A strong arm gripped hers and her watery knees offered no resistance as he forced her to the curb. But everything was happening in fast motion today. A gulp of cool, salty air and shaking fingers pressed to her white cheeks and the momentary urge to relinquish her scanty breakfast passed. She found herself looking into a pair of sardonically amused eyes, and he commented smoothly, "Somehow I think that should have been my line. Better now?"

Her teeth chattered as another shudder shook her. "J-Just s-scared half to death."

"You've got nothing on me, lady."

He was squatting beside her on the street, and her eyes, still dull with shock, would not travel farther than a pair of lean muscled thighs and calves thickly covered with light brown hair below the cut of red cotton jogging shorts. A white crescent scar was prominent on his left knee and her eyes fixed upon that in flat, unthinking fascination before moving slowly downward to encounter another round puncture scar on his shin and then to the tops of battered white Nikes that were now beginning to stain with a trickle of blood.

Beth was immediately alert. "You *are* hurt!" she gasped, getting to her feet. This she could handle. She had been born and bred on medical emergencies and adrenaline surged when she was confronted with a situation about which she was certain she could do something. The residual shakiness passed as she commanded, "Turn around."

He looked surprised when, as he was a little slow in complying with her order, she grasped his bare shoulders and turned him around herself. Her heart sank as she discovered just what she had expected. On the back of his thigh was a long, wide abrasion—about the size, she reflected sickly, of a car bumper—and a narrow cut on his ankle was rapidly turning the back of his shoe from gray-white to bright red. She said with a preprogrammed efficiency she was far from feeling at the moment, "I'll take you to the hospital. You'll need X rays."

He twisted around to follow her examination of the damage to the back of his leg, and his response was incredulous. "Hospital? For that?" He whipped off a perspiration-stained bandanna headband and knelt to tie it around his bleeding ankle.

She gasped. "That thing is filthy! You'll get blood poisoning!"

Incredibly, he grinned. "Are you implying something uncomplimentary about my personal habits? I'll have you know I showered not more than an hour ago and a little honest sweat never hurt anyone."

There was something devastating about his grin. It turned his lean golden face—which, admittedly, Beth had barely glanced at before now—from merely interesting to breathtakingly arresting. And perhaps even arresting was not quite the right word. It was more than that, somehow radiating from the high cheekbones and square chin, the slightly crooked nose and full lips, a sort of innate sensuality, a boyish innocence contradicted by the very power of its charm. The sun caught his eyes as he looked up at her and momentarily sparked crystal green from their depths. He had one crooked tooth and a small scar intercepted his light eyebrow near the temple. His lashes were thick and obscenely dark in contrast to the light brown eyebrows and streaks of gold in the damp hair that clung to his forehead, and it seemed as though an expert cosmetician had smudged just a hint of midnight-blue liner around his eyes for dramatic effect. His was a face with character, impact, totally unforgettable and for just a moment Beth was stunned by that impact before she swiftly rescued herself. It was only that she was so relieved, and perhaps there was still a bit of residual hysteria that could cause her to start reflecting on the physical attributes of a man who had almost made her the perpetrator of vehicular homicide. Yes, it was pure relief that soared through her at his matter-of-fact handling of the situation, as though being run over by cars were something that happened to him every day. He was the victim, after all, and she was the one who was flying apart. Beth decided to remedy that situation without further delay.

She shook her head firmly as he got once again to his feet, and the easy grace with which he moved did not disguise a light wince as he put pressure on bruised muscles. If there was a lingering doubt, it was dispelled. "You're going to see a doctor," she declared. "There could be internal injuries or small breaks...." Oh, if only Steve had not already left. His mother's house was barely five minutes away and time could be important in an accident case. Despite the fact that this particular victim could hardly have been farther away from displaying signs of shock or hemorrhage, there was no sense in taking chances. Her father's office was a longer drive, but it might be better than waiting for hours in an emergency room.

"Don't be ridiculous," he scoffed. "I've had worse scrapes from falling off a tricycle at age three."

"Nonetheless," she insisted, her brown eyes growing steely with a determination that only her best friends knew was dangerously impenetrable, "I'm responsible for you. I did . . . hit you, and I have to make sure you're all right. You'll see a doctor."

"I don't need a doctor." Impatience crept into his voice. "And as for your being responsible for me, while I can't say that I would object to the idea under different circumstances, it's really not necessary in this case. You were barely moving when you hit me, or," he added quickly, "when I hit you, whichever the case may be. All right," he conceded, with another grin that was designed to melt the iron in her eyes and, had he but known it, very nearly succeeded. "You can accept responsibility for the damage your bumper did to my leg. But the cut ankle is purely my fault, caused by a not-very-graceful collision with the curb when I misjudged the distance between your car and my body. My fault entirely. Satisfied?"

"I will of course pay your medical bills," Beth said coolly, staring him down.

"I'm fully insured. As a matter of fact"—he glanced back at her battered little Volkswagen, which stood with a sort of salacious smugness at the corner, its awkward midstreet angle proclaiming witness to and evidence of the crime—"I hope you are, because it looks like I did more damage to your car than it did to me."

Beth was distracted only long enough to flick a glance over the obscene vehicle. She would never trust it again. "That dent has been there over a year," she informed him, her voice steady. "Come on. I'll drive you to the hospital."

He did not move. "No broken bones, I swear. No concussion, no swelling, no internal bleeding. And if I discover any of the above at a later date," he suggested, "I'll be happy to let you know if you'll just leave your name and phone number."

"Are you a doctor?" she challenged him.

"Yes," he agreed as though on sudden inspiration. "I am."

Her obvious relief was not lost on him. He relaxed the moment she did, and there was a peculiar, almost mischievous, light of victory in his eyes. Perhaps he had already sensed that very few people ever got the better of Elizabeth Greene. "Well," she said slowly, somewhat deflated, "in that case.... At least let me offer you some first aid."

That seemed to be a proposition that came within his limits of acceptability. A slow, delicious light touched his eyes and that powerful grin threatened the corners of his lips. "Why, pretty lady," he drawled, "I think you're trying to pick me up."

She turned quickly to hide the sudden rush of color to her cold cheeks and marched to her car. "It's the least I can do after knocking you down."

He chuckled as he followed her to the car. He had an intriguing laugh, deep and throaty and more than a little seductive, and Beth could not help smiling at him as she got into the car. At the door, though, he hesitated. "I'll bleed all over your upholstery," he said dubiously.

Beth drew out an old beach towel from beneath the seat and spread it elaborately over the seat covers, which were already so stained and shredded her father referred to them as "World War II surplus." She thought the real reason her passenger hesitated was because of a certain amount of reservation over her skill behind the wheel, and she could not honestly say that she blamed him any.

He got into the small car beside her, mingling the clean smell of male perspiration with the tangy, fishy odor of the sea air and the stale mustiness of the car's interior, and for some reason having him there beside her made Beth nervous. He was not a particularly tall man, but his slender length folded into the compact space looked very out of place. She tried to justify her reaction, which began as a tingling in her cheeks and a nervous fluttering of her pulses as she fastened her seat belt and suggested he do the same. After all, how many men had she taken as passengers in her car? Only her father, and Steve, and neither one of them were quite so—so physical. And because that thought seemed almost disloyal to Steve, Beth quickly chastised herself. This man was a patient, not a date, and just because he was sitting half-naked within six inches of her was no reason to go off the deep end. *Just hold on, Bethy, old girl,* she told herself firmly. *You've got a bad case of nerves and what you need to do is find this fellow some medical treatment so you can get rid of him and quietly have yourself a breakdown. And for heaven's sake, check for traffic before you pull out into the street....*

His eyes fell upon her as she hesitated, her hands gripping the steering wheel, experiencing a moment of perfectly natural panic that accompanied getting behind the wheel of a car again for the first time after an accident. He must have read the emotion in her face, for he looped his arm across the back of the seat, half turning to her, and said easily, "Routine preflight check. Seat belts?"

She relaxed. "Check."

"Fuel?"

"Check."

"Oil?"

"Check."

"Landing gear?"

"Check."

"Ignition."

She turned the starter. "Check."

"Runway is clear for takeoff; proceed when ready."

Beth giggled and shifted the car into gear, pulling carefully into the street. Preflight jitters had vanished. She said, "My store is just up the street here. We'll find everything we need there to make you comfortable."

There was a flirtatious light in his eye. "I like the sound of that."

He was certainly taking this all very lightly—something for which she should have been grateful. It should have put her at ease, but in fact it only made her more nervous. With each passing moment he became less of an injured victim and more of a dynamically attractive man, and she supposed it was only shock that turned her thoughts to his physical attributes after what they had just been through. She ventured a glance at him. "Are you a resident," she asked politely, "or just passing through?"

"Passing through," he answered. They had pulled up to a stop sign, and he made no effort to disguise the fact that he was double-checking the traffic for her. "All clear."

Beth subdued her irritation as she pulled slowly onto the main road. She could hardly expect him to trust her driving when she barely trusted it herself anymore.

She glanced at him again in the slow-moving shadows of the quiet street. He certainly didn't look like any doctor she had ever met, but then again, she had had enough experience with the medical profession to know that doctors did not come in any particular shape or size. His hair, darkened with perspiration, was drying in straight lengths over his forehead and the back of his neck. The color was medium brown now, but she suspected when it was clean and dry it would be closer to blond. The cut was highly professional, layered ends falling into place even in its disheveled state, already

beginning to fluff up again as he absently ran his
fingers through it. That face, even in profile was...
well, sexy was the only word for it. An unforgettable
sensuality haunted every line of it, a combination of all
characteristics rather than just one: the slow smile, the
multicolored eyes, the lazy twist to his lips that hinted
of suggestive thoughts even when he was probably
thinking nothing at all, as now, the imperfect nose, the
squint-lines at his eyes, and the shaded lashes. Yes, it
was an unforgettable face and, somehow, very strangely, an almost familiar one.

His throat was strong, tall, and masculine. The chest,
still gleaming with perspiration in the morning sun, was
lean and devoid of body hair, the abdomen spare of
excess flesh, taut and flat. His arms were corded with
tight muscles and a tracing of blue veins, a light tangle
of damp hair revealed by the slightly upraised position
of the arm that was hooked over the seat. Everything
about this man spoke of compact energy, strength without frills, not an ounce of flesh wasted. There was an
uneven ridge to his collarbone, evidence to the experienced eye of a poorly mended fracture, and another
small scar near his shoulder. Apparently today's injury
had not been his first.

Beth could not help commenting, "You seem to be
accident prone." And then she flushed, because she
knew that that comment could only reveal that she had
been paying more attention to his body than to her
driving, and she fixed her eyes resolutely on the road.

"Oh, yeah? How can you tell?"

"I couldn't help noticing the scars," she admitted,
refusing to glance at him.

"Those aren't scars," he scoffed. "They're medals
of honor!"

Now she did glance at him. "War?"

She fell unexpected victim to the full impact of that
grin. "You could say that."

That incredibly sexy grin, the husky drawl, the shadowed eyes.... It all clicked together at once and she exclaimed suddenly, "Do you know who you look like? That guy on television who does those dippy deodorant commercials." She glanced at him quickly once more before turning her attention back to the road. The resemblance was truly amazing, but perhaps it was not quite the polite thing to say, and she added quickly, blushing a little, "I guess you hear that a lot."

He watched her steadily, his body twisted slightly in the seat to face her, his cheek leaning against his fist. "As a matter of fact, I do," he admitted. "Only the other day my mother came up to me and said, 'You look just like that guy on television who does those dippy deodorant commercials.'"

She slanted her eyes toward him briefly and suspiciously, but if there was a residue of laughter in his tone it was efficiently hidden in his face. His face. Unforgettable face. The man with the million-dollar face, the five million-dollar body. Where had she heard that? Her heart began to speed unaccountably. Oh, yes, it was from an article in *Forbes* her father had read to her one evening about Lloyds of London insuring this man for some excess million dollars, each part of his body catalogued separately and assessed at value. They had laughed over it and her father had made jokes about raising his medical fees to keep up with the inflationary value of the human body. Her brow furrowed in concentration, trying to remember. "Corey Fletcher." The name came to her unexpectedly. "The race car driver."

"Funny," he agreed easily, still watching her with a trace of amusement in his tone. "That's just what my mother said."

She looked at him fully for the first time. "You—you—"

He shrugged, pretending to be abashed. "Like you

said, I hear it all the time.'' He affected sobriety, his voice lowering to a sensuous bass roll. ''I hope this won't make a difference between us.''

She realized she had almost passed her store and she blindly signaled for the left turn, her head whirling. He went on, ''I mean, I realize it's not the best way to begin a relationship, my running into your car like that, but I hope you don't think it was just one of those kinky superstar things the papers are always accusing me of doing. As a matter of fact— Lady, will you please watch what you're doing?''

The steering wheel was wrenched from her grasp, her foot kicked off the brake; the little car went careening across the road within inches of a lumbering church bus filled with curiously staring youngsters, bounced over the curb, and came to a shuddering stop with its nose buried in the hedge of dwarf boxwoods that lined the front of her store. It all happened so fast she did not even have a chance to scream. She simply sat there, limp and shuddering, staring blankly at the gold script on the front plate window that announced Greene's Drugs. She was aware that he was breathing hard as he slowly moved away from her and switched off the ignition, but his voice was dry as he inquired, ''Is this where you wanted to go?''

Her head pivoted slowly and stiffly to look at him, like a mannequin responding to the jerk of a string. Beth croaked, ''Are you all right?''

He actually seemed a little pale under the tan; his breath was still ragged. ''Lady,'' he responded evenly, ''do you have any idea what it feels like to be cruising down the speedway at one-sixty-plus and suddenly have both your front wheels fall off?''

She shook her head numbly.

He informed her grimly, ''Now you do.''

He opened his door and got out, but she waited a moment longer before trusting her rubbery legs to support her on solid ground. Corey Fletcher. *The* Corey Fletcher. And she had almost killed him twice!

"You really should get a larger car," he advised her as she came around to him in front of the store. "Those models are very dangerous; no protection."

She fumbled blindly in her purse for her keys. "Oh?" Her voice was brittle with forced brightness. "What do you recommend?" For of course every word Corey Fletcher spoke on the subject of automobiles was pure gold; if she had had a recorder with her she could have sold the tape of his next utterance for a price roughly equivalent to a parcel of prime beachfront property square in the middle of Atlantic Avenue.

"A Sherman tank comes to mind," he replied mildly.

He watched her fumble clumsily with the doorhandle for a moment, then took the key from her shaking fingers and inserted it into the lock with easy competence. The brush of his warm fingers against her icy ones only made the shaking worse, and she commanded herself firmly, *Get hold of yourself, Elizabeth Greene, before you melt into a puddle right at his feet. This is no way for a trained professional and respected member of the business community to act.*

He swung open the door with a flourish and a loud clanging of the cowbell on the handle, gesturing her to precede him. Whatever fear, whether real or feigned, he had experienced over the two near brushes with death was completely gone now; he was composed and at ease. But, of course, Danger was his middle name, and flirting with death was Corey Fletcher's favorite pastime.

He followed her inside as she nervously switched on fluorescents and tossed her purse on a counter, upsetting a stack of magazines that spilled to the floor. "Nice place," he commented, rescuing the magazines and tidying the stack before returning them to the counter.

The top one was *People*, and his face was on the cover. How could she have failed to recognize him? How could she have been so dumb? But he replaced the magazine without glancing at it and inquired, "Is it yours?"

"Mine and the People's Bank of Virginia," she replied gaily. "Home of the world's last nickle ice cream cone."

"Quite a claim to fame." He stood in the center of the floor, his hands on his slim hips, and surveyed his surroundings thoughtfully. "I like it," he decided. "It's warm. Old-fashioned. Nice."

Beth was proud of her little store, and she had worked hard to establish just the atmosphere he had recognized and complimented. Beth had known when she had come home with her degree in pharmacy that she could not hope to compete with the large drug chains in the area by opening a store of her own, nor did she particularly want a nine-to-five job in one of them. When Eliot Morton, long established in the area with both physicians and customers, had decided to sell, Beth had leaped at the chance and with her father's initial financial backing she had become an independent businesswoman. Beth relied on charm and quality to keep her business showing a profit—which it did, just barely. She stocked novelty and hard-to-find items in the nondrug section, like wooden clothespins and galvanized steel buckets and oil lantern wicks. The floors and countertops were age-darkened hardwood, the rows of merchandise neat but intriguingly cluttered. Forty years ago kids had come here after school to hang around the soda fountain and drink malteds for a dime, today those same kids found the soda fountain converted for main use as a checkout counter, but malteds were still a dime and not much else had changed. People liked to come in and browse, more often than not they ended up buying something. Beth's drug customers were loyal and regular, for she knew each face, name, and prescription by heart. She loved her store and was keeping her head above water; she could not prevent a small flush of accomplishment for the compliment of a stranger.

Still, she hid her pride with a dismissing shrug and returned, "The insurance coverage on your little finger would buy a dozen like it."

"Home of the world's last nickle ice cream cone? A handful of little fingers couldn't replace *that*."

Beth almost smiled, and then she hurried away toward the first-aid supplies. What was she doing, exchanging light conversation with the man she had done her best to annihilate today? This was Corey Fletcher, daredevil, adventurer, movie star, international celebrity... *the* Corey Fletcher.

A wash of cold dread went over Beth as the full impact of that struck her. She had run down a man whose net worth probably rivaled that of the entire Commonwealth of Virginia. What if he decided to sue? What if his lawyers decided to sue? What if he ended up in the hospital with subdural hemorrhaging or developed whiplash and could never drive again? She turned to him urgently, her face abruptly white again. "How do you feel?"

Fletcher sauntered toward her at a leisurely pace, inspecting items of interest on his way. "Pretty good actually, for a guy who's just been creamed by a VW and nearly smeared all over the pavement by a church bus." He paused to pick up an egg separator. "What's this?"

Beth turned blindly back to the row of first-aid supplies. "You told me you were a doctor!" she cried in despair. "Why did you tell me that?"

He was beside her swiftly. "Lord, lady, don't cry!"

Beth clasped her hands together tightly, her eyes glittering fiercely in her chalk-colored face. "I am not going to cry," she announced slowly, trying to keep her teeth from chattering. "I'm going to call my father!"

"Even worse." His fingers closed around her arm. His grip was surprisingly gentle for its strength, the fingers smooth and warm. "Promise me," he urged. "No tears, no fathers—both of which make me incredibly nervous."

"You told me you were a doctor!" she accused again, pulling her arm away.

He tried to tempt her with a teasing smile. "I lied."

She faced him stiffly. "You did it very well."

He took a small bow.

"Why?" she demanded, shaking now more with rage than fear. "Why did you say such a ridiculous thing?"

He shrugged. "I thought it would save us both a lot of trouble."

She gaped at him. "Troub— Well, you thought wrong!" She made to push past him toward the telephone, but he blocked her way.

"Look, I've spent enough time in orthopedic wards to open up my own practice and I guess I know what a broken bone feels like. Will you believe me when I say I'm not hurt?"

She faced him squarely. "What have you got against doctors, anyway?"

"Other than the fact that the last time I saw one I ended up in a body cast?" He shrugged. "Not a thing. But there's a time and a place and this is neither." Assessing her invincible stance, he released a small breath and endeavored to explain. His eyes, she noticed, were now an amazing color of smoky blue. "Picture this: 'Internationally known race car driver victim of hit and run'; sub-title: 'Corey Fletcher critically injured by female assailant.'"

She pictured it. It made her slightly sick. "I didn't run," she mumbled.

"You will," he assured her, "once those reporters get on your tail. Now, do you want to forget all about doctors and hospitals and just give me that first aid you promised?" She hesitated. "If you don't," he warned, although there was a hint of cajolery in his voice, "I'm going to walk right out that door and you'll never see my gorgeous face again."

"I could care less about your face," she snapped. "It's your gorgeous legs that interest me."

A mischievous sparkle touched his eye and she turned away quickly. "There's a back room," Beth said stiffly, her hands blindly fumbling over bottles of antiseptic, "right through those curtains, where you can wash up. I'll be there in a minute."

His voice was close to her shoulder. "Do you have anything for shock?"

She turned, her eyes only widening as she found his face mere inches from hers. She shrank back automatically, but her voice was hardly above a hoarse whisper. "I—I can't give you anything without a prescription."

There was a softening of his eyes, as though he registered with amusement her new attack of nerves and the reason for it. "Not for me," he told her casually. "For you." He reached around her and took up a bottle of antiseptic; his arm brushed against her shoulder with a little more pressure than could have been strictly accidental and she felt her skin prickle beneath the thin cotton blouse. She was certain he noticed and was enjoying it. "It seems to me you've gotten the worst of our little encounter today. I prescribe a double Scotch straight up right away."

"It's Sunday," she murmured senselessly, moving a step away from him. Her cheeks felt hot. "Blue laws."

He smiled as he removed the roll of gauze from her hand and replaced it with a box of Band-Aids. His eyes crinkled nicely when he smiled, and he looked perfectly harmless. "Ready for surgery," he announced, stepping back and allowing her to lead the way.

The back room was actually a storage area for out-of-season merchandise and overstock, Christmas decorations and back-issue magazines. There was hardly room for all the cartons and crates it contained, but they had also squeezed in a small cot, a coffeemaker, and a card table where she and Ellie, her clerk, sometimes had lunch. Corey Fletcher edged carefully around a precariously stacked tower of Pampers and sat on the edge of the cot, bending to untie his improvised bandage. Beth knelt beside him with a damp cloth.

He glanced at her with a pretense of arrested interest as he straightened up, resting his ankle on his knee and taking the cloth from her. "Do you know who you look like?" he said suddenly. "Princess Diana." And then he gave her a crooked half smile, which she could not be certain was not a mockery, and demurred, "I guess you hear that a lot."

As a matter of fact, she did, and she quickly became irritated with people who made the comparison, which was, admittedly, shallow. Aside from the hairstyle and the shape of the face, there was no resemblance at all. Beth was shorter than the princess, her figure rounder. Her eyes were brown, not blue, and her mouth was smaller. But, most strikingly, her eyebrows were darker and thicker, lending an air of formidability to her features that no truly beautiful woman would countenance. A stubborn frown seemed to hover perpetually about the crease over her nose, and in shadow her facial expression relaxed into one of either sultry displeasure or sulkiness—when in fact, more likely than not, she was feeling neither of those emotions. The softness and charm that characterized the princess was missing in Beth, replaced by briskness and severity. And she was more irritated by the comparison today than at any other time, mostly because she was all but certain

Corey Fletcher was making fun of her—and because she knew she deserved it.

"I had my hair cut this way before she did," Beth mumbled uncomfortably, and then realized what an inane defense that was as she turned quickly to discard his stained kerchief.

"Some poor hairdresser in England must be at this moment eating his heart out." She glanced at him suspiciously, but his expression was perfectly bland as he sprayed the narrow wound with antiseptic and efficiently applied a small bandage. "There," he announced, getting to his feet. "Is that treatment to your satisfaction, or do you think I'll need stitches?" With his back to her, he twisted around to examine the scrape on his thigh, and a slow, deliberately provocative grin touched his features. "Sorry, but that's out of my range. Looks like you get to do the honors."

Beth had fully intended to do so in the first place, but all it took was that famous grin, the suggestive undertones to his voice, to make the simple cleansing of a wound sound like an exercise in erotica. She swallowed back a perfectly irrational discomfiture and braced her hand against his knee, gently cleansing the abrasion with the damp cloth. His legs were all muscle, tight and hard to the touch, raw power in an exquisitely sculpted casing. *Just think,* she told herself, *tomorrow you can tell all your friends you spent Sunday morning stroking Corey Fletcher's thigh.* Her cheeks tingled.

"So," he said, without looking at her, "what's your name, princess?"

"Elizabeth Adeline Greene," she pronounced, concentrating upon keeping her fingers away from the white piping that edged the bottom of his shorts and the tight swell of his hip beneath. *I can't believe this,* she thought nervously. *I really can't believe I'm doing this. . . .* She sat back on her heels, gulping silently to steady herself, and wondered what had happened to her professional training. The back of his leg was certainly no sexier than any other man's, but she seemed to have left her composure back at the intersection of Holly and Laskin roads.

He murmured, "Magnificent, isn't it?" and she realized that, while she had paused in her ministrations, her hands still rested about his leg. She jerked them away quickly, sprayed antiseptic, and got rather clumsily to her feet.

He turned, and there was a mild light in his eyes, which were now a peculiar off-shade of green. "Are you married, Elizabeth Adeline Greene?" he inquired.

That caught her off guard. She almost tripped over the Pampers tower as she turned quickly to recap the antiseptic. "No."

"Engaged?"

"N-no. That is, not exactly...kind of." She had to squeeze past him to take the washcloth to the sink, and came close enough to feel the heat of his almost nude body and smell the scent of drying perspiration and tangy fragranced soap.

A puzzled frown appeared as a curved line between his brows. "Kind of? Isn't that like being just a little bit pregnant?"

She spread the cloth on the sink to dry and turned to face him, clawing wildly for the shreds of her composure. "It's really none of your business," she said pleasantly.

"Sure it is. I'd like to know who's going to smash my face in when I make a pass at you."

"That's no big mystery. I will."

His eyes reminded her of the dusty antique velvet that covered a horsehair sofa in her father's upstairs study: soft and rich and ageless. The aim of those eyes was unmistakable, and she felt her lips begin to tingle as though in anticipation. *Get hold of yourself Bethy, old girl. Better women than you have fallen beneath his ax.*

An absent smile teased the corner of his mouth and he said softly, "You're very pretty."

This room was definitely not big enough for the both of them. She brushed past brightly, exclaiming in a voice that seemed a little overloud, "I guess the least I can do is drive you back to your hotel."

"Would you like to go somewhere and have some breakfast?"

They were back in the outer store now, and she turned to him, suddenly stammering. "I—I've already eaten."

We could take in the beach, sun and surf and all that."

"I have a cold," she replied inanely.

"How about a little plain old-fashioned sight-seeing?"

"I—I can't."

"All right, this is my final pitch. Will you fly to Europe with me?"

"No, I—It's Sunday. I have to go to church."

His smile was vaguely amused, his shrug casual. "I guess I know when I'm outclassed. What about later?"

"I'm having dinner...with my father."

"Love to meet him." He was teasing her ruthlessly.

"He'd make you nervous."

His eyes were dancing. His finger came forward to lightly touch her under the chin, an arm's length separating them. The brief contact left her skin tingling, and she felt sure that if she looked in a mirror the imprint of his finger would still remain. "You *are* awfully pretty," he reminded her. "Can't blame a guy for trying. However...." She couldn't believe he was starting for the door. "I guess all that's left for me now is to thank you"—the sparkle in his eyes was wicked—"for an absolutely unforgettable morning."

"I—I'll drive you!" She spoke so suddenly that her voice came out in a squeak; her hand flew to her throat in embarrassment as though to hide it.

With his hand on the doorknob, Corey grinned, slowly and beautifully. "Thanks, I'll take a raincheck." The cowbell clanged as he opened the door. "Next time I'll wear my crash helmet. See you, Elizabeth Adeline Greene."

"Yes," she said weakly, her hand still at her throat. "See you."

The cowbell clanged again, and he was gone.

Chapter Two

"Wait a minute, here it is." Dr. Adam Greene sank back into the soft, well-used leather of his easy chair and folded back a page of Friday's *New York Times*, snapping out the wrinkles. The aroma of pipe smoke—the one remaining vice the good doctor allowed himself—overwhelmed the faint scent of hyacinths that drifted in on the fluttering of a white sheer curtain covering the low window by which he sat. "'Magnum Enterprises, a division of the Fletcher Corporation, has reportedly filed suit against The Conway Company, makers of Power deodorant, for a sum in excess of three million dollars,'" he read. "'The suit revolves around the now-famous Power television commercials featuring Corey Fletcher as the whimsical, much-besieged playboy who is faced with the mind-boggling choice between a fast car and his deodorant as his last refuge against an overanxious mob of voluptuous females. In the thirty-second soft-sell spot (in which the name of the product is not mentioned once) Fletcher, trooper that he is, opts for Power rather than escape and manfully faces the music.

"'The commercial, which failed marketing tests when it was first produced in 1975, has enjoyed a recent revival due to the escalating popularity of its featured player, Corey Fletcher, who aside from his exploits on the international race circuit is most well known for his role in the Oscar-nominated film *Devlin*. Magnum Enterprises charges unethical practices on the part of The Conway Company, claiming that the television commercial is demeaning to the status of a "serious actor" and is likely to be damaging to his career.

"'Fletcher, the thirty-year-old heir to the California Verdi Wine empire, is presently ranked number four in TVQ (an index of celebrities' popularity and recognizability), just behind such household faces as…'"

Beth sighed and shifted restlessly in her seat, letting her gaze drift toward the open window and the quiet stretch of green lawn beyond. Yes, indeed, when she decided to bump into a celebrity, she didn't fool around. But an hour of silent awe over the strange twists of fortune in church and another hour over dinner reliving the episode to her father had quite sated Beth's appetite for Corey Fletcher. And she only wished that, under the prevailing circumstances, her father had chosen some other article to read aloud besides one that dealt with Fletcher's propensity for lawsuits.

She said as her father paused for breath, "Your lawn needs mowing. Do you want me to do it?"

"No, no," he murmured absently, scanning the remainder of the article silently. "I'll get around to it. Do you want to hear the rest of this or not?"

"No, thanks," Beth sighed. "My headache couldn't possibly get any worse. I just hope that if he decides to sue, it won't be for three million." She reached into the pocket of her linen vest for a tissue and blew her nose. She had used the same tissue through the church service to forestall the sniffles, and it was now damp and shredded and totally beyond further use, but she absentmindedly tucked it back into her pocket anyway.

"Taking anything for it?" her father inquired, glancing over another article that had caught his attention.

Beth assumed he was referring to her cold and she

answered, "Just your usual run-of-the-mill shock treatment this morning. You wouldn't believe how much better I felt the minute I realized I had hit him—maybe I've discovered a cure for the common cold: Scare the germs to death."

Her father chuckled as he folded the paper. "The FDA will never approve it." He sat back and tamped his pipe, easing off his scuffed slippers and stretching his toes for the hassock, which lay just out of his reach. Beth's head sloshed as she bent forward to push the hassock closer. "You've had quite a weekend, haven't you? Did Steve get off all right?"

"Five minutes before boarding." The weekend had gone by in a blur, as all weekends did when Steve came home. They never had any time to just sit and talk like they used to. Maybe that was why Beth was beginning to feel as though they were losing the closeness they once had shared... but she supposed that was inevitable. Perhaps it was simply that they had grown so used to each other with the passage of time that they no longer felt the need to exert themselves for the sake of the relationship. Beth didn't know and she tried not to think about it. It was simply that she was feeling more and more lately as though something was missing from the relationship besides the absence of an "official" engagement.

"Fine boy," murmured her father absently and unnecessarily. Beth knew how her father felt about Steve—how everyone felt about Steve. Their two families had been friends forever, and almost from the moment Steve entered medical school her father had offered him a partnership in his practice as soon as he finished his residency. That event was over a year away, but still they spent most of Steve's rare weekends at home discussing business and making plans. Had Beth been a different sort of woman, she might have almost been jealous of her father's demands on Steve's time. Or maybe jealousy was simply another thing that was missing from their relationship. A violent sneeze jolted her back from her reflective state.

Beth said abruptly, "Oh, my goodness. I almost forgot." She stifled another sneeze impatiently, groping again for a soggy tissue.

Her father frowned a little and said, "Why don't you take an antihistamine?"

"Linda called me this morning." With all the excitement, one thing right after another—Corey Fletcher not to be excluded—she had completely forgotten the most important thing she had wanted to tell her father. She blew her nose one more time and was forced to go in search of another tissue. "And I do mean this morning," she added, somewhat thickly. "Before the cock crowed." She found a box of tissues in the drawer of the telephone table. 'Before, as a matter of fact, any self-respecting rooster would even think about crowing. She's sending Jerry out."

"Parcel post?"

She made a dry face at her father's unaccustomed attempt at humor and resumed her seat, cradling the box of tissues in her lap. "Greyhound, dog sled, pony express—she didn't say and I was too sleepy to ask."

Her father, long inured to his oldest daughter's eccentricities, did not look particularly impressed. "I assume she expects me to take the boy in hand and make a man of him before the summer's out. Smart girl, calling you instead of me. I would have hung up on her."

"As a matter of fact," Beth informed him, "your name wasn't mentioned once. No, her pride and joy is being entrusted to the loving care of his Auntie Beth. Something about my having 'a way with kids.'" The only rationale Beth could find for that assumption was the two years she had spent teaching Sunday school, for other than that her experience with younger members of the species was severely limited. And what Linda imagined a group of stiffly dressed nine-and-ten-year-olds had in common with a sixteen-year-old boy— other than their tendency to throw spitballs and write dirty words in the hymnals when her back was turned— Beth could not fathom. She shrugged. "I think the real reason has a lot to do with the fact that Jerry got a vote in this, and my house is closer to the beach than yours."

Her father lifted one expressive eyebrow. "I don't suppose she gave you a reason for your suddenly being elected to her list of eligible adolescent-sitters."

Again Beth shrugged. "To tell you the truth, I didn't ask. She said she'd call me back with the details."

"Which means the boy will show up on your doorstep one fine morning, backpack in hand, and all you'll get from your sister is her answering service."

Beth's laugh was choked off with another sneeze. "Oh, Daddy, don't be so hard on her!"

"Mark my word," he warned sadly as he reached for the Norfolk paper. "Trouble is brewing. Linda has a knack for it like no woman I've ever known, and I can't help but believe her son has inherited the talent."

"I don't know," Beth mused. "The last time I saw him he was a cute little kid. Looked harmless enough to me."

"The last time you saw him," her father snorted, "he was ten years old. Cuteness has a way of wearing off with age."

"That long ago?" But Beth was talking to herself. Her father was completely immersed in his paper, and nothing and no one stood between Dr. Adam Greene and his Sunday paper.

Their Sundays together had become a ritual since Beth's mother had died. Church services, dinner, lazy afternoons talking and reading the paper, a light supper before Beth drove ten miles back home. Usually she enjoyed the tradition and would have no more moved to break it than her father would, but today her mind was too dull and her body too miserable to enjoy much of anything. She thought her father would understand if she left early for the comforts of her bed and her hot water bottle, and that was exactly what she intended to do—just as soon as she gathered the energy to make the effort.

Some time passed in the homey sounds of rustling newspaper, a dog barking down the lane and bees droning and clicking their wings against the windowpane. Beth's fatigue from the night before, in combination with the excitement of the morning, began to take its toll. She was just feeling herself begin to doze off when her father's voice dragged her back to attention.

"I wonder what he was doing here."

"Hmm?" Beth yawned, sniffled, and coughed, in that order. "Who?"

"Fletcher."

Beth shrugged, extending the gesture to stretch her arms over her head and not surprised to discover the beginning of muscular aches, the inevitable accompaniment to a cold. "Everyone has to be somewhere," she pointed out, and her interest in Corey Fletcher was beginning to wane. As long as he didn't sue, she was content to tuck the events of this morning away with other bits and pieces that would one day be elaborated into yarns to tell her grandchildren—like the time she had gotten a glimpse of Queen Elizabeth on Her Royal Highness's visit to Williamsburg. "I imagine he was cruising down the road with his Formula One in tow, on his way to some death-defying and well-publicized feat of heroism or a multimillion dollar purse, a starlet on each arm and a news crew in the backseat, when suddenly he spied a billboard saying 'Come to Virginia Beach; World's Finest Resort' and he said to himself, 'Now, that looks like a good place to stop for the night.'

So he did." Then she hesitated, frowning slightly. "Daddy, what's a Formula One?"

Adam Greene's eyes twinkled tolerantly over his newspaper. "My dear," he responded, "I haven't the faintest idea."

If it was true that the time would come when every person in the world would have fifteen minutes of fame and glory, Elizabeth Greene had already had hers. Monday was a return to the workaday routine and the brief encounter with stardom may well have never happened. And oh, what a routine it was.

Mondays were traditionally Ellie's days off, though how that insane tradition had ever gotten started Beth did not know. The store was closed on Sunday, and Monday was always their busiest day, leaving Beth to cope with the chaos all by herself. The fountain had to be restocked after the weekend, the pharmaceutical stock rotated, nondrug shelves replenished, and a stream of Monday-morning customers had to be attended to, as well as Beth's usual duties of answering the phone and filling prescriptions. Only one thing was on her side today: The prescription orders were light and mostly routine. As far as she could tell, the only person in Virginia Beach who was ill was Beth herself.

She awoke with her head feeling twice its normal size, a scratchy throat, swollen and watery eyes, and a fit of sneezing that lasted all morning without a break. She fumbled through her morning routine of opening the store with a Kleenex pressed to her face between intermittent moans of sheer misery.

For the first part of the morning the stream of customers was unending. *Customers* was a loose term, for, although most of the people who came in did buy something, pay on an account, or pick up a prescription, the main purpose of their calls was simply to chat. Virginia Beach was a transient community, its fluctuat-

ing population composed mostly of tourists and naval
personnel stationed at NAS Oceana, and the core of
permanent residents was an exclusive, close-knit one.
Something about her store made it a popular gathering
place.

Today, however, the visits were of noticeably shorter
duration. Perhaps it had something to do with her in-
ability to speak more than a few sentences without
breaking into a bout of violent sneezes that sent pa-
trons backing politely toward the door after only a
moment. The minister's wife came by to collect the
overstock and out-of-date drugs she regularly distrib-
uted to the free clinic, ended up forgetting her drugs
and buying a bottle of cough syrup and two types of
decongestant, while giving Beth yet another home remedy guaranteed to cure her cold. A neighbor bearing a
warm cherry Danish and a weekend's worth of gossip
left after two minutes, looking disappointed.

Between calls, Beth glanced surreptitiously over the
People article about Corey Fletcher. Not that she had
anything to be ashamed of. It wasn't every day, after
all, that one had a close encounter with a superstar, and
her natural curiosity was perfectly understandable and
predictable. Still, she jumped every time the cowbell
announced another customer and hid the magazine beneath the counter as though it had originally been de-
livered in a plain brown wrapper. There was no good
reason for this, except that for a split second every time
the door opened she expected to look up and see a
lanky blond figure lounging in the doorway—which
only proved how sick she really was. One might expect
to beat the odds against a person like Beth meeting a
celebrity like Corey Fletcher once in this lifetime, but
twice...never. Still, it wasn't an incident that could be
forgotten quickly, no matter how hard she tried to be
blasé about it, and she could not help being curious.

"What is it about this face that makes you look

twice?" was the caption to the cover story, and Beth, perusing the full-page close-up accompanying, agreed absently, Yes. What *is* it? And her reaction to the fourth most well-known face in the United States was much the same as it had been yesterday when she had seen it in person—nothing specific, except that when you looked away you were somehow compelled to look again, that there was something incredibly unforgettable about his features and when you tried to put your finger on what, exactly, it was, definition was elusive. The baby-fine pale blond hair in its haphazard, multi-layered cut, the youthful, deceptively innocent face, the crooked nose, the sweet grin...all of it combined to form the impression of a scruffy little boy, the kind whose battered denim pockets would be filled with balls of twine and gooey gumdrops, baseball cards and a frog or two, and a handful of cookies that had found their way into his possession the moment his mother's back was turned. Not a handsome face, not a virile face, not a face that spoke of forceful masculinity or arresting character. An endearing face. A sensual face, a somehow captivating face: the kind of face that could make female hearts beat faster wondering what guilt he was hiding behind that sweet grin, the kind of face that encouraged all sorts of imaginative exploits in trying to decipher its innocent mystery.

Corey Fletcher, second-generation product of the success of the Verdi Vineyards begun by his grandfather, was from the cradle privileged to all the advantages and idiosyncrasies afforded those of wealth and power. He was born rich; he immediately proceeded to get richer. With no real need for success, he attracted it with the inexorable pull of the moon on the tide. He was the guy with the money, the women, the cars; the man you would love to despise except he was so incredibly lovable no one could really hate him. Reading his story was enough to put any hardworking, moderately successful man or woman into a three-week depression. Beth thought there should be a law against the publication of such tales in recessionary times.

He had started driving the professional circuit at age twenty, while majoring in drama at a prestigious midwestern university. He had won his first six-figure purse at age twenty-two. By age twenty-five he was president of his own corporation that specialized in automotive design and innovation. Not content with that, he went on to pursue his original goal, acting, working into his busy schedule several guest spots on television serials and, of course, commercials, almost as a hobby. His first film, for which he had done all his own stunts, had been nominated for three Oscars, including best actor.

Between answering the phone, filling prescriptions, and lining up rows of Power deodorant on recently dusted shelves, Beth was drawn back to the magazine with a sort of guilty fascination. How could one man have so much and do so much and still have any time left over to enjoy it? When he wasn't careening down the racetrack or appearing as a favored guest on some television talk show, he was in attendance at every party of consequence in New York or Los Angeles, mixing with stars and musicians, politicians and corporate giants, producers and artists, and the just plain wealthy; rarely was he photographed alone. And his realm of influence was not limited to the borders of the United States. He had a villa on the Côte d'Azur where he reportedly kept an automobile custom-designed for the Grand Prix circuit valued at well over a half million dollars. His château in Switzerland was the winter gathering place of all the beautiful people of Europe, famous and infamous names of all nations. And in odd moments between jetting across the Atlantic Corey Fletcher could be found haunting the lots of Hollywood studios incognito playing stunt man for some of the most dangerous shots in the business, parachuting over the Grand Canyon, testing the white water of some of the most treacherous rivers in the country, dog-sledding in Alaska, cruising the Amazon in a homemade raft with a two-man native crew, climbing Mt. Everest in the middle of the winter, or flying his private plane along the face of the Andes. Good Lord, thought Beth in rising incredulity, there were only so many hours in the day. And Corey Fletcher was only two years older than she. There seemed to be something innately unfair about any man being allowed to live so well and so fully in such a short time.

But flashy life-styles seemed to run in the Fletcher family. His sister, Christine, had made her fame by bearing a love child to a British rock star and now lived in Los Angeles with her three-year-old daughter and a famous heartthrob television actor, still unmarried. She was outspoken on every controversial political and social issue that crossed her path, and embraced the label of "radical" and "incendiary" with enthusiasm. Her latest delight had been in scandalizing attendants at a governor's reception by appearing at said gathering in a partially transparent Dior gown. *Beth old girl* she decided flatly, reluctantly closing the magazine at noon, *you are way out of your league.*

She had brought a ham sandwich for lunch, but even the sight of it was revolting. She tore off a corner of the cherry Danish, and if she closed her eyes, she could have sworn she was nibbling on sandpaper. With a sigh, she poured herself another cup of coffee and took it back to the counter, halfheartedly beginning the paperwork that should have been finished two hours ago. And then Steve called.

"That cold still sounds awful," he greeted her. "That's what you get for going swimming in April."

"Is that the doctor in you speaking?"

"I'll send you my bill." His tone changed, and Beth

could see through the long distance miles the gentle smile softening his very ordinary face, the thick brown hair tousled as he ran his fingers through it, the little worry line between his brows that was really a sign of encroaching myopia for which he vainly refused to wear glasses. "Hey, kiddo, it just occured to me, we didn't have very much time together this weekend. Did I remember to kiss you good-bye?"

"I'm not sure." Beth pretended to muse. "Did you?"

"I'll write myself a note for next time."

"Which is?"

"How about next month? Meanwhile why don't you keep an eye open for a mansion on a hill somewhere, suitably impressive for Virginia Beach's most promising young surgeon and most eminent pharmacist?"

She laughed, and that precipitated a series of sneezes. "Aren't you getting the horse before the cart a little bit?" She sniffed at last. "We've got a year to worry about mansions on the hill, and I think asking me to marry you is another thing you forgot to do."

"Marriage!" He pretended astonishment. "Who said anything about marriage? I thought we'd live together for a while and see how it works out."

She started to giggle again. "You just remember it's the boss's daughter you're propositioning. Oh, it hurts when I laugh. Talk about something serious for a while."

"You don't think giving up my wild, carefree bachelor life is serious? Believe me, baby, it's serious. It's so serious it's almost funereal."

"Is *that* a proposal?" she retorted.

"Well, look at it this way, sweetheart. The longer I can put off making you a formal proposal, the more time I'll have to save for that diamond solitaire you've had your eye on."

"I changed my mind. I don't want a solitaire. I want an emerald with diamond chips."

A low droning began in the background, swiftly stifled. "You won't believe this," he groaned. "That was my alarm clock. I'm on duty in twenty minutes. Could we put the emerald and diamond chips on hold for a while?"

In response, Beth covered the mouthpiece of the phone and sneezed, three times.

"Will you take something for that cold?"

"If I get pneumonia, it will be on your conscience."

Steve chuckled. "I'm not even going to try to unravel the logic in that. Honey, I've really got to run. Take care of yourself, will you?"

"Bye, Steve." Beth's smile was a little sad as she hung up the phone. She didn't understand why there seemed to be this emptiness whenever she thought about Steve lately. She was happy with him; she liked him a lot. They were perfect together. Then why did she still feel something was missing? It was probably, she decided prosaically, just that they had so little time together—time to do the normal things engaged people were supposed to do. And it also might have a great deal to do with the fact that asking Beth to marry him was another thing Steve had forgotten to do this weekend. But, one of the most special things about their relationship was that he didn't have to ask.

After a few minutes of peering at dancing figures with teary eyes and using almost half a box of tissues, Beth gave up. She did not like to take medication, especially when she was working, but it was obvious she was not going to be able to function under these conditions. She took two antihistamines with a cup of coffee and went to attend to the persistent ringing of the telephone.

Two hours later Beth was still waiting for the medication to take effect. The sneezing had gotten so bad she could not even conduct a thirty-second phone call, and she could hardly read a label for the watery eyes. In disgust, she retrieved the bottle of antihistamine and groaned out loud when she read the expiration date. It was almost a month out of date. It was totally unlike Beth to make such a mistake, and she wondered in alarm what other mistakes she had made today, but a quick review of the day's activities was reassuring, for business had been light behind the drug counter and she had dispensed nothing of life-threatening importance. But the day was far from over, and she resolved not to take any more chances. She tossed the expired bottle in the garbage pail with the other outdated drugs, carefully checked the date on a new container, and took two more tablets. Then she began methodically going over her shelves for other items she had missed.

The second dose of antihistamine did the trick. Within twenty minutes the sneezing had completely stopped. She looked up from her work an hour later to notice she was no longer sniffling. Her head, which had felt like a water balloon for the past two days, was dry—and not only dry; arid was a better word. Positively parched. She felt good; in fact she felt absolutely marvelous. She could not remember when she had felt better. A little sleepy, perhaps, but her mind was as clear as a bell and the afternoon duties flew by in an excess of energy that completely made up for the dragging lethargy of the afternoon. The stream of customers trickled off toward the dinner hour, and little remained for her to do except the routine closing-up chores, so on an inspiration she decided to clean out the back room.

Her first chore was to organize the stack of outdated magazines into those that were to be thrown away and those that she had not yet read. Soon she was sitting on the dusty floor, flipping through volumes, and it was not too much longer before an article about Corey Fletcher caught her eye. "My, my," she murmured, settling back against the cot, "that man does get around."

Beth did not find this glowing review of the paragon's many attributes nearly as depressing as the one she had read this morning, despite the fact that it mentioned a dollar figure in connection with his latest race-car design that contained more numbers than Beth could count. The magazine was a racing publication, and most of it was above her head. She did learn that Fletcher was considered a super speedway or Indy driver and that his success on the international Grand Prix circuit was something of a phenomenon, but she did not understand why. Fletcher did not accept sponsors and drove only for himself or his design corporation. And the article mentioned that, aside from his race cars, Fletcher kept for his personal use a Mercedes, a turbo Z28—whatever in the world that was— and a restored 1956 Corvette valued at over $50,000. The automobiles were kept respectively at his three main places of residence: a New York penthouse, a Malibu beach "cottage," and a Montana ranch.

Her interest captured once again, Beth began searching through other magazines, remembering a recent issue of *Playboy* with a feature article about the man who had done as much to earn his "eligible bachelor" title as any other creature living. Just as she found it, the cowbell announced another customer. It was Albert Johnson, one of her neighbors, who merely came in for a bottle of suntan oil. Beth was extraordinarily glad to see him and kept up a stream of bright, overly animated chatter that for some reason seemed to bedazzle the poor man, who only wanted to pay for his purchase and return home to his wife. Ringing up the sale, Beth realized that the cash-register bell had quite a musical note, and she hit the No Sale button several times, just for fun.

Mr. Johnson was staring at her strangely. "Are you feeling all right?" he inquired. "You look…strange."

"Perfect," Beth assured him gaily. "I feel just perfect." She felt light, free, energetic, and very happy; she could not understand why Mr. Johnson left with such a disturbing frown on his face.

To see for herself, she went into the bathroom and checked her reflection in the mirror. She looked just like she always did, her pale caramel-colored hair with its light blond streaks cut in its distinctive style, her skin its usual shade of ivory now that last summer's tan had faded—though perhaps her cheeks were a little flushed. She looked just like she always did—except that her eyes were enormous glassy brown saucers, pupils dilated so that they all but obscured the irises, and suddenly she understood why she felt so terrific. "Whoops," she said. "I guess the eminent pharmacist overmedicated herself." That struck her as enormously funny, and she began to giggle as she went back to the storeroom to finish her article.

She had hardly settled down on the cot with her feet propped up against the wall and the magazine resting on her chest when the cowbell rang again. She took the magazine with her, scanning it as she went to greet her customer, absently hoping it was not the minister's wife returning for her forgotten drugs—who could not help but wonder what one of her most faithful parishioners was doing reading a copy of *Playboy*.

"And what does Corey Fletcher think of the infamous Power commercials?" she scanned silently, thinking it might be wise to put the magazine aside, just in case it was the minister's wife. "'I think they're kind of cute,'" responds Fletcher with a slow grin...."

"And I think *you*'re kind of cute, Corey Fletcher," murmured Beth out loud as she emerged through the curtain, tossing the magazine behind her.

"Thanks," drawled a pleasant masculine voice. "So are you."

Chapter Three

Beth gave a little squeak of total idiocy and her hand flew to her mouth, too late, to stifle it. She blinked rapidly, twice, to clear the sudden light-headedness, but it was no use. He didn't go away. He stood there as large as life in the aisle between pet supplies and cosmetics, his light wispy hair drifting like a halo around his head under the fluorescents, his lanky figure covered in soft denims and a pale cinnamon shirt exquisitely sculpted to his torso. She blinked again and cast a quick, almost frantic, look over her shoulder as though to reassure herself that the image had not stepped directly off the pages of a glossy magazine and into her shop, trying to convince herself, perhaps, that this was only part of an antihistamine hallucination. And he tolerated her disorientation with a friendly, relaxed smile in the back of those multicolored eyes, as though he was used to people having this sort of reaction to him, which, of course, he surely must be.

"What—what are you *doing* here?" she gasped.

He began to stroll toward her with his thumbs hooked into the front pockets of his jeans. "I was in the neighborhood," he suggested, "and I thought I'd drop in?"

He was about three feet from her, and there was no longer any doubt about it: solid flesh and bone. She turned quickly and bumped into a display of hand lotion samples. Righting it, she tripped over a bin of flea collars, spinning it into the middle of the aisle and knocking over a wicker basket of bathing caps in a wild attempt to regain her balance. He lurched forward to save her, but the bin of flea collars blocked the aisle and he only caught the sleeve of her shirt. She sat down hard on the floor.

For a moment there was absolute silence, and she stared at him, wide eyed and breathless. Then his lips curved slowly into a cynical, humorless smile. "Relax," he advised dryly. "Contrary to popular opinion, I hardly ever bite."

She began to giggle. "Sorry!" she gasped, scooping up the spilled bathing caps and dumping them back into the basket. They were uncommonly slippery. "I guess I did kind of fall all over you, didn't I? But you must be used to women doing that when you walk into a room."

He gave her a peculiar look as he agreed cautiously, "Sometimes. But hardly any of them have your grace."

Laughter bubbled up in her throat. "I'll have you know I was first in my ballet class! Why, my teacher said I could have been a prima ballerina in time. Of course, I was only four years old, but you can tell a lot about a child at that age, don't you think? Bone structure and all that? And who was I to argue with Madame Rivere? I mean, she had a genuine French accent and everything!"

A suppressed smile twitched at the corner of his lips even as his brow creased with a frown. "Yes, indeed," he murmured, and moved the metal bin out of the aisle. He knelt beside her and deftly swept the remaining packages off the floor, righting the basket and replacing it on the counter.

"There!" exclaimed Beth in satisfaction, dusting off her hands. "That wasn't as hard as it looked, was it?

Now, the real trick is going to be getting *me* off the floor!'' And she began to giggle helplessly again.

But her laughter died in her throat as he reached out and grasped her chin lightly between his thumb and forefinger, turning her face to his. She felt a leap of her pulses beneath the unexpected touch, hardly intimate, yet strangely exciting. There were little yellow dashes in the depth of his brown-green eyes, and spots of turquoise that fascinated her. Beneath his steady, intent gaze her breath began to quicken, so that she had to part her lips to maintain its rhythm. And gradually, as he studied her face, the puzzled frown between his brows smoothed out, the murky disturbance in his eyes faded. "Lady," he demanded softly, "what are you on?"

She blinked once, slowly, and it took all her willpower to move her face away from his gentle grasp. It was suddenly very difficult to swallow. "O-oh," she said, and took a firm hold on her few remaining cognitive powers. "Oh," she repeated with more energy, for now that the physical contact between them was severed, it was much easier to think. "You must mean because my eyes look funny. There's an explanation for that." She pushed herself to her feet. He caught her arm lightly to assist, but she stepped away quickly, feeling very self-assured now and perfectly in control of the situation. "You see, I have a cold—or at least I had— and I was sneezing all over the place. Well, you know in my profession that's not very sanitary and even though I don't usually take medicine I couldn't really go on like that, so I did. Take something. Only the date on the bottle was expired and I didn't notice it until I had already taken it, and I figured the tablets were old, you see, because they weren't working, so I took some more. Fresh ones. Only I guess the first pills weren't really old because although I'm usually a very responsible person I was just feeling so *rotten* I guess I overdosed...." She ventured a not-very-hopeful glance at him. "I don't suppose I'm making much sense, am I?"

Warm humor sparkled lazily in the depths of his eyes. "Having a nice trip?" Corey inquired mildly.

Beth frowned. "Trip? I'm not going anywhere, I—" Then understanding dawned, and she smiled, pleased with herself. "Yes," she agreed happily, totally at peace with the world. "I am." And then she looked at him with acute perception. "What *are* you doing here?" she demanded again.

There was amusement in his voice as he replied, "Well, I'll tell you. There are two things I promised myself I wouldn't leave Virginia Beach without tasting: Smithfield ham, and the world's last nickle ice cream cone. The ham was quite good, but I have a feeling the ice cream is going to be absolutely unforgettable."

"Oh, it is," Beth assured him airily, and led the way to the counter. Corey sat on one of the two stools as she went around the counter and took a cone from the stack. "What flavor would you like?"

How many choices do I get?"

"One."

His eyes were twinkling. "I'll have vanilla."

Beth put the cone under the spout and pressed the lever, watching in wide-eyed amazement as the soft-serve ice cream quickly filled the cone with a slick mountain and then began to spread its glossy white ropes over her hand and into her palm. She released the lever in bafflement and stared at the cone in one hand and the ice cream sans dish in the other. "Whoops," she said.

The sound he made was a stifled laugh, and she grinned at him impishly as she thrust the cone toward him. "That will be five cents please."

He dug into his pocket and plopped a nickle on the counter. "Worth the price already." He took a napkin from the counter and wrapped the dripping cone in it, then pulled out another and offered it to her.

She debated for a moment, then elected to forgo the napkin. She began to lick the ice cream from her fingers. "Good," she announced, her eyes sparkling with diamond-chip brightness as she wiped a trace of ice cream off her upper lip with the back of her hand, succeeding only in spilling another dribble on her chin. "Messy, but good."

"Is it?" His eyes were merrily devilish. She offered no resistance as he took her wrist and drew it toward him, close to his face, his lips. But a shiver of hot shock went through her as she felt his tongue penetrate the cold film of ice cream and flicker with electric warmth across her palm; her fingers curled involuntarily and she caught her breath. "Umm," he murmured, his eyes hooded. "Delicious." And his lips fastened against her palm in a gentle sucking motion; her knees went weak and something horrible was happening inside her chest, she couldn't breathe.

She stood in a state of suspended paralysis as his lips, his warm, rough tongue, travelled slowly over her palm in a delicious tickling circle, short, teasing flicking motions and luxurious sensual tasting ones. Her heart was thundering and the flush that began in her cheeks and rushed like lava down her arms and to the tips of her fingers was surely hot enough to make the ice cream boil.

It was the pills. She was having a bad reaction to the pills and she was certainly on the verge of a heart attack or a stroke at the very least if he did not stop. His thumb, braced lightly against her wrist, must surely register the dangerous level of her pulse as he took her index finger slowly, oh, so very slowly, into his mouth, sucking, releasing, teasing the nail bed with his tongue. Another finger was drawn inexorably into the warm wet recesses of his mouth, and she closed her eyes and swayed a little against the sudden surprised quiver of awareness deep within the secret core of her abdomen.

God, how did he turn the eating of ice cream into a torrid sexual experience without even trying? And then she felt his teeth lightly capture her finger at the midpoint and it was all she could do to stifle a moan. "I—I thought you said you didn't bite," she whispered hoarsely.

He held her finger willing captive between his teeth for just another moment before releasing it. "I lied," he responded huskily. His eyes were a very, very deep green.

She could feel her heart pounding in her throat, surely he could see it. But his eyes were fixed with unmistakable intent on her lips; his hand, warm and rough, moved gently against the back of her neck, a subtle pressure urging her forward as he leaned over the counter toward her. Her own hand, free now, did not seem capable of movement, and her fingers rested against his face as he slowly closed the distance between them, only the space of her folded arm separating them. She felt the mingling of their breaths, the flicker of his tongue across her chin where ice cream had spilled, the roaring in her head, which was the desperate clamoring of subdued senses begging for release, then the gentle biting motion, which took her lower lip between his, and she jerked her face away.

Beth turned away quickly, gulping for breath, feeling like the lone survivor of a shipwreck rescued at the last moment by unexpected fortune. All circuits on overload, erratic sensory bleeps shooting down her arms and legs and—and other places, her mind a blurred muddle of jelly, totally helpless. She turned the water on full blast and rinsed her hands thoroughly under the cold spray, shocking the heat out of her face by splashing away the remnants of ice cream and drying it vigorously with a wad of paper napkins.

When at last she ventured to look back at him, he was leaning back on the stool, licking his ice cream cone, looking totally relaxed and at ease. She took hold of herself and cautiously caught his eyes. He smiled at her, a friendly, totally unthreatening smile; she let herself relax by stages. It was the pills. She had imagined the whole thing.

After a time of silence broken only by the slow passage of automobile tires outside her storefront and the occasional earth-shattering whoosh of test fighters from the nearby air station, she once again felt in control of the situation. Comfortable and at ease, she folded her arms on the counter and watched him soberly. He sipped and savored the ice cream cone as though it were an exotic and highly potent drink, making delicate paths and curlicues in it with his tongue, caressing it almost, just as he had with— Again she flailed for the remnants of her self-control. Where was it that she had read that the way a person ate an ice cream cone was an index to his sensuality? Dangerous ground, there.

After a time, hardly oblivious of her scrutiny, he folded his arms across the counter, assumed her air of wide-eyed gravity, and said mildly, "Hi, there. Come here often?"

"You have pierced ears!" she exclaimed abruptly, straightening a little to better examine them.

With his tongue he flicked the top curl of the ice cream mountain into his mouth. "A leftover of my antisocial days," he admitted negligently.

"Antisocial?"

"Sure." His teeth flattened the pointed top of the mountain. "You know, the period all kids go through just to put a little gray in their elders' heads: stealing cars, breaking into liquor stores, doing their best to overcrowd the county jail.... Well, it's pretty hard to get arrested when your Dad is worth forty-two million, so I compensated by piercing my ears and trying to jump my Harley Davidson over the family pool."

"Good Lord," she said softly. "What happened?"

He shrugged. "The bike made it through okay; I damn near drowned."

She giggled. "So you threw away your earrings and parked your motorcycle."

"Nope." He crunched into the cone, licking upward with the flat part of his tongue to catch the drips. "I traded my gold hoops for a pair of metal skull and crossbones and joined a gang."

Her eyes, if possible, grew even wider.

"It lasted almost a whole summer," he went on, in an almost bored tone. "We used to tear through the valley, sixty deep, stealing what we wanted and burning what we didn't. The women were the best, though. Those that didn't come willingly we tied to the back of our bikes and took out into the desert. Sometimes it took a little persuading, but they all eventually came around. Nobody could stop us, see, because we were too powerful. Rape, murder, vandalism, terrorism, we did it all. We made our mistake, though, when we lifted five dozen M-Sixteens and a couple of hundred hand grenades from the army base and put Burbank under siege. Couldn't hold out, you see, because—"

Suddenly Beth caught on, and the relief that rushed through her was like a gush of cold air. "You're making it all up!" she exclaimed.

He grinned, slowly, deliciously, savoring her reaction with the same slow luxury with which he had the ice cream: unreservedly, with utter delight. "Princess," he said, "you are entirely too gullible."

"Oh!" she cried, stupefied and more than a little annoyed. She couldn't think of anything else to say.

Corey leaned over and dropped the remainder of his ice cream cone in the sink. "Absolutely delicious," he announced, and the slanting, dancing eyes made her blush a little. "But next time I think I'll order it without the cone. What time do you close up?"

"Not until seven."

He glanced at his watch. "It is exactly seven forty-two."

Beth couldn't help staring. The gleam of the one piece of jewelry that adorned his wrist was unmistakably solid gold, a spaceage hexagonal design with two small windows displaying digital readouts and a multitude of minuscule control knobs. Time, date, weather forecast, and horoscope, no doubt. *So how long has it been,* she asked herself, *since you served ice cream to a man whose watch was worth more than your car?*

He followed her gaze in some perplexity, and she flushed a little. "Nice watch," she commented lamely.

His glance was oddly puzzled. "It has a minicalculator and plays Tchaikovsky's Piano Concerto Number One every hour on the hour in full orchestra."

"Oh, yeah? Where's the miniature TV set and folding shuffleboard?"

He regarded her mildly. "Sorry, I must have left it in my other suit. Are you ready to go?"

Beth blinked a little, feeling very light-headed now. Was he suggesting they leave together? The man with the million-dollar watch? "I—I told you," she stammered, "I don't close until seven."

"And I told you, it's seven forty-two—three. You're on overtime."

"But—" She floundered in confusion. "I have to do my drug count. I'm not finished yet."

He smiled patiently. "Lady, in your present condition I doubt seriously whether you could count to three." He took her hand and drew her around the counter. "Be a sensible girl now, and call it a night. And, gentleman that I am, I'll even drive you home."

She hesitated, then shrugged philosophically. "Well, you can be a gentleman if you like, but I don't know what you'll drive. I didn't bring my car."

"Thank heaven for small favors," he murmured under his breath. "Do you have a coat?"

She shook her head and he went unerringly for the light switch as she found her purse. She locked up under the dim glow of the security lights and they stepped out into the cool, tangy night air. The wind tickled her hair and invigorated her senses, brushing to life forgotten nerve endings with the taste of salt and sand and fish. She tilted her head back and took a deep breath, drowning in the dazzling canopy of stars and the pulsing radiance of a platinum crescent moon. "Look at that sky!" she breathed, stretching her arms overhead to embrace it. "On nights like this I feel like I could touch the stars."

"On nights like this I don't doubt that you could," he responded dryly. Gently he lowered her arms back to her sides. "Don't do that, princess, you're so high now I'm going to have to find some guy ropes to tie you down. You keep flappin' your arms that way and you're liable to take right off into space."

She giggled. Somehow his arm was around her shoulders and her head was snuggled quite naturally into the hollow of his shoulder. "I guess you're right." She sighed, luxuriating in the feel of his warm arm around her, the finely textured fabric of his shirt beneath her cheek and the tough muscle it encased. "My, this is nice."

She felt his head bend toward her, sensed a smile beneath the shadows that hid it. "The night, the company, or both?"

"Both," Beth replied, and when his fingers pressed her shoulder a shiver of pleasure ran from the base of her neck right down to the tip of her spine. She felt marvelous. "Colds always remind me of Christmas," she said suddenly. "Red and blue lights and tinsel making light patterns on the ceiling. The smell of spruce and carolers singing 'We Three Men.' Do you know 'We Three Men'?"

His thumb caressed the edge of her collarbone indulgently. "Umm-hmm. You're not going to sing it for me, are you?"

"Not if you already know it," she shrugged. "When I was six I was really sick at Christmas, and my father gave me codeine syrup. It made me all warm and woozy and...good feeling, like now. I guess that's why. Funny the things that kids remember, isn't it?"

"Sure is. Would you happen to remember where you live?"

"Oh." She straightened up, suddenly realizing that they had been standing aimlessly on the sidewalk in front of her store. "Sure I do. Would you care to take the scenic route?"

He stepped back with an imperious wave of his hand. "I'm yours to command."

The scenic route was via the deserted boardwalk, five blocks away. He held her hand as they walked and it warmed her to the very tips of her toes. She felt happy, expansive, utterly content. When another jet rattled the night sky she explained importantly, "They're from the naval air station. You get used to it after a while."

He squinted toward the sky. "If you don't go deaf first."

"Oh, I think it's kind of nice." Tonight she could have found kind words for Godzilla. "It's part of the character of this place. The uniforms, the beach boys, the funny men in striped robes who walk down to the surf at sunrise chanting and making temples with their fingers, the fog horns, the planes.... This is a town with personality, you know? Always changing, always staying the same. I was born here, and I never wanted to live anywhere else."

Sand on the cement boardwalk crunched under her feet, and she went to lean on the rail, inhaling deeply of the rich night air as she watched the rolling whitecaps meeting the beach. Long angular shadows stretched like fingers toward the tide, and the swelling sea was a study in royal velvet, which broke into prisms of white moonlight as it met the shore. Its powerful rush and roar whipped at her hair and tingled her nostrils, filling her ears like the masterful percussion of a world-class orchestra. "You know" she breathed. "I really love it here. Especially when it's quiet and empty, like tonight. Or after a storm, when the sky is still purple and the light is yellow, and the sea is churning and foamy, like an angry god just starting to settle down after a temper tantrum. Steve and I used to come here after storms and watch the rain move out over the ocean, like a sheer curtain that went straight up to heaven. Sometimes you could even see a rainbow in it."

Corey was standing very close behind her, not touching her, but close enough so that the heat of his body blocked the wind and fell over her backside like a warm shawl. It was a nice feeling. "Steve, is that the fellow you're almost, but not quite, kind of engaged to?" he inquired.

"Hmm-hmm," she replied absently, drinking in the sea with her eyes, her ears, absorbing it through her skin and the flare of her nostrils. Its power filled her, transported her, made her feel free and adventurous and more alive than she had ever felt before. She could embrace it all. "We were voted couple of the year at our senior prom," she added.

His fingers fell upon her arms, brushing a path of bare skin, warm, tingling, lovely. "Is he in the Navy?"

"Steve? No, he's a doctor, like my dad. He's in Boston now, but next year he's coming home."

She felt the softness of breath caress the back of her neck, whispering over her jaw. His touch was warm, titillating, secure. Nice. "Turn around, Elizabeth Greene," said a husky voice in her ear. "I'm going to kiss you."

She was turned into the circle of his arms, whether through his effort or hers she did now know. Lazy eyes caught the reflection of moonbeams and floated like a velvet cloth over her, filling her vision. Warm breath fluttered on her parted lips. And slowly, very slowly, his face descended toward hers.

She gasped because she had not really expected it to happen. His open mouth took hers gently, exploring and savoring, urging a response she was too startled to give. It was tentative at first—a cautious testing of untried waters, an assault on her senses of warmth and softness and burgeoning awareness—and then with a parting and a breath, Corey turned his head a little, and angled Beth's to allow his mouth full possession of hers in a bolder exploration.

Her head was bent back into the crook of his arm, his other hand supported her at the waist and she sagged against it, totally unprepared for what the feel of his lips against hers did to her. Heat surged to her face and she shivered as unexpected sensations coursed through her, a weakness, a breathlessness, an utter senselessness. The symptoms of an impending heart attack were back again, only in spades; the force of it shook her entire body, and her ribs constricted like an iron band against the desperate pumping of that life-sustaining organ. The roaring in her ears was no longer the ocean; her fingers, resting uselessly against the soft fabric of his shirt, felt numb but perversely aware of every rippling motion of the muscles of his arm, the heat of his body, the fine weave of the material. And when he lifted his face, just a fraction, and just for a second, she whispered, "You shouldn't. I'm contagious."

"Now you tell me," he murmured huskily, his lips brushing hers. Deliberately he moved his other hand to her waist, drawing her with a firm pressure of his fingers against the hardness of his pelvis as once again his mouth covered hers. Shocked heat pulsed in secret regions with the intimate pressure of his fingers against her buttocks, and his tongue flickered over her lips, seeking entrance. Somehow she managed to keep

her teeth determinedly locked. His palms pressed into
her waist, holding her prisoner against his lean thighs
and his hard chest. Newly sensitized nipples strained
against the scratchy fabric of her shirt and sought the
heat that pressed against them. Her fingers curled
around his biceps and though her mind told her she
was pushing away, what she was really doing was
drawing closer. *You are being manipulated by the master,*
she thought. *You don't know what you're doing...you'd
better stop this.*

Patiently his lips closed over hers, kissing her sweetly, tenderly, then moved to the plane of her face, softly
against the corner of her eye, to her ear where his
tongue played a three-second dance that left her shivering violently and arching helplessly against him, then
back to their original intent. "Open your mouth, princess," Corey murmured throatily against the corner of
her lips. "It won't hurt."

"N-no," she whispered, but when next they met, his
tongue passed through her easily. A low moan was
dragged from the center of Beth's throat and she was
swept away just as surely and as completely as if the tide
below had swelled up over the boardwalk and carried
her out to sea. Her breasts, crushed against his chest,
were heavy and aching for his touch. Somewhere deep
within the control center of her brain violent signals
were being fired off and glands were busily secreting
little-used hormones in preparation for receiving him
and that, above all things, was what she had no intention of doing. Elizabeth Greene, a woman of the
eighties, moderately sophisticated, expecting few surprises in her life, had not been prepared for this. No
one had ever moved her like this, touched her like this,
known all the proper buttons to push. There had been
Steve and the few boys she had dated in high school—
boys, all of them boys. None of them had known the
secrets this man did, possessed the consummate skill of

a practiced lover. It was too fast, too sudden, and she was way out of her league.

His hand slipped between their bodies and moved inexorably upward toward the breast that yearned for his touch, and all the strength her ennervated body possessed was concentrated into one feeble attempt to resist, to preserve her sanity, to gather her reason. "Don't," he soothed, gently clasping her lips. "Don't."

His fingers brushed across the fullness of her curve, stroking, reassuring, then cupping, clasping gently, seeking with one exploratory finger its stiff center. The sound that caught in her throat was like a whimper, and she turned her face helplessly to his. *Oh, yes,* she thought as her trembling arms slipped slowly around his neck, *this is entirely too sudden....* And there was an urgent, demanding pressure low in her abdomen, her weak legs longed for a reclining position, the heady taste of him and the maddening things his fingers were doing were sending bubbles of fire through every vein in her body. Delight and torture. She knew she was sinking fast.

"Darling." His breath was unsteady and hot against her cheek, the hands that rested around her waist were urgent. His voice had an odd, hoarse tone. "I hope you won't take this the wrong way...but my hotel room is only a five-minute walk from here."

She sank against him weakly, trying not to gasp for breath, her fingers curling into helpless little fists against the fabric of his shirt. Yes, she thought. Oh, yes.... "No," she whispered, moving her head slowly back and forth against his chest. "I don't know what kind of girl you think I am...." *Don't be an idiot, Elizabeth, you know perfectly well what kind of girl he thinks you are. A quick pickup in a Navy town he can chuckle about over cozy ski gatherings in St. Moritz.* She tightened her fists against his shoulders and tried to push away. She succeeded by a few inches. Her eyes were like great glass globes in the pale starlight as she looked up at him, the expression deep within them somewhere between terror and brilliant radiance. "But I d-don't go to...strange hotels with men I...hardly know."

His smile was somewhat strained. Now she could feel the rapid pounding of his heart against her breast; she tried to move away because it was only an echo of the turmoil that had invaded her own body. "How long," he suggested, placing one affectionate finger beneath her chin, "will it take you to get to know me?"

Beth swallowed hard. "You move awfully fast, don't you?"

He answered soberly, "I lead a fast life."

"I want to go home now."

She stepped away; he released her. But as they started moving down the boardwalk in the direction from which they had come she was grateful for the support of his arm around her shoulders. The brisk wind was no longer stimulating, simply cold. Her limbs were heavy, her eyelids started to droop. The night pulsed and strobed wearily around her, bringing the rushes of the sea into deafening focus and letting it fade out to the dim coursing of her heart, highlighting the fluttering of a candy wrapper trapped against the rail, but muting their footsteps. She felt strange all over, her mind in a sort of perpetual free-fall weighted down only by her heavy limbs, and if she was aware of anything in the meaningless expanse of time that passed as they walked it was his arm around her shoulders, his body close to hers. It was a good feeling, a right feeling.

They were on solid asphalt again before he pointed out, "We're going back to your shop."

"I know," she said wearily. She wanted nothing more than to sink down on the grass and go to sleep. All told, they had already walked ten blocks, and her legs ached magnificently. "I live on the same street. Three blocks down."

He gave her an amused look, but made no comment.

The white picket fence that surrounded her little rented house sagged with the weight of rose bushes not yet in bloom. It was shadowed by a distant streetlight and bathed in the silvery glow of the moon; it had never looked more inviting. Because she was simply too tired to do it, he took her keys from her to open the door, then reached inside to turn on the interior light. She hesitated on the threshold, looking up at him, and he did not invite himself in. She was so very tired. His face began to dance before her eyes, and she blinked hard to keep it steady.

"Elizabeth." His hands rested firmly on her shoulders. His voice sounded very sober, but his expression, to her capricious vision, was unreadable. "I'm trying not to move too fast. But I have to leave for Europe tomorrow and I'm going to risk repeating my previous invitation. Will you come with me?"

She stared at him, blinking owlishly, until his face literally began to dissolve before her eyes. "I think," she said in a small, very faraway voice, "I'd better go to bed first."

She closed her eyes and sank gratefully into the support of his arms.

Chapter Four

Elizabeth opened heavy-lidded eyes the next morning wondering why her neck was so stiff and her head hurt so badly, wondering what she was doing in bed fully dressed and why her pillow was so hard, why her legs were entwined with a pair of fully clothed male ones, why her arm was curved around a partially bare torso. A face turned, a male nose only a fraction of an inch from hers; heavy lashes shaded lazy brown-green ones. "Good morning, princess," said Corey Fletcher. "You snore."

She gasped and sat up straight, her head screaming a protest as she did. Fletcher straightened up more slowly, wincing as he stretched and rotated the arm upon which she had, presumably, slept all night. Pinpoints of morning light bored through the drawn shade like miniature laser beams, spotlighting little circles on her rumpled poster bed and turning fractions of his hair to sparkling silver. Had he done that, then, placed her half-swooning form on the bed and crossed to draw the shade that should have been replaced years ago, then returned? *Why?* In the dusty half light of morning with his light, fly-away hair falling about his face, the rumpled cinnamon shirt unbuttoned midway down his chest and untucked from his jeans—who had unbuttoned it? Oh, no, had *she?*—and the look of exquisite pain on his face as he rubbed his shoulder, he looked disheveled, boyish, completely harmless. But oh, no, her memory wasn't that bad, and she recalled the pounding surf and the torrential sensual assault with a leaping flame of color that sent her springing off the bed.

Corey smiled up at her easily. "How're you feeling?"

"I—I have to go to the bathroom," she blurted and scurried across the room toward that very useful facility, which aside from its utilitarian functions possessed the only workable interior lock in the entire house.

Once there, Beth leaned against the door and pressed her hands to her hot cheeks, a shame of wanton memories flooding her. Had he really asked her to go back to his hotel room with him, and had she really almost said yes? And worse yet—oh, far worse—had she really reached for him from the drowsy, misty depths of her bed last night and drawn him down beside her, and had she really fallen asleep with the touch of his lips on hers? She would have been grateful at that moment if a gaping hole had erupted in the worn linoleum tile and swallowed her whole. Elizabeth Greene did not give her body shamelessly to fast playboys, movie stars, and Grand Prix drivers. Elizabeth Greene did not share her bed with them or become tempted by wild invitations to Europe or strange hotel rooms. Elizabeth Greene, pillar of the community, dispensed therapeutic potions by day and watched television by night, went to church on Sundays and meetings of the Better Business Bureau the first Thursday of every other month, minded her own business, and never caused any trouble. Elizabeth Greene was almost, practically, engaged to another man. So who was that abandoned woman Corey Fletcher had held in his arms last night?

She groaned out loud and made her way to the sink, bracing herself with a few splashes of cold water on her face and a vigorous brushing of her teeth. She couldn't postpone it forever; she had to go out there and face the music.

When she eventually, after much procrastination, crept back into the bedroom she was relieved to find it was empty—and surprised to find that the bed was made and the window shade raised. So, he was a man of good manners and fastidious personal habits. Why did it amaze her that Corey Fletcher was capable of making a bed?

Sounds from another part of the small house told her that he had found his way to the kitchen, and she took advantage of the opportunity to swiftly change her wrinkled clothes for a clean pair of slacks and a fresh blouse. When she joined him in the kitchen, he was aimlessly opening cabinets, reminding her acutely of the fact that neither of them had eaten the night before—and that, in fact, she had not had anything to eat in the entire preceeding twenty-four hours. Which, of course, would go a long way toward explaining her unorthodox reaction to the overdose of antihistamine yesterday. But the less she thought about that, the better.

"Can you cook, perchance?" inquired Corey Fletcher, closing the cupboards which were, admittedly bare.

"Not a lick." He had buttoned his shirt to just below the collarbone, but still it was atrociously wrinkled and untucked. He had made an attempt to straighten his hair with his fingers, and there was a soft bristle of pale beard on his chin. He looked all of seventeen, strangely, almost frighteningly at home in her cramped kitchen with its small red-lacquered wooden table and ladder-back chairs, the gingham-checked curtains and scuffed white linoleum.

"What do you do when you get hungry?"

She shrugged. "If it's not frozen, canned, or instant. I do without."

"Aha," he agreed, "a woman after my own heart." She assumed that meant he could not cook either, but what was the big surprise in that? A man like Corey Fletcher had no need for such banal domestic accomplishments, and she was still recovering from the shock that he actually knew how to make a bed.

He opened the freezer and found a carton of butter pecan ice cream. "Got a bowl?"

She took a cereal bowl from the cabinet, but it was chipped. He took it from her before she could put it back. "You must be a real nut for ice cream," she commented, trying not to sound as nervous as she felt.

"It's a recently acquired taste." He replaced the carton and took his bowl over to the table, licking the spoon. "This, however," he pointed out with a twinkle, "is not nearly as good as what I had last night."

She found she could not take her eyes off the way the soft denim jeans embraced his thighs, skintight, flesh and fabric blending together without a breath to separate them. How did a man walk in jeans that tight? How did he— She jerked her eyes away quickly. "What exactly did you have last night?" And the horrifying words were out before she knew it.

His eyes traveled up her length with the slow, dazzling insinuation of his grin. His elbow on the table, the spoon resting in his hand like a baton, he drew his tongue around it once before replying, "Nothing, I assure you, that you did not give willingly."

She swallowed hard and turned quickly to fill the coffeepot with water. Her face was brilliant. *Hold on there, Bethy, anything you say can and will be held against you... Ice cream, stupid. That's what he meant. Ice cream.*

She put bread in the toaster and took butter and jam from her small white twelve-year old refrigerator, noticing in chagrin that it needed a good cleaning. The paint was peeling in one corner over the sink, and why had she never noticed before how worn and faded the linoleum on the floor was?

She tried not to glance at him too covertly as she busily spread the toast with butter and a sloppy measure of homemade strawberry jam that Ellie had put up for her last season, and she took her plate over to the table across from him with as much casual ease as she could muster. She gave him a small smile as she sat down.

"Why are you looking at me like that?" he asked.

Her eyes widened. "Like what?"

"Like I'm going to plunge a knife into your back the minute it's turned."

She took a hasty bite of her toast, chewed and swallowed without tasting it. "I'm looking at you," she replied pleasantly, "the same way I would look at any man who has butter pecan ice cream for breakfast."

He had chameleon eyes, she realized suddenly, that changed color not only according to the shade he wore, but with his mood as well. Today they were a clear mixture of brown and green reminiscent of mossy riverbanks, bright and verdant on the surface, murky secrets lurking just below. He said casually, "You never did get around to answering my question last night."

She swallowed hard on nothing. She knew very well what he meant. "What question?"

"Europe."

Beth got up slowly, crossed to the counter, and poured herself a cup of coffee. She brought it carefully back to the table, sat it down, took a breath, and began deliberately. "Mr. Fletcher—"

"Oh-ho." His eyes were twinkling, and he made that disconcerting little circle around the spoon with his tongue again. "So now it's 'Mr. Fletcher.'"

Beth's hands tightened in her lap. She repeated patiently, "Mr. Fletcher, I think you may have gotten the wrong impression about me last evening—"

"You mean because you were higher than a Georgia pine and not, shall we say, to be held accountable for your actions?"

Beth released an uneven breath. She couldn't have put it better herself. "Y-yes. You see, I'm not the kind of woman who—"

"Goes to strange hotels with men she hardly knows," he supplied for her, spooning up more ice cream, "or flies to Europe with them or even"—a wicked light danced far back in the depths of his eyes—"goes to bed with said men on first date. I believe we've established that." And then he added thoughtfully, "Figuratively speaking, of course."

Tingling color tinged the flesh just beneath Beth's cheekbones, but she outstared it manfully. Her voice was as calm and as controlled as she could possibly make it. "Aside from all that..." Corey spooned up the last of the ice cream and slid it into his mouth. Beth dragged her eyes away from his lips and focused on a half-open cabinet. Why hadn't she changed that shelf paper last month as she had planned to?

"Aside from all that..." he prompted, and Beth glanced back at him quickly.

"I've been trying to tell you," she continued patiently, her nails digging into her palms, "there's someone else. So you see I'm really in no position to—"

"Ah, yes." He pushed his bowl away and leaned back in the chair, one arm hooked negligently over its top rung. "The infamous Steve." His expression was mild, his tone lightly interested. "If I ask you a question, will you promise to leave my face in relatively the same condition in which you found it?"

She took a quick, burning gulp of her coffee. "What question?"

He regarded her frankly, in a friendly, casual, ultimately nonthreatening sort of way, in no way preparing her by his expression for what he was about to say.

"This Steve—the fellow who, if what you've indicated to me is correct, can't quite get up the nerve to ask you to marry him—"

"It has nothing to do with nerve, it—"

"Do you sleep with him?"

Beth gulped, choked, coughed, and clattered her cup into the saucer, spilling half the contents onto the checked vinyl tablecloth. "What a question! I—it's none of your business! How dare you! I don't have to answer that!"

"No," he agreed mildly, watching her. "You just did. Very interesting," he added, and his tone dropped to musing as his eyes remained steady upon her scarlet face with no more than a purely detached interest.

Beth couldn't help it. Even though she knew she should be outraged and indignant, even though her face was on fire and her heart was beginning that ridiculous pounding again, she had to demand, though in a somewhat choked voice, "Why—why would you ask such a thing? What business is it of yours?"

He smiled, bringing a hidden light to the surface of his eyes, and drawled, "Now I *would* be pushing my luck if I answered that." And then he straightened up. "I have to be at the airport by eleven. What time is it?"

She got up from the table, suddenly irritated with him, and not for his presumption as much for the fact that he had so easily embarrassed her with it. Oh, what a locker room tale she had given him to share with his cronies next time out! "What happened to your fancy watch?" she snapped, bringing a sponge back to the table and beginning to mop up the spilled coffee with short, jerky motions, "Did it blow a gasket?"

He gave her one odd look before glancing at his watch and murmuring, "Just making conversation." He stood and politely took his bowl to the sink. "My fancy watch tells me I just have time to get back to the hotel to shower and shave before I have to leave. Are you going to wish me luck in Belgium?''

She turned, the damp sponge clutched in her hand, staring at him. ''Belgium?'' she parroted. ''Should I?''

He came toward her, an easy smile on his little-boy face, arms half-extended to touch her. ''It never hurts.'' Oh, how innocent he looked with that sweet smile and tousled hair, but what grave danger that rumpled exterior disguised.

''Corey, don't,'' she whispered as his hands rested on her upper arms.

''For luck?'' he prompted and bent his head toward hers. His midnight-shaded lashes dropped over steadily darkening eyes, the face of a river when the sun goes behind a cloud.

''N-no,'' she whispered. The sponge slipped out of her hand and plopped on the table.

His lips were cold from the ice cream, and then warmer as they gently moved against hers, eliciting a response she was totally incapable of subduing. Her vertabrae dissolved into a slippery column of jelly, she swayed against him, her hands moved to his waist for support. Firm masculine flesh seemed to surge beneath the material of his shirt and tingle her fingertips. Her head spun. Her ears pounded. Her breath was a thin stream far deep in her throat and all she could think about was drowning.

Corey drew his lips away, very slowly; he nuzzled her cheek. ''That, by the way,'' he said softly, ''was the third thing I promised myself I wouldn't leave Virginia without tasting.''

Her breath was a whispering flutter against his mouth. ''You—you said there were only two.''

He smiled. ''I lied.''

And then, before she could prevent it, his lips found hers again, clasping, tasting, caressing with brief, unmistakable finality. All too brief. All to final. He stepped back, holding her shoulders for just another moment. His eyes were a very warm brown. "Good-bye, Elizabeth Greene," he said.

And that was how the brief encounter between Elizabeth Greene, small town druggist, and Corey Fletcher, international legend, came to a very predictable end.

Or so she thought.

Two things happened in May: Corey Fletcher won the Grand Prix in Belgium, and Jerry Fields arrived from Phoenix, Arizona. Of the two, the arrival of her nephew Jerry had by far more significance for Beth.

He arrived one bright morning in a slick black Trans Am with gold snakes painted on the side, a can of beer in one hand and, yes, his backpack in the other. No phone call, no letter, nothing but the roar of dual chrome exhausts whipping into her driveway and shattering the peace of the quiet spring morning. The sound of the mighty engine almost caused Beth to fall off the step ladder upon which she was standing while painting the kitchen because for one brief, utterly ridiculous second she thought it might be—well, someone else. In a paint-splattered T-shirt and faded denim shorts, she went to greet her summer guest.

She described it to Steve via long distance this way: "You know the old running gag, 'you know you're in trouble when?' Well, you know you're in trouble when the kid you last saw in a Little League uniform with two front teeth missing gets out of a car that sounds like the landing pattern of the Concorde, wearing a razor blade and a coke spoon on a chain around his neck."

"Glad it's you and not me, hon," replied Steve generously.

Beth had never before believed in the Generation Gap, but she needed to look no further for evidence of its existence. The front of her nephew's black T-shirt read Put Something Exciting between Your Legs. The usual rearview conclusion of that popular slogan was Ride a Motorcycle. But when Beth found herself walking behind him up the walk, she blushed. The shirt was apparently custom designed. His thick black hair fell lankly over one eye and he was as tall as she was. He wore faded denim cut-offs and no shoes, and there was a pack of Winstons tucked into his front shirt pocket. He was not yet seventeen, but he looked much older. Oh, brother, did he look older.

The way he looked at her, a nasty little grin flickering in his eyes, made Beth wish suddenly she had worn a bra under her white T-shirt, made her wish her shorts were not quite so tight and not nearly as short. And his first greeting confirmed the practiced leer. "Hello, sweet thing. Been getting any lately?"

Their relationship was off to a rocketing start.

He did carry his own backpack and duffel bag inside, but after that he did not volunteer his services for anything. He plopped down on the sofa and lit a cigarette while Beth went to clean out the extra bedroom which had been used for storage as long as she had lived there. She could feel his eyes on her retreating backside as she left the room, and it gave her the creeps. The first thing she did was change into a pair of jeans and a very conservative, button-to-the-collar shirt.

When she asked why he wasn't in school, he laughed and flicked ashes on her freshly dusted end table. She exclaimed over the fact that his parents had let him drive all the way from Arizona alone, and he swung his leg up over the back of the sofa, grinning. "Auntie, it was their idea!" At the very first opportunity, she closed her bedrom door and called her sister long distance.

The only thing Beth had against her sister was her choice of a husband. David Fields was a demigod in the world of corporate law; he held himself in great esteem and never lost an opportunity to persuade others to do so as well, playing the big frog in the little pond for all the role was worth. He thrived on power, and what he could not control he ignored. He was the type of man who would give his sixteen-year-old son a suped-up Trans Am and let him drive halfway across the country in it, for out of sight was out of mind as far as men like David Fields were concerned. The only thing Beth could not understand was why Linda let him get away with it.

Her sister's voice sounded strange at first, tight and somewhat strained. "Oh," she said weakly. "He made it. I'm glad."

"You're glad!" Beth's voice was high with incredulity. "Is that all you can say—you're glad? You let your only son loose on a continental highway with a sports car that could be classified as a deadly weapon and all you can say is you're glad he made it okay? Weren't you the least bit worried?"

"Of course I was worried!" snapped Linda. "And I didn't 'let him loose,' I—" Here the voice faded, and Beth could not be certain what she heard next was not simply the result of a bad connection. "I couldn't stop him."

"What?"

"Oh, Beth." Linda sounded tired. "You don't understand."

"Now that I agree with." Beth settled back on her white chenille bedspread and kept a cautious eye on the door. "Why don't you explain it to me? Start with why this child is not in school in the middle of May."

"He's not a child, that's why," answered Linda sadly. "He's dropped out."

The silence on Beth's end of the line ticked off precious long-distance dollars. Then Linda began cautiously, "Beth...there was some trouble.... That's why we thought this summer with you would be such a good idea. A change of environment, you know."

Why did Beth get the impression that that was only a nice way of saying the kid had been told to get out of town before sundown? "Trouble?" she ventured. "With the law?"

"Well...yes. Very minor."

"How minor?" Beth's hand tightened around the receiver and she straightened up.

"Oh, just the usual pranks. Really, Beth, it's nothing to get concerned about, it's just that he was hanging out with the wrong crowd and we thought the best thing to do was to break it up before it went too far. The court thought so too."

"Court?"

There was a long and ominous hesitation. "You see," Linda began at last, "David was able to get the charges dropped only on the condition that Jerry be remanded to the custody of a responsible relative for three months. It wasn't his first offense, I'm afraid. Jerry wouldn't stay with Dad," she went on in a rush. "He would have run away within a week. But I thought with you.... The only reason you haven't received the official papers yet is because he wasn't supposed to leave until the first of June. I was going to fly out with him and explain it all to you, but then he took off—it was only three days ago, Beth. I've been worried sick, but I didn't want to alarm you unnecessarily, and Jerry is basically a good kid, I knew he would come to you. You'll have to keep in touch with his probation officer through the court system there, but that will all be explained in the papers from Judge Harley's office. I did write you, Beth." Beth could not be certain whether it was remorse or accusation she heard in her sister's voice. "I guess you didn't get the letter yet."

Beth's head spun. Custody, first offense, probation officer.... "God," she said out loud. She struggled for a grasp on the situation. After all, it happened in the best of families...but why did it have to happen to hers? "Wait a minute." She took a deep breath. "Are you trying to tell me—Do you mean to say that the courts have taken Jerry away from you and David and given me full custody?"

"No, nothing like that," Linda assured her quickly. "It's just a formality, because he's a minor living out of state, and on probation—"

Probation. Beth's mind was jumping like a cricket from one shock factor to the next. "What, exactly, if you don't mind my asking, was the nature of Jerry's offense?" If she was going to house a jailbird, she might as well know his record.

"Well, just little things...at first. Driving without a license, public intoxication, breaking curfew, shoplifting...." These, thought Beth in horrified amazement, her sister considered "little things"? "Then there was breaking and entering, carrying a concealed weapon, threatening a police officer...and this last time—"

Linda was telling her far more than she wanted to know. "That's enough," choked Beth. "I get the picture. But, Linda—" She felt as though she were drowning in a whirlpool with no rescue in sight.

"You will take him, won't you?" Desperation stabbed in her sister's voice. "You said you would over the phone. I was counting on you...." And then Linda's voice broke in what may very well have been a sob. "Oh, Beth," she whispered. "My marriage is in trouble—bad trouble. With all this with Jerry—You have no idea what it's like, what a strain it can put on—But I thought this summer, if you could help us out, there might be a chance—Beth, I know it's a lot to ask. Please don't think I don't know. I know I haven't been fair to you, but it's just because I was so scared. Beth, you're the one person in the world I can depend on right now. You won't let me down, will you? Because if you do, I just don't know what—"

Beth sighed. If there was one thing no one could

deny about her sister, it was her persuasive abilities. So Beth would spend the summer playing warden to a juvenile delinquent and never think of refusing her sister in her time of need. Beth was generous, tolerant, kind to small animals and underprivileged youths, and a pushover for a good sob story, all of which her sister knew very well.

Beth was also, as the weeks progressed, growing a little desperate herself.

Beth tried to be patient. She raised only the most sensible objections to the liquor stains that gradually began to appear on her furniture and carpet and silently collected enough beer cans to start her own recycling plant. The pattern of cigarette burns emerging on her sofa was a little harder to deal with, but when she tried to explain to Jerry about the harmful effects of cigarette smoke on preadult physiology, he only leered at her. "Yeah, we don't wanna stunt my growth, do we, mama?" His eyes went over her once strippingly. His voice was soft and somehow threatening. "Don't you worry, baby, my body is in fine shape. Just fine."

Jerry had two passions: the beach and his car. It never ceased to amaze Beth that, while *slovenly* was too mild a word to describe his personal habits around the house, not one speck of dust was allowed to appear on that automobile before it was diligently polished away. Every spare moment was devoted to the vehicle, tuning, adjusting, applying potions and rubs to the exterior, flicking dust off the chrome engine, polishing the whitewalls. He even covered it up at night with a shroud of plastic and tucked it in like a baby.

One typical Friday evening Beth was repainting her kitchen chairs and Jerry had his head buried beneath the hood of the car. She could have really used some help with the painting, for it was hot and sweaty work and two hands would have been faster than one, but Jerry did not allow himself to be volunteered for anything remotely resembling work—as evidenced by his flat refusal to take a paying part-time job in her store cleaning and sweeping and stocking shelves. He wasn't interested. It wasn't his fault, Beth tried to rationalize as she paused to wipe a grimy hand across her forehead. With a father like the one he had been stuck with, what could anyone expect? All he needed was a little patience, understanding...and a lot more charity than Beth was capable of feeling right now.

Her relationship with her nephew was deteriorating rapidly. For the first few days he had made an effort to placate her—it was anyone's guess why—but now he no longer made any effort to disguise his drinking, smoking, and other disagreeble habits from her. He kept his own hours and drove that monstrosity of a sports car with a suicidal mania that made Beth cringe and hold her breath every time he peeled out of the driveway. Why the police hadn't caught up with him yet she had no idea—he must have a guardian angel somewhere—but that was her biggest fear. One probationary offense and he would go straight to jail and she would have failed her sister and her nephew and, in some yet undefinable way, herself. Reasoning with him did no good. Threatening him was even less effective. He rarely acknowledged her presence except to leer or make some very suggestive remark, and that particular habit disturbed her more than she liked to admit. He looked at her in a way that constantly made her want to fold her arms across her breasts or button her shirt to the neck—further, if possible—and she even became uneasy about having no lock on her bedroom door. It was something she could not discuss with Steve, or even her father, but it was the most intimidating aspect about her relationship with Jerry. Was it her imagination, or did her sixteen-year-old nephew have sexual designs on her?

Watching him work so intently now beneath the

hood of his car, she thought without much conviction that anyone possessed of such industry, such single-minded devotion for an inanimate object surely must have some redeeming value. And then she straightened up a little, squinting curiously into the slanting late afternoon rays of the sun, as another vehicle came into sight, cruising slowly down the street, then pulled to a stop at the curb in front of her house.

It was the strangest car Beth had ever seen. In fact, it was positively weird. It was painted a dull silver gray, and seemed to be built in one smooth piece, without a seam or a protrusion. It was snub-nosed and sleek, like a bullet, so low to the ground it glided rather than rolled. It was futuristic and other-worldly, like something straight off the set of *Star Wars*, and Beth gasped as it seemed to sprout wings right before her eyes. Of course it was not a wing, merely a door that opened up rather than out, but another gasp was wrung from her as an unforgettable figure unfolded himself gracefully from the cockpit and climbed onto the sidewalk. In fact, she could not have been more stunned if Luke Skywalker himself, complete with light saber, had materialized before her eyes. It might even have been more rational.

Three days after he had left her, presumably for good, Corey Fletcher had called. Her heart began to thunder so loudly she could hardly hold the phone as soon as she recognized the voice, and all she could stammer was, "I—I thought you were in Europe!"

"Funny thing," he replied cheerfully, in a voice that sounded just the slightest bit hoarse. "I got as far as New York, and then came down with the worst coid."

She giggled in spite of herself, sinking to the bed before her legs gave up their valiant effort to continue to support her. "Don't say I never gave you anything."

There was an interruption, loud music and voices, and Corey yelled, "Close the damn door, will you? I'm on the phone." He was back with her. "Sorry, princess. There's a party in the next room. Some people have no consideration."

"Why don't you call the management?" she suggested easily, just as if long-distance telephone calls from men like Corey Fletcher were something that happened to her every day.

"Can't," he responded. "The party's mine. As a matter of fact, that's what I called you about. Would you like to come?"

Her eyes flew open wide. "To New York?"

"I'll send a jet. You can be here in three hours."

She frowned suspiciously. "Are you drunk?"

"Not very" was the bright reply. "What d'you say? Will you come?"

"No, thanks."

"Okay," he agreed. "Will you marry me, then?"

She tried very hard not to smile. "Sorry, I don't marry drunken playboys with pierced ears and private jets."

"You're not very much fun after midnight are you?"

The smile broke through. She should have been furious. How was it that he could make her smile at twelve thirty in the morning, dead drunk, and over eight hundred miles of telephone wire? "Good night, Fletcher," she said firmly.

"I'll be seeing you, princess."

But of course he wouldn't. He would not even remember the call in the morning. So what was he doing standing on her front walk, running his hand casually over the high gloss of the Trans Am, turning to greet her nephew?

Beth was aware that her hand had crept to her throat as though to prevent what little breath she had left from escaping. And she simply stared.

She had thought about him a lot during those first

two weeks, justifying defensively that it was only natural. It wasn't every day of a woman's life, after all, that she was kissed by a superstar, invited to Europe, New York, and received a marriage proposal from said superstar, all within a one-week period. What she decided, after much cool and rational thought, was that she really did not like him very much. He was high-handed, conceited, very full of himself, and he had an awful lot of nerve. He came on much too strong. Beneath all the tinsel and glitter there was only more tinsel and glitter, a man whose soul was composed entirely of one-line come-ons and single-dimensional sensual appetites. Oh, it had been an experience meeting him, an exciting experience, even, but she considered herself well out of it.

That, of course, did not explain why the mere sight of him ten yards away set her ears to roaring and her face to tingling, why her normally excellent muscle tone had been reduced to that of a bed-ridden invalid and why she was having such extraordinary difficulty catching her breath.

The phone rang, and it was the magic chime that broke the mesmerist's spell. She rushed to answer it. It was just shock, that was all, surprise at seeing him again, at seeing him at all.... What was he doing here?

The screen door banged loudly behind her as she snatched the phone off the hook. She had been intending to replace that broken spring for two years, but there never seemed to be time.

"Beth," said Ellie breathlessly, "you'll never guess who was just by the store, not in a million years, you'll never guess."

Beth turned slowly to face the window, swallowing hard. "I know," she answered with difficulty. "He just got out of a space capsule and is walking up my driveway."

Chapter Five

In ten rather frantic seconds, Beth looked down at her stained jeans and rumpled workshirt, tried to scratch the paint off her hands with a fingernail, touched the unattractive cotton scarf protecting her hair, resigned herself to her appearance, and went rather haltingly to the screen door. Corey Fletcher smiled at her.

"H-hello," she said rather weakly. "What are you doing here?"

He lifted an eyebrow. "If you let me come in, I might tell you."

She was aware of Jerry's curious gaze from farther down the driveway, and her hand fumbled with the latch. "Oh sure. I mean, I guess you may as well." The door swung open and he stepped inside.

He was wearing a tan doeskin shirt that was molded to his body like a second skin and a pair of shiny brown pants that had the same effect. Rawhide laces criss-crossed over patches of golden chest, and a small silver medallion nestled into the hollow of his throat. The soft blond hair was streaked with champagne-gold and his eyes today were a misty mixture of blue-greens, sea-watching eyes, lazy and undulantly changeable. He lounged before her with supple, loose-limbed grace, every inch of him radiating wealth, confidence, and success. He no more belonged in her haphazardly furnished little living room—which was more haphazard than usual, now that Jerry had made his daily trip from front door to back—than did a Bengal tiger straight from the wilds of India.

He withstood her scrutiny with unembarrassed patience, as he always did, as though he were aware of the effect he had on her every time they met and had grown accustomed to it. When at last she jerked her eyes away somewhat uneasily, he simply commented, "Nice kid I met outside. Is he yours?"

She stared. "Jerry? Nice kid?" She did a double-take out the window, convinced they must be talking about two different people.

There was a very small dimple near the left corner of his mouth when he smiled. She had the feeling he could make it appear and disappear at will, depending on exactly how devastatingly disarming he chose to be. It made her uneasy, and she refused to look at it. "Not giving you trouble, is he?"

"Jerry?" She shrugged. "For a kid who apparently made up his mind at age thirteen to pursue a life of crime, I suppose he's not too bad. He belongs to my sister," she informed him. "He's only mine until the end of the summer. What are you doing here?"

The abrupt change of subject seemed to amuse him. There was nothing she could do about it as his hand came up slowly and his forefinger lightly traced the path of her jaw. She had not realized until then how close they were standing. "I don't suppose you would believe me if I said I came down just to see you?"

She shook her head firmly.

His fingers moved downward and around to gently caress the back of her neck. "All right then; I was out testing the new car. What do you think of it?"

She glanced out the window, and then, with some trepidation, back to him. "Did you design it?"

Warm fingers traced the ridges of spinal column at the back of her neck, gently molding the flesh. It was a deliciously relaxing sensation. "No, one of my engineers did. Like it?"

Yes, she thought, automatically sinking into the luxury of the soft kneading motions of his hand against her neck, Oh, yes. Then she realized he meant the car and she stiffened melting muscles to look at him. "I think it's the ugliest thing I've ever seen in my life," she informed him flatly.

He laughed softly, and his forefinger tickled her earlobe. What a disturbing sensation that was. Why was she standing here in broad daylight with all her senses about her letting him take liberties with her body this way? "It wasn't built for beauty, princess, but for power and, believe it or not, economy. It's the sports car of the future."

"That I gathered." She tried to move away from his touch, but succeeded only in moving his hand so that it gently swept off the scarf that covered her hair. A slow, enigmatically amused light reflected in his eyes and made her feel as though she had just been stripped naked.

"It's good to see you again, by the way," he said softly.

Beth swallowed hard, vainly attempting to free herself from the luxurious, sensual sensations creeping down her spine from the magic of his touch. Was this an integral part of his renowned charm, then, to make any room look like a bedroom the moment he walked into it? But she refused to let him know how effective his technique was on her, and she met his eyes evenly. "I'm really surprised you remembered me at all," she said negligently.

Blue sparks danced in his eyes as he laughed. "A man doesn't forget a woman who tries to kill him twice in one day, or who takes him to bed and then falls asleep while he's kissing her." Color sprang to her cheeks and she lost the battle to maintain eye contact.

"You are many things, princess," he assured her soberly, but she knew he was still laughing with his eyes, "but forgettable is not one of them."

"Well." Her voice sounded thin. "That's reassuring, I suppose."

Corey looked at her intently. "Do I make you nervous?"

Nervous was hardly the word. "No, of course not," she lied brightly, but something in her eyes made him frown. She turned her head quickly away, trying both to escape the light pressure of his hand against her collarbone and to discover some fresh, innocuous topic of conversation. Her eyes fell on a length of smooth brown wrist sprinkled lightly with pale blond hairs; she said the first thing that came to her mind. "Where's your fancy watch?"

In only a moment the slight murkiness that troubled his features disappeared. "I got the impression it offended you," he told her, "so I took it off."

She stared at him. "Why should it offend me?"

"That," he replied with a quirk of the brow, "I have yet to figure out." Both his hands slid to her waist and rested there firmly. She had never been fully aware of how sensitive the flesh around a woman's waist could be until now. "Now, pretty princess," he announced, "I'm in town for the rest of the weekend; how do you want to celebrate?"

She blinked. The weekend! Celebrate the entire weekend! Warning bells began to go off.

"I suggest," he continued, taking matters in hand with his usual masterful lack of indecision, "that you change your clothes and let me feed you. Your choice of restaurants, of course. After that—"

"N-no." In a second, it all flashed through her head. She, Elizabeth Greene, going out on the town with Corey Fletcher. Where would they go, what would she wear, what would her father say, or, for that matter, what would everyone say when they saw their plain little Beth hanging on to the arm of an international celebrity? Did photographers follow him around like a courtly entourage? They must, otherwise why was his picture everywhere she turned? No, it did not sound like Elizabeth Greene's scene at all. Not at all. She cast a frantic eye toward the side porch. "I—I have to paint my chairs."

"All right, then," he agreed equitably, "we'll paint chairs."

She looked at him, wide-eyed, and in that moment she really believed he would. She really believed he would sit down amidst the newspapers and cans of red paint cluttering her porch in his doeskin shirt and sharkskin breeches and spend the evening painting her kitchen chairs. The picture almost made her giggle. She lowered her eyes and took a firm grasp on his hands while she still had the courage, moving them away from her waist. "Corey—"

"Oh-oh." His voice was soft. "You're not about to turn me down, are you?"

She faced him evenly. "That's exactly what I'm about to do." It was much easier, now that he was no longer touching her. Now she could remember who she was and who he was and this was really absurd.

There was a speculative gleam in his eye, but it did not intimidate her—or at least, not much. "I'm not used to being turned down, Elizabeth Greene," he warned mildly.

A flash of anger sparked in her eyes. "I'll just bet you're not."

And then, disconcertingly, he smiled. His hand moved again to touch her face and his eyes rested determinedly on her lips. *Oh, no*, she thought. *Wake up, Elizabeth. What happened to your survival instinct?* But the touch of his fingers on her cheek made her shiver and when his finger brushed the corner of her lips they parted without volition. A hurricane could have blown the house to matchsticks around them and she still would have been rooted to the spot.

The banging of the screen door announced Jerry's entrance, and, although Beth was convinced Corey Fletcher could have cared less what the teen-ager saw or thought, it was to his credit that he moved away. A rush of hot, quivery relief—or was it disappointment?—coursed through her, and she folded her arms across her chest, taking an automative defensive step backward, which, of course, was what she should have done in the first place. She was great with the hindsight.

Jerry sailed through the room, tossing an oil-stained rag on the sofa as he passed. "Jerry," she began her programmed speech, "will you please put that filthy thing in the outside trash where it belongs?"

Jerry caught himself against the door leading to the hall, and glanced at Corey with a nasty little wink. "Cute little piece ain't she? Mouthy, though." And he swung out toward the bathroom, leaving a greasy handprint smeared across the doorframe.

Corey frowned and glanced at Beth. "Does that sort of thing happen often?"

Beth knew he wasn't referring to the grease smear, the oil rag, or the bathroom towels, which would never be usable again once Jerry finished with them. So she turned away, pretending to straighten a fold of drapery, and answered, "Is once every ten or twelve minutes often?"

"Does it bother you?"

She shrugged, still unable to look at him. The light note she tried to force into her tone sounded a little shaky. "Sticks and stones may break my bones.... He's just a kid."

Beth bent quickly to pick up the oil rag and was aware of Corey's silent, watchful gaze following her as she went to dispose of it in the kitchen. When she returned, Jerry was there, drying his hands on a once-white towel, which he irreverently tossed into a corner when he was finished. He plopped into a chair, swung his legs over the back and demanded of Corey, "Say, man, when're you gonna let me drive that mean-looking mother of yours?"

Jerry was impressed by no one, awed by nothing. It was obvious by the hard gleam of challenge in his eyes that he did, indeed, know whom he was addressing, that he knew who Corey Fletcher was and what he represented, but perhaps it was his method of showing respect to show no respect at all. Beth held her breath and waited for the explosion.

Corey glanced at Beth, briefly, but there was absolutely no change of expression on his face. He reached into his pocket and took out a set of keys, holding them loosely between his thumb and forefinger before him. He said mildly, "How about right now?"

Jerry's eyes narrowed suspiciously; it seemed to Beth he sat up a little straighter. "I'm going to need some wheels, though," Corey continued easily. "How about us just switching keys?"

Beth could not believe what she was hearing. She opened her mouth to protest, but in a glance that was so swift and sharp it was almost indiscernible, Corey silenced her. She was aware, as Jerry got slowly to his feet and eyed with wariness on his face and tension bunching in his muscles the tempting set of car keys, that something very exclusive was going on between the two men—a testing and a challenge, a cautious trying of unfamiliar ground. It was a scene in which she played no part, and it fascinated and confused her.

Then Jerry reached forward slowly and took the keys. The look in his eyes as he met Corey's was like that of a male animal prepared to fight for his territory but preferring to accept a truce. And then, beneath Corey's steady, unwavering gaze, he reached into the pocket of his grimy jeans and dug out his own keys.

Jerry left without another word, and Corey turned to Beth, smiling. "See what happens when you turn me down? I find someone else to play with."

Beth took a breath to reply, but he was already leaving, calling after Jerry, "Say, do you know any good places to eat around here?"

Beth simply sank to the sofa, feeling as though she had been caught up in a whirlwind, whipped about a few dozen times, and deposited in her original place none too gently. She always felt that way whenever Corey Fletcher left her.

Beth tried to finish up her painting, but her eyes and ears were constantly straining for some sign of their return. Obviously the fact that they had exchanged keys indicated neither one of them intended to make a simple cruise around the block and it could well be hours, or more, before they returned. That made her furious. What was Corey thinking of, giving a sixteen-year-old hot-rodder the keys to a very expensive hot-off-the-assembly line experimental sports car? He may as well have given Jerry the combination to the vault of the People's Bank and told him to help himself. And by taking Jerry's car he had virtually given the boy permission to stay out as long as he liked, to do whatever he pleased with his new set of wheels. Did Corey have any idea what a dangerous thing he had done? Did he care? If the car came back in one piece it would be a miracle; if Jerry came back at all Beth would be greatly surprised.

By the time Jerry pulled into the driveway at nine thirty Beth's nerves were as mangled and shredded as a skein of yarn after a bout with a playful kitten. It was all she could do to keep herself from flinging herself on her nephew in hysterical relief and gratitude. She was terrified to look at the car, she did not dare reveal to her cynical charge how worried she had been, so she simply took a deep breath and inquired as negligently as she could, "How did it handle?"

Jerry replied offhandedly, "Smooth machine," tossed the keys onto the coffee table, flung himself into a chair, and turned the television on full blast.

It was another couple of moments before Beth could register surprise at the fact that he was home early. Jerry had not been in at nine thirty in the entire two weeks he had lived with her. What was this? Had the boy been given the keys to the candy store and made himself sick on the merchandise? Or was she seeing something in him she would have never, ever suspected existed, something suspiciously like—she almost cringed at the word—responsibility?

In the ensuing hours she vacillated between mounting amusement and churning rage. Jerry tried to keep his cool, tried very hard, in fact, but eventually even Beth began to realize that only half of his attention was focused on the blasting television, the other half was alert for signs of the return of his own car. By eleven o'clock he was no longer content to sit before the flickering screen and cast a glance of carefully disguised anxiety toward the door every now and then; he began getting up and looking out the window every ten minutes, finally taking a permanent post there with his eyes fixed searchingly on the empty street.

Beth felt a pang of sympathy for him, tempered quickly by amusement and followed almost immediately by anger. Jerry had entrusted his only child to the hands of a stranger and they were late getting home; she knew the feeling. And then there was the anger. What in the world was Corey Fletcher trying to pull? And how dare he! She was at a loss to explain the rationale behind it, but this entire situation smacked of some sort of nasty trick. He had no right to sail into their lives with his high-handed methods and plummet them into this kind of turmoil. Although Jerry would commit hara-kiri before admitting it, he was worried sick. At the very least, the brilliant path Corey Fletcher's appearance had cut across the day had ruined their evening; at most, he might have well destroyed Jerry's trust in the adult population forever. How dare he! And where was he?

Nervous exhaustion forced Beth to bed at twelve thirty, and her heart went out to the lone figure maintaining his vigil at the window, suddenly more of a little boy than an arrogant young man. She did not know what time he finally gave up and went to bed, but when last she looked at the clock it was two thirty and the television was still on.

Beth was up, dressed, and making coffee when Corey tapped on the screen door at nine o'clock the next morning. She glared at the lanky figure casually encased in white denim and blue chambray for a full ten seconds before crossing the kitchen to unlatch the door; he entered at an easy, relaxed gait and placed the keys to Jerry's car on the kitchen table. "Good morning, princess," he smiled.

Something happened to her scowl beneath the gentle coaxing of his smile; she fought determinedly to regain it. "Just what do you think you're doing?" she demanded.

"Returning a borrowed car," he answered, turning toward her with a lazy light in his eyes, "hoping to bum a little breakfast, and about to kiss a beautiful lady."

Real panic assailed her and she turned quickly out of his reach. "Oh, no, you don't!" Busily she opened the café curtains over the window and added, her cheeks hot, "And you can forget about breakfast too. I'm all out of ice cream."

She could feel him very close beside her, and she half stiffened, half melted in anticipation of his touch. But all he did was reach casually around her to take a

mug from the stand on the counter, his arm brushing
her shoulder with just the lightest feathery touch as he
did. She thought it was deliberate, and she tried not to
shiver.

He did not speak until he had helped himself to a cup
of coffee and crossed back to the table, where his hand
paused above a freshly painted chair. "Are these dry?"
he inquired.

A malicious instinct urged Beth to tell him that they
were. At that moment nothing would have given her
more satisfaction than to see Corey Fletcher with red
paint smeared all over the back of his designer jeans
and fifty-dollar shirt. But he caught her expression just
in time, acknowledged her near one-upmanship with a
gleam in his eye, and elected to sit on the counter instead. She tried not to notice the way the muscles of his
thighs strained against the denim, almost at eye level,
as he lounged upon the counter, sipping his coffee as
though he had every right in the world to be sitting in
her kitchen at nine o'clock in the morning doing so. To
distract herself, she turned on him with that never-
failing resource: anger. "Do you mind explaining yourself?" she demanded. "Just what were you thinking of,
giving a sixteen-year-old road maniac the keys to your
car? Are you crazy? Do you have any idea what might
have happened? Did you think at all?"

Corey regarded her mildly over the rim of his cup.
"Well," he answered thoughtfully, "since the car tops
out at one fifty-five and I was pretty sure Jerry
wouldn't be able to resist ascertaining that fact for
himself, I had a few ideas about what could have happened—ranging from his blowing the engine to wrapping a half-million dollar piece of equipment around a
telephone pole or sailing it off the end of a pier. Yes, I
thought about it."

She felt weak. One fifty-five! Only now did she know
how worried she should have been. "Did you—did you

look at your car this morning?" she managed, for she had not yet gained the courage to do so.

"Not a scratch on it," he assured her. "Were you worried?"

She gaped at him. "Weren't you?"

He sipped complacently from his mug, watching her. "No need. The kid has as much respect for a fine piece of machinery as anyone I've ever met, and he would no more have totaled out that car than I would."

"Hah! You've got a few things to learn about my nephew, Mr. Hotshot. He would have done it just for kicks."

Corey slowly shook his head. "Nope. There's a sort of code among car lovers, you know, and there are certain things you just don't do."

"Honor among thieves?" she suggested dryly.

He grinned slowly. "Something like that. I'll tell you something, princess, that's a pretty talented kid in there and you shouldn't underestimate him. Did you know he supercharged that engine all by himself? I checked it out; it's a damn good job. As a matter of fact, everything he's done to that car is first rate. I wouldn't be surprised if he didn't have the makings of a brilliant career on his hands, all he needs is a little self-discipline."

Beth eyed him speculatively, her arms crossed over her stomach, her head tilted slightly. "Is that what your little game last night was all about? Some kind of new twist on child psychology?"

He grinned and slid down from the counter. "That's enough of the saga of Jerry Fields. What I really want to know is what you and I are going to do with the rest of the day."

"I am going to work," she informed him airily. "You can do whatever you like." She glanced at him darkly. "Just take your own car."

There was laughter deep in the golden-green eyes as

he approached her. She knew she was lost when his hands rested on her shoulders. "Your very efficient assistant can manage without you for one day, I'll venture to say. And as a member of the business community, you owe it to the commerce bureau to keep a lonely tourist happy. We'll go sight-seeing—is that innocent enough for you?"

What was it with this man? Had he made it his quest to tempt, torture, harass, and otherwise make the life of one Elizabeth Greene miserable? Hadn't she made her position clear when last they met? What was he pursuing? "What do I have to do to get rid of you?" she demanded.

"Spend the day with me" was his immediate answer.

On the other hand, it occurred to her as his thumbs began a sensuous massaging motion against her collarbone, what was one day? A little innocent sight-seeing.... She grappled for her reason. "I—I can't just go off and leave Jerry." That was good, and true enough. After last night he might just take off and never be heard from again.

"How much trouble can he get into around here?" insisted Corey.

Beth's laugh was sharp and strained. "If only you knew! Besides, it's not around here that I'm worried about. It's what he might do when he leaves the premises that gives me nightmares."

"On that score," replied Corey, slipping his arm around her shoulders, "I can reassure you." His eyes twinkled soberly as he led her toward the door. "Jerry won't be going anywhere today. I left his car on empty."

She stared up at him and, against her best efforts, laughter broke through. "Corey Fletcher," she decided, eyes dancing, "you have one incredible nerve."

"It's a trademark," he agreed modestly, but as he began to lead her toward the silver car, she stopped.

"Just one thing," she said, eyeing the space capsule warily. "If we're actually going to be driving around town, do you think we could go in my car? Yours is so—"

"Ugly?" he supplied, deadpan.

She dimpled with the effort to remain in command. "I was going to say conspicuous." Beth went inside and dialed Ellie's number to arrange to have the other woman attend to the store for the day.

Corey hesitated before her dented and rust-stained little Volkswagen, and she thought, vaguely and very briefly, that this was where he would draw the line. A man like Corey Fletcher would surely die before being seen behind the wheel of such a limping, bedraggled vehicle. But then he simply opened the door for her and pronounced generously, "The princess wants to go incognito, we'll go incognito. You do, of course," he queried her meaningfully, "intend to let me drive?"

She could not prevent a smile of resignation as she handed him the keys. "You have to coax her up the hills," she warned, "and first gear grinds, but don't let that bother you. You have to jiggle the key a little to get it started, and keep your foot on the accelerator when you stop." She felt very powerful, giving Corey Fletcher advice on driving. "The clutch slips, and you have to pump the brakes."

He glanced at her dryly as he slid into the cramped space behind the wheel. "A car with personality?"

She smiled in satisfaction. "Yes."

He slipped the key into the ignition, jiggling it as she had told him. "I think," he pronounced to the dashboard of the car, "that we are going to be great friends." She wasn't certain whether he meant the two of them, or himself and the car. The question made her heart speed a little.

Very official in her capacity as a tour guide, she directed him to all the prominent spots of Virginia Beach.

He listened with a pretense of polite attentiveness as she gave him the formal lectures of the history of the Cape Henry Cross, which marked the first ground touched by the Jamestown colonists, and patiently climbed the stairs of the old lighthouse with her, though the day was overcast and the wind chilly. There, however, with the glassy gray sea stretching endlessly before her and the wind biting through her cotton blouse, she dropped her formal lecturer's tone. Like most natives of any city or town, she did not visit the tourist spots very often. Steve had brought her here once just before high school graduation, and she had always promised herself she would come back. They hadn't climbed the lighthouse that bright, warm summer day, but strolled along the beach, holding hands, talking about college. They had both been a little frightened of the new lives that lay ahead of them, both already missing each other, yet too excited by the unfolding adventure of adulthood to give it much thought. Other girls in their class had been rushing into marriage, other boys rushing into the Navy, and Beth remembered thinking on that day how nice it would be to have a lover to whom she would be saying a tearful good-bye or with whom she would be making ecstatic wedding plans—it didn't matter which one, for this place had been made for dramatic scenes. But of course her relationship with Steve did not lend itself to such flashes of drama. They had walked along the shore that day missing the days of their carefree youth, remembering the time he had given her a bunch of daisies at age eleven and how they had made pledges of undying love at age six, knowing that in the years ahead there would be other boys for her and other girls for him yet feeling no jealousy—knowing, even then, that in the end it would be the two of them together again. All part of a well-ordered plan, secure, predictable, perfectly pleasing to both of them.

She stood at the top of the tower and looked out over the sea and the past and the future seemed to roll together like the unfolding tide. Misty shadows of barely moving ships blended in to the horizon and she imagined all the places those ships had been—China, Italy, Spain, Gibraltar, the Bering Strait. She imagined other ships from other times, bringing home their cargoes of exotic goods, weary passengers, noblemen and renegades. Days like this were made for flights of fancy.

As though reading her thoughts, Corey said, "On a clear day you can see forever, but on days like this I think you can see even more."

He was standing with his arm around her shoulders, and she was grateful for the warmth. Corey did not seem to be able to be near her without touching her, and at first it had annoyed and alarmed her. Then she began to realize that it was something he did automatically, without thought or real meaning, he was simply one of those very touchy people. What Beth did not understand was why she had been fighting the urge all day to reciprocate—to slip her arm around his waist or entwine her fingers through his or to brush away the hair from his eyes or touch the corner of his mouth when he smiled. Beth was not a demonstrative person, as he was; a touch or a gesture was not elicited from her unless there was genuine emotion behind it—except in the presence of Corey Fletcher. With him it seemed the most natural thing in the world to let her body say things she was far from feeling or meaning, and that was a rather disturbing discovery to make about herself.

She glanced at him, her eyes for a moment entranced by the way the wind whipped his straight hair about his head and molded his shirt to the muscles of his arm and his flat stomach. His shaded eyes were narrowed against the reflection of infrared rays on the dull sea, giving them a dreamy, faraway look. She inquired, "Like what?"

"Oh, memories and daydreams, pirate ships and golden shores, sea serpents and treasure chests." He smiled down at her. "What do you see?"

She leaned her head back into the hollow of his shoulder, and the tangy wind played with her hair like an ardent lover. "Indians fishing on the shore," she answered immediately, "shaggy beasts roaming the forest. White sails of a clipper ship and a boy in stockings and knee-breeches with a telescope looking toward shore."

"Looking at us," supplied Corey.

"Yes, looking for the lighthouse to guide them home."

"And a storm is building offshore, the sea is swelling, and the wind is cracking the sail."

"Lightning flashes and foam splashes over the deck." A sudden blast of wind added authenticity to their story, and she shivered.

Corey moved behind her, blocking the wind as he wrapped both arms around her waist, the warmth of his pelvis cradling her buttocks and his chin resting on her shoulders. Automatically her hands moved to rest over his wrists, protecting the warmth of his arms against her stomach and his strong length against her back. "Thunder cracks, and sailors slip and slide across the pitching deck, shouting orders."

"That boy," advised Beth soberly, "had better get down out of the crow's nest, before lightning strikes the mast."

He laughed, low and throatily against her ear. It was as though her eardrum had magnified the vibration of his laugh and sent the impulses scurrying down every nerve path in her body, a sensation very much like placing one's hand against an amplifier with the volume on maximum. Daydreams receded into a tingling awareness of the here and now. "Do you think they'll make it?"

She twisted her head to look at him, her eyes wide with the uncertain return to reality and her lips parted somewhat breathlessly. "Who?"

Gentle laughter faded from his eyes and it seemed to be an instinctual movement that turned his face to close the fraction of an inch of distance between their lips. Her heart gave one magnificent lurch of alarm, and his lips had barely brushed hers before she turned her face away, releasing herself from the gentle imprisonment of his arms in the same moment, and she called brightly, "I'll race you down!"

Tripping and leaping over the tall sea grass, gasping and laughing into the wind, she reached the parking lot one step ahead of him. He caught her around the waist, in the same motion lifting her a few inches off the ground, and declared, "I let you win, you know."

"I know!" she gasped, struggling to regain her footing and pressing a painful stitch in her side. His eyes were dancing like sparks of sunlight on golden sea spray and he was barely winded. "But it's not very chivalrous of you to tell me so!"

"Chivalry is not my long suit," he retorted, catching her hands, "which you no doubt would have discovered before too much longer anyway." His hands tightened their grip and he began to pull her slowly toward him, the sensuously shaded eyes moving once again inexorably toward her lips.

The new leaping and pounding of her heart, in addition to the rigors of the unaccustomed exercise, was unbearably painful. She pulled her hands away quickly and started for the car. "I'm hungry."

He drove back toward the beach, and, although she knew it was ridiculous, she had to quell a small sense of disappointment that their time together was over. She should have been relieved, for she still had not figured out why he had come back or why he had insisted upon spending the day with her, and Beth did not like questions without obvious answers. She would be well rid of the mystery of Corey Fletcher.

But, rather than turning the car toward her house, he drove to the beach and parked near the boardwalk where they had gone that first night together. She swallowed hard and glanced at him suspiciously, wondering if there was a significance to his bringing her here. But he simply said, taking her hand to help her out of the car, "You said you were hungry, and I smell hot dogs. Shall we?"

Only a few of the boardwalk attractions were open before Memorial day, among them a couple of greasy fast-food shacks and the arcade. Still, the boardwalk today was quite different from the way it had been that night. The sun tried vainly to illuminate the slate sky and the water was murky and heavy. A few tourists from the nearby hotels strolled along the shore or chatted at the railing of the boardwalk, glancing at the sky and complaining about the weather. No, there was nothing exciting or romantic about this atmosphere, and Beth began to relax a little.

She could not believe he was serious about the hot dogs, and she grabbed his arm as he approached a vendor. "Are you crazy?" she whispered, for it was something that had been ingrained into her by an overly cautious father since childhood. "Never buy food at these places. Do you want to get food poisoning?"

His eyes twinkled at her. "Come on, princess, where's your spirit of adventure? Don't you ever take chances?" He turned back to the vendor. "Two with everything."

Taking chances was something Beth rarely did, but of course with him it was a way of life. She shrugged philosophically as he handed her a hot dog, figuring that any man who ate butter pecan ice cream for breakfast must have a cast iron stomach and she could do as well as he could. They strolled toward the arcade, eating their lunch and holding hands, listening to the sound of the surf, the occasional snatches of conversation about them, the music, and the explosion of pop guns from the arcade. Once there, Corey handed her the remainder of his hot dog—which she discreetly deposited in the trashcan, along with most of hers—and demonstrated his skill at Space Invaders. And skill was a mild word. He played the game with an intense, unshakable concentration, eyes flickering across the screen with lightning rapidity and the swift, perfectly timed motions of his fingers and hands in perfect coordination. She could very well imagine that same expression on his face as he came down the straightaway on the final lap, every ounce of psychic and physical energy focused on one goal, one purpose—winning.

It was an awesome thing to watch, this fierce warrior's battle with mental discipline and physical coordination, and Beth fell back a little, feeling excluded and a little uncomfortable. It was not long before a crowd began to gather, murmuring first over his skill and then, after a time, speculating on his identity. Corey's concentration was not broken. He and the machine were in a world of their own—mortal enemies—and he was winning.

Beth was embarrassed. She wasn't certain why, except that the more his name was whispered about, the more uneasy she became. Corey Fletcher was used to drawing a crowd, to being the center of attention and making a spectacle of himself—in fact, he thrived on it—but Beth was not. She began to edge unobstrusively away, starting for the exit. At that moment, oddly, he looked up. It was as though a part of his attention all along had been directed at her, so that he was aware immediately when she made that small move to leave. He forfeited the game, but even so, the high score drew enthusiastic applause from the crowd. Corey grinned at them generously and started for Beth, then some brave soul approached him with the question, "Aren't you Corey Fletcher?"

Murmurs of agreement and curiosity rippled through the arcade above the sound of pinging bells and rattling machine guns. Corey glanced at Beth, then back to the young man who had addressed him. "Who?" he said blankly.

"I guess I was showing off," he apologized when they were outside. "I didn't mean to embarrass you."

"Embarrass me?" she returned lightly, walking very fast. "Goodness no, I was impressed! If you drive a car as well as you do a spaceship, you must be some terror on the roadway."

He hesitated for just a moment, then smiled. "I'm glad you were impressed. It's a lot easier than turning cartwheels on your front lawn or riding my bike past your window with no hands."

In spite of herself, she laughed.

They walked down the steps to the beach, and Beth kicked off her sandals and cuffed up her jeans to go wading. Corey sat on the sand to unlace his own shoes, the same battered and faded Nikes he had worn that first day. She shivered at the memory.

Immediately in tune with her, he glanced up. "What are you looking at?"

"Oh." She swallowed hard and tried to disguise her train of thoughts. "I was just thinking you look like the kind of man who could afford a new pair of shoes every once in a while."

"I'll have you know," he retorted, stripping off his socks, "these are my lucky shoes. They're irreplaceable."

"Sure," she returned dryly. "Everytime you wear them you get mowed down by a woman in a Volkswagen. Who could ask for more?"

His eyes twinkled at her as he cuffed up his jeans. "Right."

As much as she tried not to, she could not help looking—and she found it, on the back of his ankle, a small pink scar. The one she had put there. "You see why I can't forget you?" he said, noticing her gaze. "You've left a permanent mark."

"I should be honored," she replied, a little weakly, "to be included among all your other trophies."

"Indeed you should," he agreed and took her hand as they walked into the surf. "Of course you realize the mark you left is much more special than any of the others."

She did not know what he meant by that, and she did not care to pursue it. "Are all your scars from racing?" she asked.

He touched the uneven ridge of his collarbone. "Indy, 1975." He showed her his forearm, where a long, thin and jagged line was etched into the tan. "Road Atlanta, 1980." He stretched forth his leg. "Monte Carlo, 1979. Shall I go on?"

She stared at him, wide-eyed. "Are you one of those people who's broken every bone in his body?"

"No, I still have a few pieces of original equipment left. I do, however, have enough hardware holding the pieces together to set off the metal detector at any airport in the country."

She laughed, although there was really nothing funny about it. She laughed simply because she knew he had meant to make her laugh, and because somehow he could make even such a maudlin subject as a flirt with death sound entertaining. She looked up at him, and, without volition, touched the tiny scar that separated his blond eyebrow. That was something she had been wanting to do all day—touch him. "And what about this one?" she inquired teasingly. "What victory does it represent?"

His eyes danced, and his hands came around to take her waist lightly. "That," he informed her, "I got when I fell out of a tree when I was eight years old."

He stood there, his hands warm upon her waist and his eyes laughing down at her, his silky brow smooth beneath her fingers, and all she could remember was the way his lips had felt upon hers, the way he had tasted and felt and smelled. Her senses responded to the memory as to the fact, with an alertness, an anticipation, a rising need. She dropped her hand and turned to walk casually beside him again.

The sucking sand tickled her feet with an oddly sensuous motion and the cold spray invigorated her bare legs. His hand was very warm over hers. "Why do you do it?" she inquired curiously, after a time. "Race, I mean."

He seemed to think about it. Then the corner of a grin played with his lips and he suggested, "Maybe because I don't want to be remembered by posterity as the guy who does those dippy deodorant commercials?"

She refused to blush. Had she actually said that to him? "And what do you want from posterity?" she demanded lightly, kicking at the wet sand.

"Easy. A bunch of little Fletchers to carry out the tradition of driving their parents insane."

She snorted with laughter. "You'll never live that long."

He stopped and took her shoulders and slowly turned her to face him. "I will live," he assured her very seriously, "as long as it takes to get what I want."

The depth of his gaze took her breath away, and she stared at him, helpless, spellbound, utterly lost in the pull of the tide against her feet and the pull of his eyes against her soul. She was convinced in that moment that he meant it, and more. This was the man who had the power over death; what chance did Elizabeth Greene stand?

The moment prolonged between them, becoming entirely too intense. It took all of her willpower to break it and to start walking again. This time he did not take her hand, but rested his hand lightly atop her shoulder instead. "I think you have a death wish," she said abruptly.

He was silent for so long that it surprised her. When she ventured a glance at him, his face was very thoughtful. "Maybe you're right," he admitted after a time. "Maybe it's a way of looking for attention—love— I've never had in my life. Maybe I'm trying to prove to the world, or myself, that I'm worth something." He took a breath, and she stopped, fascinated. He didn't look at her as he spoke. "I guess I'm the classic example of the poor little rich kid. My father was always so busy running his empire I sometimes think he forgot he had a son. When I was little and would try to sit on his lap, he would give me a ten-dollar bill and tell me to go away and stop ruining the crease in his trousers. My mother—" He shrugged uncomfortably, his eyes on the ground. "I never saw her unless she was so drunk she didn't recognize me. She didn't like kids. I was raised by a slew of nannies and governesses, but none of them ever lasted long because of Mother's drinking. They sent me away to boarding school when I was twelve and they were glad to be rid of me. I suppose I should have been glad to be away too, but I wasn't. I missed them. They wouldn't even let me go home for Christmas." Beth's heart went out to him, she wanted to hold and comfort the neglected little boy who was trying so hard not to be bitter. Then he took a breath, and his tone changed. Still he did not look at her. "But when I'm on that track," he said slowly, intensely, with a fierce pride and a barely maintained ardor for the memory, "when I feel the power of that engine surging in my hands—I know I'm *somebody*, I'm doing something no one else can do. And when I win—" His voice fell to a dreamy whisper. "When I win the crowd cheers; they love me. Then I'm important, then everyone notices me. Then I'm loved."

Her hand fluttered up to touch his cheek, her eyes brimming with sympathy. At last he looked at her, and something in his expression made her hesitate. She took a step backward. "Corey Fletcher," she demanded suspiciously, "was that another piece of fiction?"

"Darling," he laughed, "my dad is the finest man I ever knew. He never missed a Little League game and helped me build my first go-cart out of packing crates and old lawn mower parts. My mother is so perfect she ought to be bronzed. If she ever drank anything stronger than sweet sherry, I don't know about it, and I never had a governess in my life. I had a relentlessly boring, blissfully happy childhood. I've never seen a boarding school in my life and we've all spent every Christmas together for the past thirty years. I was breast-fed until I was a year old and toilet-trained by age three. I don't harbor secret hatred toward my father or unresolved sexual feelings for my mother. Shall I go on?"

"Oh!" The exclamation was choked in fury and outrage, but in truth she was not certain whether to be indignant over his ruse or impressed by his talent. This was Corey Fletcher the actor, and he could pull emotional strings a person did not even know she possessed without trying. She was furious, insulted, amazed—and a little disturbed by his ability to manipulate her so easily.

"I'm sorry, princess," he said, still laughing. "It's just that I've been psychoanalyzed by the best in the business and some of the complexes they've hung me with would make Freud turn over in his grave. They ignore the obvious answer: I live the life I do because it's fun. I like it. No other reason. Is that enough for you?"

Of course. Nothing complicated about this man. He took what he wanted because he wanted it; he did what he did because he enjoyed it; he sought pleasure wherever he could find it. What could be simpler?

She turned away, folding her arms across her chest and looking out over the sea. Simple, shallow, one-dimensional. That was Corey Fletcher. A huge billboard promising everything and delivering nothing, all theatrics and bright colors. There was nothing alarming in that. Then why did he intrigue her more every time they met?

He had stopped laughing. His hand came out to brush her cheek gently. "Are you mad at me?"

There was tenderness in his voice, and she hardened herself against it. Maybe that was why, because every time she thought she had him figured out he did something unexpectedly thoughtful or sweet or funny. She focused her eyes determinedly on the miniature etching of a ship on the distant horizon, and she said conversationally, "Did you know one of those aircraft carriers is large enough to house a small town? It seems impossible to believe, doesn't it? They look so small from this distance."

"Then that's next on the agenda," Corey said, catching her hand. "A visit to the pier."

She protested it was growing too late to drive to Norfolk, the weather was not getting any better, and she really should check on Jerry. Forty-five minutes later they were walking through a misty rain with the gray-green waters of the Elizabeth River slapping the pillars below them and gargantuan monsters of steel and iron blotting out the sky above them.

There was activity along the pier, but it was muted by the fog that swept around them, muffling voices and shadowing movement. Beth always felt a little reverent in this place, overwhelmed by the sheer size of these monuments to man's industrial ingenuity and by the vastness of the sea, which, in comparison, made even the ships seem small. But on this gray, wet day there was an added quality of loneliness, of secrecy, as though the day hid whispers of sadness and the very air about them oozed tears.

Corey said, close to her ear, "It's awesome, isn't it?"

They were standing in the shadow of a hull, looking straight upward, and still they could not see the top. "Don't tell me you've never seen a ship before." Something about the quality of the atmosphere constrained her to keep her voice low, and it had an odd, muffled, and slightly echoing sound in counterpoint to the crack and splash of water beneath their feet.

"Not at this distance," he admitted. "I travel by road or air. I had a place in San Francisco once, and we used to go to the wharf. Of course, it was nothing like this."

She turned her head to look at him. His eyes, in contemplation of the mysteries of the sea and the vessels that sought to tame it, had taken on the quality and the color of the sea itself, misty gray, murky green, vast and bottomless. Even his eyes were an illusion, she thought suddenly. Always changing, never stable, nothing real or permanent. If the eyes were the windows to the soul, what lay within the depths of Corey Fletcher? Only more illusion. . . .

She shivered, and once again he slipped his arms around her from behind, cradling her head against his shoulder, shielding her from the dampness with his warmth. She settled into the embrace easily, for the atmosphere seemed to demand it—misty secrecy, shrouded intimacy, the strength of two bodies together to ward off the uncertainties of the future. "Days like this," she said softly, holding his hands against her waist and gazing dreamily over the endless water, "remind me of good-byes. The sailor parting from his lady. Will he come back? Will she still be there when he does? What will he find on the other side of this sea? What will she find in the lonely nights while he's away? On days like this"—she drew in a breath of heavy, salty air, half closing her eyes—"you can taste the tears of all the women who have ever wept for missing their love."

He turned her slowly in the circle of his arms. There were pearls of moisture on his face and clinging to his straight hair, his eyes were very intense, as gray and as secret as the air surrounding them. "Elizabeth," he whispered, "let's not ever say good-bye."

Guarded by the shadows of the giant ship and wrapped in the caressing embrace of the fog, he kissed her. A little moan formed in her throat and when she moved to pull away, her arms instead crept around his neck. There was a quickening in his muscles as he felt her hands there, against his damp hair and the cords of his neck, as her taut breasts brushed against his chest and her stomach flattened against his. It was instinct, nothing more, nothing less. How could she help responding when his lips were turning her veins to little rivulets of fire and her limbs were melting and her hands seemed to have a mind of their own, wanting to touch him, seeking entrance beneath his collar, wanting to feel bare skin and explore hard muscles? What could she do when her head was swimming and the only thing keeping her on her feet was the hard grip of his hands against her back, except open herself to him, letting him, wanting him to...?

He moved his hand to the back of her neck, cradling it yet holding it steady, as though afraid she might break away. She gasped at the shock of his tongue darting through her parted lips and at the sudden pulse of awareness in secret regions—warm, moist, surprising, wonderfully pleasurable, opening herself to him even as she fought against him with the last of her remaining reason. Corey Fletcher was not real; she was playing with a fantasy, and he was drawing from her things she never would have given willingly. Yet her head roared and her breath thinned and the strong muscles of her thighs weakened and it was all she could do to try to turn her head.

He retreated gently, sensing the struggle she did not have the strength to form, and his tongue traced a light, burning pattern on the outside of her lips, then, with a rush of hot breath that ignited flames, to her ear. Her arms were heavy, no longer able to maintain the strained position around his neck; they slid to his biceps. She clutched at him, digging her fingers into his arms for support, arching her neck to better receive the gentle nibbling motions of his lips even as she whispered in protest, "Corey...."

He looked at her, and deep within the magnetic gray eyes was a light of passion, of wonder and contentment, urging her to follow him into the world of pleasure only he had the power to create. His hands were on her shoulders now, gently spanning her neck while his thumbs performed a light, mesmerizing massage upon the points of her collarbone. She was entranced by those eyes, when held by those eyes all she could think was yes...yes, anything...anything.

Then he bent his head to let his lips replace the working of his thumbs, moist kisses against bare flesh, and his thumbs moved lower, his hands following her curves—across the ridges and indentations of three ribs, over the material covering the swell of her breasts. There was a pinpointing pressure where aching nipples sprang to life and then she felt moist hot breath through the material of her shirt. His teeth sought and gently took fabric and flesh, rubbing but not hurting, and electric currents of new sensation shot out in all directions; she moaned out loud.

"Don't." It was hardly more than a breath as she tried to pull away. "Stop."

Slowly, he lifted his face, warm moisture brushed

her lips, then penetrated the fog of perspiration and mist that clung to her cheek. He smiled at her tenderly. "Did I hear you say don't stop?"

She turned her head away weakly, only to find herself cradled in his embrace, his lips against her temple. "Princess," he murmured soothingly, "don't be afraid of me. I'm not going to make love to you here in the cold and damp in full view of the dock workers." He moved away a little, looking down at her with a gently encouraging smile. "But I must admit, I'm beginning to get a few interesting ideas about what is possible in the backseat of a Volkswagen."

She twisted her head away, biting her lip to control a sudden unsteady quivering that seemed to be affecting every nerve of her body. *Look what he's done to you, turned you into a shivering mass of sexual jelly without even half-trying. You're supposed to be so smart, but all he has to do is push the proper button and your backbone is ready for the glue factory.* She tried to move out of his embrace, but that was a task requiring entirely too much willpower. So she simply looked up at him and requested with quiet dignity, "Let me go, please."

The smile lingered about his eyes and the corners of his lips. He knew very well that was the last thing she really wanted. He knew entirely too much. He bent to kiss her again.

At the very last moment, some deeply reserved resource of strength leaped out to save her. She pushed against him, her heart slamming against her ribs and her breath coming in little gasps. "Corey, don't...you don't understand. Just don't."

He looked at her intently. "Why? What don't I understand?"

The question caught her off guard. "It's—it's not fair," she floundered. No, what he did to her was definitely not fair, the odds were stacked against any woman who came into his reach and he knew that perfectly well. "You can't just. You have to stop doing this to me. It's too fast, too sudden, and I...." She trailed off, helpless.

He looked puzzled. "Isn't everything?" he inquired.

She looked at him and managed a deep breath. Her voice was much firmer now. "Please take me home."

The tension between them was as thick as the fog in which they walked as they went back to the car. She got inside and huddled far against the passenger door as he got behind the wheel, trying not to think what a fool she had made of herself. Why was he doing this? Corey Fletcher could have any of the world's most beautiful, glamorous women—and probably had had most of them—why did he persist in the pursuit of one small-town druggist who never bothered anybody and only wanted to be left alone? Or perhaps it wasn't a pursuit at all, maybe she was overestimating herself. It was the old if-you-can't-be-with-the-one-you-love-love-the-one-you're-with syndrome. He saw a woman and he only knew one thing to do with her. Give and take. It was what made the world go round.

He got behind the wheel and looked at her for a minute. "You don't have to fall out the door," he said. "I've decided not to rip your clothes off and commit rape after all."

She straightened up a little. "That's reassuring."

He smiled—that damned adorable, innocent, sweetly caressing smile that made everything right with an upside-down world in the space of a few seconds. "Come on," he said soberly. "A little closer. I promise I won't touch you. Just don't be mad at me."

She looked at him and was convinced in that moment that he meant it. Incredible as it seemed, Corey Fletcher really cared what she thought of him. "There's only one problem with your promises," she said in a moment. She shot him a glance beneath slanted lashes. "You lie."

He grinned as he started the engine and made no reply.

An early darkness had fallen by the time they reached her house, and lights glowed warmly from the living room windows. As she hesitated over inviting him in, she noticed Jerry's car was in the driveway, safe in its plastic shroud, and to her surprise, her father's car was at the curb.

"It's my dad," she explained, when Corey noticed with a questioning glance the extra car parked behind his.

She turned to him, planning to say a polite goodnight as he turned off the engine and the headlights, but he interrupted, "That's great. I've been wanting to meet him."

There was no way to tell him to go away as he came around to open the door for her, but this was definitely not a scene to which she was looking forward. Jerry and her father together in the same house was bad enough — and who knew how long they had been there without her presence as referee? — but what would her father think of Corey Fletcher? She opened the door with some trepidation and Corey followed her inside.

The tension in the room was thick before anyone said a word. Beth tensed herself for an unpleasant scene and was even for a moment grateful for Corey's presence close behind her as a distraction. And then she stopped on the threshold, staring, as three men looked up at her — Jerry, her father, and Steve.

Chapter Six

They regarded one another for a long moment like
wary motorists at a four-way intersection, no one quite
certain who was going to make the first move. Somehow it was not surprising that Corey should break the
silence.

He went to Beth's father with his hand extended and
greeted him pleasantly, "Dr. Greene. I've been wanting to meet you. I'm Corey Fletcher."

So, he remembered her father was a doctor. Score
one for him. Somehow it was just his style to take over
an uncertain situation with easy mastery, to walk into
her living room as though he belonged there and they
were the strangers, to approach her father with every
confidence of having already won him over—which of
course he had. Was it also part of his charm to be able
to snow even uneasily impressed and skeptical fathers
with a smile and a word? Apparently so, for her father
was responding just as pleasantly, "It's the other way
around, I'm sure—I've been wanting to meet you.
Jerry told us Bethy was probably out with you."

"Steve." Beth came over to him, stammering and
confused. "I—What are you doing here? I didn't—" But
she bit her lip before she could finish that very con-
demning sentence, utterly chagrined. She had known
he was coming down this weekend. How could she
have forgotten? They had planned it for weeks. But

Corey Fletcher sailed into town and turned everything upside down, and she had simply forgotten. She looked at Steve with mute apology in her eyes.

Steve glanced at Corey, waiting for the introductions. She made them rather clumsily. Corey shook his hand with his charm in low-idle, just as he had with her father, subduing whatever initial animosity there might have been with an easy smile. Beth felt some small and rather petty satisfaction to notice that Steve was the taller of the two men by several inches and, as normal male physiques go, the more well built. Certainly he was the more attractive by conventional standards, with his dark, wavy hair and soft brown eyes. Then why, she wondered with a sense of deflation and helplessness as she watched the two of them side by side, did Corey inevitably seem to be the more powerful?

"I was passing through town this weekend," Corey was explaining to both men in general, "and found myself at loose ends. Elizabeth was kind enough to give me a guided tour of some of the local spots of interest." Beth stared at him. In precisely thirty seconds he had transformed himself from a free-wheeling road-jockey into a polite young man carefully schooled in drawing room conversation, and every detail of the role—from his mode of speech to the way he held his shoulders—was polished. He knew exactly what Steve and Adam Greene were accustomed to meeting in Beth's friends, and that was what he gave them. It was called working an audience.

His eyes twinkled at her briefly as though catching her thoughts, but he added with every vestige of polite concern, "I hope we didn't keep you waiting too long."

"Too long for me," Jerry muttered, and Beth glanced at him. For a moment she had almost forgotten his existence, which expressed better than anything else the havoc Corey Fletcher had wreaked with her mind. He remained sprawled out in the armchair, wearing dusty denim cut-offs, no shoes, and a sleeveless gray sweat shirt that had been cropped above the midriff. He glowered at the assembled company in general, and from time to time reserved for Corey a glance that was laced with particular malice, mistrust, and just a trace of respectful caution, as though he did not know quite what to make of the episode with the car and was almost afraid to leap to any conclusions. For Beth, that attitude more than anything else signaled panic. She had been programmed to expect the worse from Jerry, and not knowing what to expect from him was enough, in the present circumstances, to send her over the edge. Her only hope for salvation obviously was to separate all of them—to somehow get Corey out the door, Jerry to his room, her father back home where he belonged, and Steve— How was she to explain all of this to Steve?

With that course of action in mind, she had no earthly idea why she suggested brightly, "Why don't we all sit down? Can I get anyone coffee or—"

"Nothing for me, love," replied Corey, and she stared at him. *Love?* He had never called her that before. What was he trying to pull? "I won't stay." But his hand was lightly, possessively, on her elbow, guiding her to a chair, and when she sat he perched upon its arm with his hand still resting against her shoulder, denying his previous statement. "Obviously we have kept your father and Steve waiting, and"—he smiled quickly and disarmingly at Steve—"I have a feeling I'm going to make an enemy if I take up too much more of your time."

Beth felt a shaft of acute disappointment that Steve was so easily taken in by Corey's phony charm. He said quickly, "Not at all. As a matter of fact, we've been having a nice talk with Jerry."

"Like hell," Jerry muttered. Beth winced at the viperous glance the young man shot Steve, and she could feel her father's tensing anger. It must have been worse than she had imagined. "They've been picking me apart like a couple of buzzards since they walked in the damn door." Jerry's language always deteriorated when he became defensive. His eyes darkened as he turned them on Beth. "You ought to be more careful about the kind of creeps you hand out your front key to. If I want to hear all about what a piece of crap I am, I can damn well do that at home. I sure as hell didn't have to travel two thousand miles to get it."

Dr. Greene was literally livid, obviously not trusting himself to speak. It was left to Steve to explain, rather wryly, "Unfortunately, we got sidetracked on the advantages of a high school education." The glance he sent Beth was rich with both apology and sympathy. He obviously felt he had failed her in being unable to soothe the obstreperous Jerry and did not envy her the twenty-four-hour task.

The sudden shrewd look that passed over Jerry's face generated a sick tightening in the pit of Beth's stomach. The young man had been outrageously abused in the past twenty-four hours—having been the victim of a tasteless lesson in responsibility by someone wearing the guise of friendship, grounded by an empty gas tank, and then forced to submit to a barrage of lectures by two men he now despised. The moment of vengeance would be sweet.

"Mechanics don't need no high school diploma to be good," he said and directed his malicious attention to Corey. "Ain't that right, Fletcher? Ain't that just what you were saying to me yesterday? You wouldn't turn down a guy who could do the job just because of a piece of paper, would you?"

The boy was truly Machiavellian. He had picked up on some innocent comment Corey had made yesterday and was now twisting it so that he would either have to admit he was a liar or antagonize the three adults he was trying to impress. Beth was ashamed of the vicious sense of amusement she felt at seeing Corey Fletcher bested at his own game.

But Corey did not seem the least bit intimidated. He regarded Jerry thoughtfully before admitting, "None of my mechanics has a high school education. And as a matter of fact"—he swept a glance from Dr. Greene to Steve—"Jerry's got a point. He's a talented kid and I would hire him today if he could do the job."

Beth was aghast and she saw indignation and disapproval register simultaneously on both her father's and Steve's faces. It ceased to be funny when Corey's offhand techniques could sabotage a summer's hard work of trying to convince Jerry to return to school and could possibly ruin his whole life. She glared at Corey as Jerry chortled with satisfaction and declared, "You got yourself a deal, man! When do I start?" Whatever doubts had lingered in Jerry's mind were erased, and Corey had made a friend. But at what cost?

"Soon as you prove you can do the job," replied Corey mildly. With easy grace, he leaned across Beth to scribble something on the telephone pad near her. Beth pressed herself back into the chair to keep his arm from brushing across her breasts, for even in this high-voltage situation he emanated sexual awareness that must surely flash like a beacon across the room. She felt her cheeks burning.

But he was totally nonchalant as he passed the pad to Jerry and straightened up. Beth watched as Jerry's expression turned from puzzled to stormy, and he demanded, "What the hell is this?"

"A simple calculus problem," replied Corey. "We use it all the time to measure air-flow dynamics."

Jerry glared at him. "What's this got to do with a high school diploma?"

"All of my men have college diplomas," answered

Corey mildly. "Plus masters and doctorates in engineering and design. It's a buyer's market, old man."

Palpable admiration and amusement from the other two men formed a subtle background for Jerry's temper as he flung the pad to the floor and leaped to his feet. "You son of a bitch."

The violence that might have erupted at that moment was forestalled by Corey's graceful movement of rising, and by the easy lack of concern in his voice as he said, "I've really got to be going. I'm sure you all have dinner plans and I won't hold you up any longer."

Smooth, Beth thought in amazement, as they all rose to see Corey out. In a second he had diverted attention from Jerry to himself, and Jerry without an audience was a deflated balloon. An old actor's trick that he knew only too well. Her father was saying, with real enthusiasm in his voice, "Can't we persuade you to join us? It would be a real pleasure."

Corey glanced at Beth, seemed to find something amusing in her face, and replied, "Not this time, I'm afraid. But it's been an honor meeting you, sir, and I hope to see you again soon."

Damn him, Beth thought. *He's even got my own father eating out of his hand.* But as Steve came forward, hand extended and a look of real admiration on his face, she knew her father was only one half of Corey's triumph this night.

"I can't tell you how glad I am to have met you," Steve said. "I've heard so much about you."

"I've heard a lot about you too," Corey responded, smiling. "That's the second thing we have in common."

The flattery in Steve's face turned to puzzlement as his affectionate glance left Beth. "The second thing? What's the first?"

"Elizabeth, of course," responded Corey, and the glance he gave her was unmistakably proprietorial.

Steve seemed to withdraw a step, but the small frown that puckered his brow was not so much disturbed as it was confused. "What does that mean?"

"Only," replied Corey pleasantly, "that I've decided to do everything in my power to see that she doesn't marry you—nothing personal, you understand." He turned to Beth, smoothed the hair near her ear with an affectionate touch, and smiled, "Later, princess. Thanks for a great day." He nodded once again, courteously, to the two flabbergasted men, and was gone.

The stunned silence that followed his departure was broken in a moment by Jerry's low chuckle. "Right on, man," he murmured, and bolted out the door after Corey's car and the two of them drove off, and then she had to face the two witnesses of her humiliation.

"He's—he's a nut!" she gasped at last, and a mixture of consternation, outrage, and utter embarrassment warred on her face as she looked at Steve.

"Maybe so," mused her father, still gazing out the window at the point where Corey had driven off with his young charge. "But you've got to admit, he sure knows how to handle that boy."

"Oh, he knows how to handle people, all right," returned Beth bitterly and looked anxiously again at Steve.

Steve looked somewhat like a man who has just been caught by the tail of a hurricane—an analogy that constantly occurred to Beth in describing Corey Fletcher's effect on people. But gradually the look of puzzlement on his face faded into a smile, and he admitted, "He's quite a character, all right." And he quirked her chin affectionately. "Don't let him bother you, honey. Flamboyance is a trademark with people like that, just like dramatic exit lines." An eyebrow lifted in amusement. "Hey, you're not afraid I'm jealous, are you?"

Jealous? No, she and Steve did not have the type of relationship that would ever lend itself to jealousy.

They were both too mature for that. She was just humiliated and angry and she would have cheerfully wrung Corey Fletcher's neck if he ever dared to show his face again.

"It should be quite an experience for you, getting to know a man like Fletcher," added Steve with his usual magnanimity. "You're not likely to meet many more like him in your lifetime."

"With luck," ground out Beth, still seething. And then, more out of curiosity than a real desire to flirt, she looked up at him. "Do you really mean to say you don't mind in the least that I'm keeping company with Corey Fletcher?"

He laughed, just as she had expected him to. "I say live it up while you have the chance, sweetie." And he winked at her. "Just don't start making comparisons." He brushed her lips with a light kiss and sent her off to the bedroom to change for dinner.

Steve's reaction did not really surprise her. He knew her too well to think she would ever be attracted to a man like Corey Fletcher. He knew, just as she knew, that she had everything she wanted from life right here, and it was sweet of him to encourage her to have a little fun. The most special part of their relationship was that they had never tried to exercise control over one another or to tie one another down, each knowing that when wings were tried and new adventures grown old, they would come home where they belonged.

But what, she wondered with a growing uneasiness as she dressed for dinner, would Steve think if he knew that Corey Fletcher had kissed her and turned her blood to fire, had touched her and made her quiver with helplessness? Steve would find a way to understand. That was what made him Steve. He would understand even if she could not, and that was one of the most wonderful things about him. Yet disappointment nagged at her all through an otherwise extremely pleas-

ant dinner that she did not even have a jealous boyfriend's rage to protect her from Corey Fletcher. And
there was also alarm, because that was the first time she
had ever thought of herself as needing protection.

When Beth arose the next morning and made her way,
bleary-eyed and yawning, to the kitchen for coffee, she
was shocked to almost stumble over the prone figure of
Jerry sprawled out over the living room couch. She had
long since given up waiting for him to come in at night
as a necessary concession to her sanity, and wondering
what he did and where he went in those late night
hours was another pursuit she had been forced to aban-
don for health reasons. As long as he was home by the
time she got up in the morning, she felt she was better
off not knowing how he had passed the intervening
hours. But now she was forced to face a graphic encounter with reality, and she was horrified and sickened
with residual concern.

The reek of alcohol and other unpleasant substances
permeated the room with a heavy cloud of corruption.
He was shirtless, and on his left shoulder blade was a
brand new tattoo—the Trans Am eagle. Visions of the
filthy dockside dives he must have frequented during
the night swept her and left her weak with fear, and
then were replaced by a killing rage. He had left with
Corey. While presumably in the company of a responsible adult he had returned in this condition. No doubt
Fletcher had paid for the tattoo and whatever other
filthy amusements he had provided for the boy. Yes,
she would have killed at that moment. Happily.

It took her almost ten minutes to get him to his feet.
When she did his knees buckled and he sagged against
her heavily. The eyes that looked out at her from a
tortured man's face belonged to a confused little boy,
and her heart broke for him as she half dragged, half
led him toward the bedroom. But then she caught the

change of his expression and quickly changed direction for the bathroom where she held his head and wiped his brow with a damp cloth as he heaved and swore incoherently. Kill, she thought mercilessly, conjuring into vision Corey Fletcher's smiling face. Kill.

It was only a stroke of luck that she got him to the bed before he passed out again. She made him as comfortable as she could before Steve picked her up for church services, where they were to meet her father. She could not tell Steve what had happened. She was too upset.

The thoughts she had on that pew between her father and Steve definitely did not belong in church. They centered mainly around Corey Fletcher and various forms of medieval torture, with a few imaginative variations brought on by the advent of twentieth-century technology. She shuddered every time she thought of Jerry, recalled the sickening odor of alcohol that had oozed from his pores, and pondered the contaminated needle that had made that hideous drawing on his shoulder. Oh, yes, Corey Fletcher was a great one for sight-seeing. He had no doubt found the day's activities too mild for his taste, but Jerry had been only too happy to explore with him the infamous red light district of Norfolk, the porno houses and massage parlors and bars where even hard-core sailors were too wise to go. Grown men wandered into those bars every night of the week and were never heard from again; what chance did a sixteen-year-old boy have? Instead of the more appropriate soul searching and meditation, Beth's mantra was, "Just let me get my hands on him. Just let him dare show his face one more time. I'll kill him. I swear I'll kill him."

Beth's concentration was broken by an inconsiderate late-comer who was making his way down the pew, stepping over feet and bumping knees and murmuring apologies. People began to whisper and stare, and Beth looked up in annoyance. He paused beside her father, who cheerfully moved over to make room for him, and Corey Fletcher sat beside Beth.

"Sorry I'm late," he whispered to her. "I had to go to four churches before I found you. It would have been simpler if you were Jewish."

Beth's face flooded with purple color, then whitened with anger. Still people were turning their heads, casting discreet glances their way, and looking quickly back again, eyes widening with excitement. She was torn between the urge to crawl under the pew and to rip his throat out with her bare hands. Not content with humiliating her before her boyfriend and endangering the life and corrupting the morals of her nephew, he now had to make a public spectacle of her—in church, of all places! The rack was too good for him.

She sat with her lips tightly pressed together and her attention rigidly fixed upon the pulpit, determined to endure. But how could she ignore him, sitting so close beside her their shoulders and knees brushed, the tangy scent of his after-shave wafting her way, the heat from his body setting her nerves on edge? She moved closer to Steve, but Steve was looking at Corey with a mildly amused smile, which, although she did not trust herself to look, she was certain Corey returned. He was wearing an exquisitely cut sand-colored suit, a pale pink shirt, and a silver-and-pink striped silk tie. His hair glistened in the reflection of the sun that poured through the stained glass windows, and his face was composed into sober lines as he fixed his attention on the minister. She wanted to strangle him.

At last the interminable service was over. Silver sunlight spilled over the steps where Beth stood with her father, Steve, and Corey, wondering when the excited, curious crowd that was gathering behind them was going to attack. Corey was telling her father, "I have to leave this afternoon, but I wanted to get a chance to tell you all good-bye.'' He looked at Beth. "Could I drive you home? I believe I left my sunglasses at your house yesterday, and I'm going to need them for the trip back.''

Beth knew, and Corey knew that she knew, that he had not worn sunglasses yesterday. She said with smugness, "I'm afraid not. We're all expected by Steve's mother for dinner.''

Steve spoke up quickly. "I'm sure she'd be more than pleased to have you." He was obviously only seeing the fun in the situation; his mother would be bowled over to have a celebrity like Corey Fletcher unexpectedly arrive for Sunday dinner, and Steve would derive immense enjoyment from the fluttering chaos that would inevitably ensue. He could hardly be blamed. After all, he did not know what a menace Corey Fletcher really was.

Corey was looking at her, and she realized what a neat trap he had plotted. She must now either endure an impossible dinner with Corey the guest of honor in her future mother-in-law's house or give him his way and let him drive her home. "We'll go pick up Corey's glasses," she told Steve with poorly disguised ill-grace, "and I'll meet you at your mother's in a few minutes. Give her my apologies.''

On second thought, she decided, seething, as curious eyes followed them down the stairs, maybe this was the best thing. She still had a few things to say to the grandiose Mr. Fletcher before he swept so blithely out of their lives.

But she did not speak until they were inside the house, and then it was Corey, turning to her with his hands outspread and a look of staunch resignation on his face, who had the first word. "All right, shoot. I'm ready." She glowered at him, and he explained, "It doesn't take a complete idiot to see that you're furious with me about something. The suspense is killing me.''

Beth's eyebrows flew up in mock surprise as she replied poisonously, "Furious? With you? Now why should I be furious? Just because you humiliate me within an inch of my life with that ridiculous comment you made to Steve last night. How dare you! Just who do you think you are?"

His lips curved into an abashed smile. "Ah, that."

But she gave him no chance for rebuttal as she heaped crime after crime on his head, her temper mounted as she realized how much she truly had to be angry with him about. "And then you come sauntering into church this morning just as if you had every right in the world to be there—just to make a spectacle of me and set tongues to wagging, knowing that you're the last person in the world I wanted to see this morning, or ever, for that matter!" Her eyes snapped and her cheeks flamed, for Beth in a temper was an awesome sight to behold. Her hands curled and uncurled into violent fists and claws, and her nostrils flared with rage. "What kind of man are you, anyway? You come cruising into town in your million-dollar car and thousand-dollar set of threads and act like you own the place—telling me what to do, telling Jerry what to do, and telling us we ought to be grateful for having you around to do it! Putting on that phony act for my father and embarrassing Steve, and as for what you did last night, hanging is too good for you! If there's not a law on the books to have men like you put away, there should be!"

He endured her tirade until she had to pause to catch her breath, and then he loosened his tie and slipped off his jacket, saying mildly, "Since I have a feeling you're just getting started, you don't mind if I make myself comfortable?" He folded the jacket on the back of a chair and added, "Now, as for what I said to Steve last night, I'm not going to apologize. If I embarrassed you by coming to church this morning, I do apologize, but I'm protected under the right to freedom of worship.

After that, I'm afraid you've lost me, but don't let that stop you. Please continue.''

The blood vessel on Beth's temple threatened to pop. She glowered at him for a moment, too enraged to form a coherent sentence, and then stalked toward the kitchen. Midway there she whirled, the exercise having cleared her head enough for speech, but the words became tangled before they ever left her throat. She had to pause to take a breath.

Corey was making himself comfortable on the sofa and seemed very interested in something he had discovered beneath one of the cushions. He drew it out slowly, holding it between thumb and forefinger, and glanced at her blandly. "Why, princess," he drawled, "I didn't know you indulged."

Angry accusations evaporated, and so, for the moment, did the emotion. She stared at the thin brown cigarette he held between his fingers for a long moment. Her voice was weak and rather thin. "Is that... marijuana?"

He brought it to his nose and sniffed. "It ain't rolled cornsilk. One hundred percent grade-A Colombian, if you ask me."

In two swift steps she snatched the incriminating evidence from him. "You should know," she snapped. "He probably got it from you!"

The silence pulsed about them as she stared at the small scrap of illegal goods in her hand. Horror sank in the pit of her stomach. How could she have been so blind? Was she really naive enough to think this was the first time he had brought something like this into the house? She was supposed to be a pharmacist, she knew the look and the symptoms, but she had totally ignored what was going on right under her nose. She had the feeling suddenly that things were escalating out of her control, and she couldn't cope. She wanted to cry. It was just too much.

Corey said quietly, "I've been known to do some stupid things in my life, but giving drugs to kids is not one of them."

"Oh, no!" she cried furiously, blinking back tears of rage and frustration. "You just get them blind drunk and take them to tattoo parlors and whorehouses and heaven knows what else! Spare me a defense of your morals, Corey Fletcher!"

A look of utter bafflement crossed his face as he stood. "Tattoo parlors? Whorehouses?" He repeated the word as though it astonished him that she even knew it. In truth, she could not recall ever having used that particular phrase before and a rush of color compounded her misery. "What are you talking about?"

"You know perfectly well what I'm talking about!" Angry tears only pushed her further toward the point of hysteria and she blinked them back, shoving the offending cigarette into the pocket of her light jersey skirt and turning blindly toward the kitchen again. "He was with you last night—and I, foolishly, thought for once he would be safe!" Her laugh was high and bitter. "Had I but known!"

He had followed her into the kitchen, and she whirled on him, bracing herself against the counter to stop the trembling that threatened to break in her voice. "Are you aware," she demanded furiously, "that that boy is on probation? Even being seen in places like he was in last night could land him a jail sentence even his father couldn't get him out of! Didn't it occur to you that he could get hepatitis from that filthy needle? Or were you too drunk yourself to even care? Do you realize he could have been killed in that part of town for nothing more than the change in his pocket? Are you completely crazy?"

He stared at her scarlet face and glittering eyes in increasing puzzlement. "Look, I'm beginning to think we're getting our wires crossed somewhere along the line. I know you don't approve of Jerry's drinking and for that I'm sorry, but let's face it, princess, the kid is going to drink. I had rather it be a few beers in my hotel room than in some sleazy back-alley bar where they don't check IDs, but of course you have every right to argue with my judgment. As for the rest of it, I have no way of knowing what Jerry did or where he went after he left me last night. Why don't you back up and tell me exactly what's going on?''

She gasped in astonishment, half believing him. ''You left him?''

''I turned my back and he was gone,'' he corrected. ''Even I,'' he explained patiently, ''have to answer the call of nature every once in a while. Now, will you please tell me what happened? What's all this about needles?''

She turned away abruptly, flinging open a cabinet and clattering about for a coffee cup. ''When I woke up this morning Jerry was passed out on the sofa, and from more than a few beers, I can tell you that. There was a fresh tattoo on his shoulder and his shirt was missing. He was a wreck. Three stages past drunk and closer to dead than sick. For that,'' she declared, slamming closed the cabinet door and opening another, ''we have the famous child psychologist Dr. Corey Fletcher to thank, who treats adolescent anxiety with a few beers in his hotel room.''

''Damn.'' Corey said softly.

''Don't swear on Sunday!'' she snapped, banging closed the cabinet door.

His smile was faint and wry as he took her arms gently. ''First of all,'' he said, ''stop banging around those doors. If Jerry's in half the shape you say he is, his head's going to feel like a nuclear holocaust as it is, he won't need the sound effects.'' She tried to twist angrily away, but he held her firm. ''Secondly, your point is taken. Next time I'll know not to let the little renegade out of my sight.''

"There won't be a next time!" she cried hotly, succeeding in jerking away. She marched over to the counter and sloshed into the cup a measure of stale coffee that she had no intention of drinking. "Just stay away from us, leave us alone! We'll be fine if you just leave us alone!"

There was a silence, and Beth rested both palms stiffly on the counter, staring out at the scraggly row of daffodils bravely lining her cracked walk. Corey said quietly behind her, "I know you're mad. I don't blame you. I feel rotten about what happened to Jerry, okay? It won't happen again, if I have to break every bone in his punk macho body. Now, can we stop fighting for a minute and talk about something else?"

She whirled on him, and the nearness of his face to hers startled a blaze of color to her cheeks. She pressed against the counter, feeling trapped. "No!" she cried. "Will you just go away and leave me alone?"

His hands were on her waist, and a smile played lazily in the back of his eyes. He knew exactly what his touch could do to her. His fingers caressed the small of her back and his thumbs slid upward to the point of her ribcage. "I'm not going away," he told her. "And if you don't stop shouting at me I'm going to kiss you until your lips are too swollen to talk, much less utter expletives. Still want to fight?"

"Let me go." It was meant to be a command, it came out more as a plea. She stood immobilized by the promise in his eyes and the gentle circular motions of his thumbs against the points of her ribs.

He said, "I'm going to be in North Carolina next weekend testing a new car for the track. I've asked Jerry to come with me. Now I'm asking you too."

"Forget it," she snapped, turning her face away from the mesmerizing gaze. If only it were as easy to break away from what the absent movement of his fingers was doing to her body.

"Okay," he shrugged, not dropping his hands. "If you're sure you trust your nephew for a whole day in my unsupervised company."

"I don't trust either of you as far as I can throw you," she retorted. "I'm not going and neither is he."

"I'm not breaking a promise to a kid. You're going."

"You're using Jerry to get to me," she accused, incredulity mixed with anger as she stared at him.

He thought about that for a moment. "Maybe I am."

Her eyes widened in disgust and amazement as she tried to wrench away. "That's cruel! That's crazy! You're a crazy person and I'm not going to North Carolina or anywhere with you! You—"

Making good his threat, he closed her mouth with a kiss. For a moment she struggled, but it was just to the point that she became aware of the softness of his lips, the warmth he seemed to be pulsing into her body with each breath, and then she was melting against him. His kiss seemed to draw from her all the anger and frustration festering inside and replace it with fresh air and roses. His kiss eased away the shock and the pain of the day, which was ridiculous because he had been the cause of both. Or had he? She didn't know any more. She didn't care. She only knew that when he kissed her everything else suddenly seemed very far away and nothing was unsolvable.

She felt her body ease into full contact with his, her stomach against his, her arms folded helplessly against his chest, her thighs molding themselves against his, and she thought vaguely, *Oh, no,* while the delicious sensations spreading inexorably throughout every nerve fiber whispered back, *Oh, yes.*

"Pretty princess," he murmured against her ear, stroking her hair. "You worry too much. When are you going to stop fighting and just let it happen?"

She was dazed and tingling from his kiss and she simply let him cradle her in his arms, not wanting to ever move, ever. The warm lethargy that enveloped her was like the effect of a mild soporific, she felt stupefied, helpless, and good. "Damn you, Fletcher," she whispered against his shoulder, struggling against the urge to close her eyes and seek his lips again.

He smiled down at her. "Don't swear on Sunday."

She stepped back. It was a tremendous effort. "Why are you doing this?" she demanded soberly. "You know I'm engaged to another man. Why did you say such a stupid thing to Steve? Why do you keep coming on to me and complicating my life? What is it with you?"

He smiled at her rather vaguely and caressed the hair that fell over her forehead. "Would it reassure you to know that the attraction is purely physical?"

"That's all it ever is to you, isn't it?" she replied tiredly. "What feels good, what looks good, what gives you a thrill. You risk your life on a racetrack and do crazy stunts and jump out of airplanes over frozen wastelands because it gives you some sort of perverted physical satisfaction. Even the way you eat a stupid ice cream cone. Pure sensual pleasure. It's the measure of your whole life."

He looked at her for a moment without replying, then turned and went back into the living room for his jacket. She followed him aimlessly. "Don't worry about Jerry," he said, shrugging into his jacket. "I'll do what I can about him. He's got some problems, but he hasn't reached hopeless yet." He stood close to her, and the light in his eyes was gentle, reassuring. She met his gaze evenly, ready for anything. "As for this...." His hand slipped into her pocket and brought out the forgotten cigarette, and she tried not to shiver at the brush of his finger along her hip. His lips tightened dryly. "Either smoke it, or put it back where you found

Harlequin reaches
into the hearts and minds
of women across America
to bring you

Harlequin American Romance

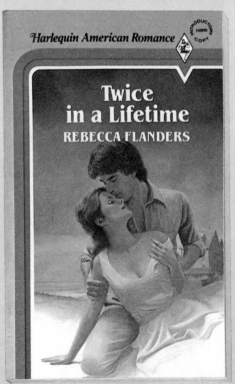

Enter a uniquely American world of romance with
Harlequin American Romance.™

Harlequin American Romances are the first romances to explore today's new love relationships. These compelling romance novels reach into the hearts and minds of women across America…probing into the most intimate moments of romance, love and desire.

You'll follow romantic heroines and irresistible men as they boldy face confusing choices. Career first, love later? Love without marriage? Long-distance relationships? All the experiences that make love real are captured in the tender, loving pages of *Harlequin American Romance*.

What makes American women so different when it comes to love? Find out with *Harlequin American Romance!*

Send for your introductory FREE book now.

GET THIS BOOK FREE!

MAIL TO:
Harlequin Reader Service
2504 W. Southern Avenue,
Tempe, AZ 85282

YES! I want to discover *Harlequin American Romance*.

Send me FREE and without obligation, "Twice in a Lifetime."
If you do not hear from me after I have examined my FREE
book, please send me the 4 new *Harlequin American Romance*
novels each month as soon as they come off the presses. I
understand that I will be billed only $2.25 per book (total
$9.00). There are no shipping or handling charges. There
is no minimum number of books that I have to purchase. In
fact, I may cancel this arrangement at any time. "Twice
in a Lifetime" is mine to keep as a FREE gift, even if I do
not buy any additional books.   154 CIA NARM

Name	(please print)	

Address		Apt. No.

City	State/Prov.	Zip/Postal Code

Signature (If under 18, parent or guardian must sign.)

This offer is limited to one order per household and not valid to
current Harlequin American Romance subscribers. We reserve
the right to exercise discretion in granting membership. If price
changes are necessary, you will be notified. Offer expires
December 31, 1984.   PRINTED IN U.S.A.

Experience *Harlequin American Romance*...

with this special introductory FREE book offer.

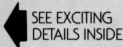 SEE EXCITING DETAILS INSIDE

Send no money. Mail this card and receive this new, full-length *Harlequin American Romance* novel absolutely FREE.

it. There are worse things, princess," he advised her, "and our young friend is going to lose no time discovering all of them if you start jumping down his throat. Just try to hang loose for a few days, okay? I'll see you next weekend."

She stood there with the marijuana cigarette in her hand and watched him until he reached the door, then she remembered to call out, "I'm not going!"

He winked at her and closed the door behind him.

Chapter Seven

"I'm not going," repeated Beth stubbornly six days later as she calmly sliced cheese for the sandwiches she was making for lunch.

Corey popped a piece of cheese into his mouth and replied, "We don't have time to argue about it now, princess. I'm already six hours late."

"That should worry you," she retorted. "Doesn't the world stop at your command?"

He was straddling a kitchen stool at the counter where she worked, and it was a great effort to keep herself from cutting her eyes constantly toward him in an effort to reassure herself that he was really there. Despite his parting words, she had been convinced she would never see Corey Fletcher again, and she had spent an entire week telling herself how glad she was. She read that he was in Los Angeles, beginning filming on a three-part television miniseries, and she thought that settled it. He had found diversion in a small Virginia naval town while he was at loose ends, but now he was on a tight schedule again and no one made transcontinental flights for a weekend. She told herself she was relieved and was happy to get on with her life and forget about him.

Only it was not so easy to forget about Corey Fletcher. She was reminded of him every time she turned around. She saw a photograph of him flashed on the screen of a nightly entertainment-business television show. His arm was around the shoulders of a gorgeous female country-western recording star, and the caption read Making Beautiful Music Together. There was a replay of the race in Belgium which of course Jerry turned on at full volume, and although Beth told herself she had no intention of watching—auto racing was crude, barbaric, mindless, and held no interest for her whatsoever—curiosity kept drawing her back. At last she sat on the edge of the sofa, a dish towel drawn between her hands, and stared at the screen in wide-eyed fascination.

She listened to the commentators praise Corey's skill and awe over the speed, their voices rising in excitement and approaching hysteria as danger points were reached and surpassed within a hair's breadth of catastrophe. She watched Corey's car and found herself holding her breath as he scraped a wall and sparks flew and the car fishtailed wildly, as he cut in front of another vehicle at two-hundred plus miles per hour and then had the same done to him not half a mile down the track. Tension started aching in her muscles and her throat felt dry, though of course it was ridiculous because the race had been run and won weeks ago.

Then there was the point where the car in front of Corey went off the track and burst into flames. The driver was killed instantly. She had not been prepared for that. Of course she must have seen film clips of events like that dozens of times in her life, but she could not have known how different it could be when she knew someone who had actually been there, when, except for a number of split-second variables, it could have been Corey Fletcher's car going up in flames. She was sickened with horror and residual anxiety. What kind of fool would do such things? He didn't need the money, he didn't even need the fame—he had that from his acting. Then why?

She read an editorial in the sports section decrying the excessive speeds to which auto racing had grown and claiming that increased technology had surpassed the human element. The writer pointed out the outrageously high number of deaths attributed to the sport in the last two years alone, a toll, he claimed, that should make any enthusiast think twice. Even the most skilled driver could not be expected to control a vehicle capable of the speeds modern tracks were expected to see, yet designers continued to build cars for more and more speed, directly affecting the odds against survival once a driver climbed behind the wheel. Corey Fletcher was named as one of the culprits who continued to escalate the sport beyond manageability.

If there had been any doubts about going to the track with Corey and Jerry—or even allowing Jerry to go—they were erased. Not, she assured herself, that it would be a decision she would have to make. He simply wouldn't show up. And now he was sitting in her kitchen, thigh muscles straining against faded jeans and shoulders molded into an equally tight and faded blue T-shirt, his eyes twinkling at her tolerantly. "See anything you like?" he inquired.

She jerked her eyes away irritably and pulled out bread for the sandwiches. "I've heard that wearing jeans that tight can have a damaging effect on the male anatomy."

He grinned slowly. "No one's complained yet."

She swallowed back the heat in her face and began to plop cheese onto the bread. "Do you want one of these?"

He patiently removed the cheese and replaced it in the square of aluminum foil from which it had come. "We'll eat at the track, where, at this moment, there are at least six burly men waiting to put my butt in a sling because we've already lost half a day's work. Are you procrastinating, princess?"

With great concentration she spread mustard on the bread. She asked calmly, without looking at him, "That driver in Belgium—did you know him?"

He did not respond immediately, and she thought for a moment he had not understood to what she referred. But a quick glance at him assured her that he did, indeed, understand. A mask had come down swiftly over his features and he replied briefly, impersonally, "Yes. I knew him."

She turned to him, the knife dripping mustard, a question forming on her lips. But he said shortly, "Let me save you the trouble. I felt like hell. I spent the first two days so drunk I didn't have to think about it and the second two trying to figure out if there was anything I could have done to have prevented it or that I had done to cause it. I went to the funeral, got drunk again, and then tried not to think about it at all."

She said softly, "It's not the first time."

He dropped his eyes. "No. It's not. And if you're wondering how much sleep I lose worrying that the next time it might be me, I'm not going to answer that. The truth would surprise you." He looked up, the mask gone, took the knife from her hand, and dropped it with a clatter into the sink. He placed his hands on her waist and drew her slowly between his knees, the sweet, persuasive smile gradually lightening his features. "How many nights did you stay up trying to figure out ways to distract me?"

She was aware of a definite increase in her pulse rate. She watched with as much detachment as possible as her blood pressure rose about twenty points. Her thighs pressed against the rounded edge of the stool only inches from full contact with his body, and she tensed her muscles until it hurt. The worst part was, he was making *her* crazy. He was making her forget her responsibilities, her carefully ordered routine, all the things that were important in her life. Last weekend she had left the store to Ellie for an entire day and had been hearing from disappointed customers who had prescriptions to fill all week. In five years she had never taken a vacation or a day off. People depended on her, she couldn't just run off with Corey Fletcher whenever the whim hit him—or her. She braced her hands against his forearms in preparation for stepping away and said firmly, "I don't have to distract you. I told you I'm not going. You know perfectly well I have a business to run."

He bent his head and drew a gasp of surprise from her with the warm tickling motion of his tongue upon her forearm. She tensed and drew her arms away; he recaptured them and placed them upon his waist. "And you know perfectly well," he told her, just as though nothing had interrupted the conversation, "that I've talked to Jerry twice this week. I know exactly what the state of your business is."

Of course. She had been deceiving herself into thinking that a man who made regular long-distance phone calls to a teen-ager on the East Coast would not fly the same distance to keep a promise to said teen-ager. And of course he would have ascertained from Jerry that her store was no longer a valid reason for her to refuse to see him.

Partially because of the episode last weekend, and partially because her father insisted she was beginning to show signs of stress, Beth had accepted his persuasion to hire an assistant. Naturally, her father had just the man in mind. He was a twenty-six-year-old licensed pharmacist who, because of the present job crunch, had been working in a Suffolk factory for the last two years. Beth could only afford him part-time, but he was happy to get it, and he kept his job on the night shift at the factory. Beth had been uneasy about leaving him alone because he had not worked in a pharmaceutical capacity since he had shipped out of the Navy two years ago, but he seemed competent enough. He still had a lot of catching up to do on the latest drugs and dosages, and the hardest part had been learning to read the local doctors' handwriting, but finally today she had felt confident enough to leave him on his own for a Saturday afternoon. The thing that made her that confident was knowing that she was only a phone call away if he needed her. How could she expect Corey to understand that she couldn't just run off and leave?

His lips shocked a tremor out of her as they clasped the sensitive flesh in the hollow of her throat. One forty over ninety and rising, she thought, and turned away. "Stop that." Her voice was hoarse, almost a croak. Someone should do a study on the effects of sexual excitement on the human vocal cords.

His eyes were bright, like sunshine through a windowpane, as he looked up at her. "No," he said huskily and bent his head again. His teeth lightly pinched the bare flesh on her chest, and his tongue flickered provocatively over the area where the low neck of her T-shirt scooped against the swell of her breasts. He nibbled at the inviting curves daintily, with leisure and deliberation, and he murmured, "Tell me when it hurts."

Her fingers tightened against the firm muscles of his waist. She gasped, "Then will you stop?"

His low chuckle fanned a wave of hot breath over her chest, making the flesh crawl. "No. Then I'll make it hurt better."

"Sadist."

"I've been called worse." His teeth discovered the sensitive flesh of her inner arm, exposed by the sleeveless shirt and at eye level due to the position of her hands on his waist, and a prickle of goose bumps shot from the pressure of his teeth all the way down to her toes. "Who needs lunch?" he murmured.

Not content with torturing her front side, his fingers now began a firm, exploratory search of her back, traveling without hesitation over her buttocks, scratching a shockingly vibratory pattern along the seam of her jeans, moving lower.... Her knees sagged. Her breath was hot and rapid. How to Discover a Woman's Erogenous Zones in Three Easy Steps, she thought, and his fingers brushed between her thighs.

She gasped out loud and her heart slammed against her throat. "Stop it!" she whispered, wondering why a one-hundred-twenty pound woman in relatively good physical condition should find it so extraordinarily difficult to break the hold of ten fingers exerting no more than two ounces of pressure per square inch.

His eyes were so bright they practically shone, yet at the same time so dark they were completely unreadable. "Don't blame it on the jeans," he said huskily, tightening the fingers that now held her thighs just below the curve of her buttocks. "You're the one who's damaging my anatomy." He stood slowly and drew her to him, and just as his lips hovered over hers the screen door slammed.

She twisted away, turning the water on full blast and commanding automatically, "Wash your hands before lunch, Jerry."

Jerry leaned against the doorframe and sent a lewd glance in their direction. "You too, Fletcher," he advised with a nasty wink. "We all know where *your* hands have been in the past half hour."

Beth flushed scarlet as Jerry swung out of the room, and Corey murmured dryly, "Don't I wish."

He turned to her with rueful amusement as she turned off the water and began to busily mop off the counter. "Was that insult directed at me, or at you?" But then he caught her expression, and amusement faded into a troubled frown. "It does bother you, doesn't it?"

She couldn't look at him. How could she discuss with a virtual stranger what she could not confide to her father or her boyfriend, both men of medicine and both with enough experience to put what Beth was convinced were Jerry's incestuous inclinations into their proper perspective? How could she discuss it with anyone, when her guilt and embarrassment made it a taboo subject even in her own mind? She was convinced she must be doing something to encourage her nephew's perverted fantasies and she lay awake nights trying to figure out what it was. Yes, it upset her. More than she was willing to admit to Corey Fletcher or anyone else.

He was silent for a moment while she hurriedly retrieved the cheese and began slapping it blindly onto slices of bread. Then he said quietly, "He's just trying to scare you, you know. Looks like he's doing a pretty good job of it too." She felt his hands lightly on her shoulders; gently he turned her to face him. His smile was quiet and reassuring. "Princess, that boy is no more interested in the, er, admittedly appealing aspects of your sexuality than he is in winning the next Miss America Pageant. It's a power play, that's all. Kids that age tend to house most of their brains below the waist anyway and when he found out he could intimidate you by coming on to you, naturally that's exactly what he did. This is one time that I can absolutely assure you that if you ignore it, it will go away."

She looked up at him in mute gratitude and felt a burden swept quietly away by the calm confidence in his eyes. Perhaps it was because when he said it, it made perfect sense. Perhaps it was simply relief to be able to share it with someone, someone who understood so easily and completely. When he smiled at her, she returned it, and though the tightening of her lips was reluctant, the gratitude in her eyes did not fade.

He smoothed a strand of hair behind her ear and resumed his seat on the stool. "Otherwise, how's he been this past week?"

Beth had watched Jerry carefully since the discovery

of the illegal cigarette, acting on Corey's advice to say nothing mostly because she couldn't think of anything better to do. At first she had been panicked into thinking the only reason she had not previously noticed the signs of Jerry's drug abuse was because she had never seen him sober, but gradually she regained faith in her diagnostic abilities. He was stoned a lot, it was true, but he was also straight occasionally—perhaps more than occasionally. She shrugged, and Corey became more specific. "Do you think he has a drug problem?"

"I'm not sure." She frowned a little. "Probably no more than any other teen-ager in the country."

Corey nodded. "As long as he's not hitting the hard stuff, we still have a chance." Her eyes flew to him in surprise because he said that so easily—"we". As though it were his problem too, as though he were committed. Reading her thoughts, he gave her a dry little smile. "I've already admitted I'm using Jerry to get to you, haven't I? I hardly think my cause would be furthered if I let the kid slip into the depths of depravity and moral corruption just when the end of the chase was in sight."

As she turned away quickly to begin putting together the sandwiches, Corey went on casually, "He just has an excess of energy, that's all. I think next weekend I'll take him up in my glider. And today"—he took her waist and turned her around firmly—he's going to be so busy being pushed around by my pit crew he won't have time to even think about getting into trouble."

"I'm not going," she told him, pushing against his shoulders.

Thirty minutes later Beth's white knuckles were gripping the velour upholstery of her seat while Tidewater Virginia receded into a bas-relief map below her and her teeth chattered as she croaked, "You—you didn't tell me you were going to f-fly!"

"Time is of the essence, princess," he shouted over the roar of the engine. He grinned at her behind mirrored sunglasses. "You didn't tell me you were afraid of flying."

"I'm not!" She was sitting next to him in what was presumably the copilot's seat, and she had a bird's eye view of every gory detail of the diminishing landscape. She would have much preferred to be sitting next to Jerry in the back of the four-seater craft where she could have put her head between her knees and squeezed her eyes shut and moaned to her heart's content. "I just prefer to do my flying in a plane, not a lawn mower!"

He grinned at her and banked sharply; Beth left her stomach somewhere near the border of Surrey and Sussex counties.

Beth did not know exactly what to expect at the track; after the flight down—which she was convinced had aged her two years at the minimum—she should have been prepared for anything. She had hardly had a chance to find her land legs before they were whisked into a chauffeured limousine for the ten-minute drive from the airstrip to the track. That should not have surprised her. Somehow she had assumed that when he said he was testing a new car that was exactly what he would do—get into the car and drive it around the track a few times. She was not prepared for the spectators who milled around the infield, the reporters who descended upon them the moment they climbed out of the limousine, the dozens of cars and campers that lined the grassy banks, the important-looking men who flocked around Corey with querulous voices demanding where he had been. In the pit area two Silver Stream trailers were drawn up next to a portable building that Corey told her was the factory machine shop. Any deficiencies in structure or design could be corrected right on the spot, he explained to her, and so, he added, casually, could any parts he might damage during today's trial. For once, Jerry was impressed enough to keep his mouth shut; Beth already wanted to go home.

He led them inside one of the trailers, where hard music vibrated the foundation of the earth for miles around and deafened the eardrums of perhaps forty people who were crowded into the small space. There was a long table at the entrance spread with sandwiches and hors d'oeuvres and an open bar, which, judging from the condition of some of the room's occupants, had been open for some time. A round of applause mixed with shouts of "There's our man!" and "Where you been, baby?" greeted them as they walked in, and Corey answered with a mocking bow.

"Broads and kids! Of all things, this I don't believe!" This from a big man with a gray-streaked beard, and someone next to him, a ramrod of a man with a mole on his chin who glowered dangerously and bellowed, "What the mother-lovin'— Where the hell have you been?"

Corey slipped his arm around Beth's waist and drew her forward. "Princess, may I present two very dear friends. On your right there, looking like Grizzly Adams, is Nick Holloman, my head mechanic and personal albatross. Right next to him, the mousy-looking one, is Robbie Marinara, just like the sauce. We call him Stretch for obvious reasons. He's my personal manager and head pain in the butt. These two earn their pay by arguing about whether I'm worth more alive or dead." He tightened his arm around her shoulders and urged her forward another step. "This is my Elizabeth. You'll be nice to her," he added pleasantly to the man who had made the comment about broads and kids, "or I will personally slit your throat and hang you up to drip-dry."

Nick Holloman was taken aback for the space of one

startled blink, and then he began belligerently, "My man, you've had us wearing holes in the carpet and chewing our nails to bloody stubs for half a damn day and then you show up with this pretty piece of baggage— no offense, sweetie—and what the hell are we sup- posed to do? Break into the Hallelujah Chorus? I think whatever brains you've got left after that Daytona crash are stuffed into your front pocket for spare change! You wanna know the absolute truth—"

"Corey, I need to talk to you for a minute about the specs—"

And from another side, "Corey, how about an open- er for tonight's edition?"

"Think you'll break two hundred today, Corey?"

Corey leaned forward and brushed Beth's cheek with a kiss. "I've got to go, princess. Have one of these char- acters get you something to eat. Stretch, keep your hands to yourself. And Nickie"—he smiled at him sweetly—"enjoy yourself. It's later than you think."

For the space of about two seconds after he was gone the two men looked at her as though neither one of them was quite sure what should be done with her, and then the one called Nick muttered gruffly, "You want a drink?"

Without waiting for a reply, he shoved his way to the bar, and she was left with Stretch, who smiled down at her benignly and rather smugly. There was a hair sprouting from the mole on his pasty white chin and Beth tried not to stare at it. "Don't let the bear scare you," he soothed as if to a child. "His bark—or growl, as it were—is worse than his bite." It occurred to Beth that he could afford to be generous. He had been as angry with Corey as Nick was, but, obviously the smarter of the two, he had let Nick vocalize and antago- nize Corey while he was pleased to accept the role of the protagonist in the bad-cop—good-cop bit. "There's a sort of superstition about women at a racetrack," he went on magnanimously, "like women on board a ship. They're supposed to be bad luck."

Beth gazed around the smoky room at the women in every size, shape, and imaginable variety and found that hard to believe.

"Don't you let him kid you," Nick growled and thrust a drink into her hand. "He's just worried about our baby boy messing up that pretty face of his and he'll hang all over any woman who looks like she could make Corey settle down and forget the track. Well, let me tell you something, baby—"

Beth took a sip of her drink in self-defense and almost choked. She did not know much about liquor in its various forms and flavors but she could tell this was straight ninety-proof something, without so much as an ice cube to water it down.

Stretch glared at him. "What're you trying to do, poison her? Can't you tell this is not a drinking lady?" He snatched the glass from her. "It's okay, sweetheart, I'll get you some tomato juice. You want something to eat?"

Beth opened her mouth to reply, but he was already gone. "Look, baby," Nick was saying to her seriously, "you're not one to hold a grudge are you, and like I said before it's nothing personal—hell, I think you're kinda cute, myself—but you got to understand where I'm coming from, you know what I mean? Corey, he's got his women and ain't none of us complaining, as long as he don't wear himself out the night before the race." His grin was friendly. "But he's got better sense than to bring them to the track," he went on more seriously, trying to fix her with an intimidating gaze and doing a pretty good job of it too. There was something highly unnerving about being stared down and lectured to by a two-hundred-pound man while being jostled by strangers and trying not to cough against the sting of cigarette smoke, especially when they both knew Corey would not really slit his throat. "There's a reason for that and it's important, so are you with me, sweetheart? The reason is that there's something damn spooky about knowing there's a woman waiting in the pits worrying about you. Can you catch my meaning, hon? It makes a man think twice about taking chances, it slows down his reflexes, it makes him want to look over his shoulder, you know what I mean? It's a proven damn psychological fact and let me tell you, sweetheart, half a second can be fatal out there on the track, you know what I mean?"

A hot hand crawled around her shoulder while another pressed a glass into her hand. "Stop trying to scare her, Nickie," Stretch crooned. "She's just along for the ride, aren't you, baby?"

"You know damn well he's never brought a woman to the track before," Nick glowered.

"Hell, it's just a test run. After a weekend with lover boy she could probably use the fresh air, right sweet thing?"

"Just so long as she don't get any ideas about a house in the country with Corey sitting on the front porch while she knits little things."

Stretch roared with laughter. His hand slid down to her waist. "Hell, our boy's too smart to fall for that one!"

"Look at her, damn you! She's got apple pie written all over her face. And don't tell me you wouldn't be dancing at the damn wedding."

"You think that's what I want! Hell, his TVQ would fall right off the scales. A married Corey Fletcher is as good as a dead Corey Fletcher and he knows it as well as we do, so give the boy a break, will you?" He grinned at her. "Can't say's I'd mind giving this one a ride myself, would you?"

"You'd better watch your damn mouth," growled Nick, and downed his drink in a single gulp.

Stretch's fingers dug into her ribs. "So. Where're you from, sweet thing?"

Beth sipped her drink. "I hate tomato juice," she said.

A roar of whistles and catcalls announced Corey's entrance. He was zipping up a shiny silver coverall and pulling on gauntlets of the same material while balancing a heavy helmet in the crook of his arm. He grinned as he came over to her, and she could feel the adrenaline humming through him like a high-voltage electric cable. His eyes snapped and his cheeks were flushed and he walked as though unaware that his feet ever touched the ground. "All right, boys, let's hit it." He brushed his lips across Beth's mouth, and his touch left a trail of sparks. "Enjoy the party, princess, but when Stretch tells you it's quieter in the back room, slap his face."

She touched the material of his coverall hesitantly, and looked up at him. "Asbestos?"

He grinned at her. "An ounce of prevention...."

But Beth was no fool. A pound of cure was hardly needed unless there was something that could have been prevented, and no one wore an asbestos suit unless he was expecting a fire. She felt slightly ill.

Corey found Jerry, who was partaking liberally of the buffet and the bar, tapped him on the arm, and commanded, "Let's go, Ace." Beth snatched the drink out of his hand as he brushed by, but he was too busy trying to keep up with Corey to protest.

Nick left with Corey, and Beth was not sure whether that was good or bad. She spent the next hour and a half trying to keep Stretch's hands away from the more private parts of her anatomy—she thought he might have earned that nickname for more reasons than his height—and peering through the haze of blue-white smoke at the assembled menagerie, nibbling on soggy hors d'oeuvres and sipping tepid Coke and wishing to heaven she had stayed at home.

Some of the room's occupants had left with Corey, and for a while it was easier to breathe. But after a time they wandered back in and others left; new faces mixed with old in a constantly changing potpourri. Women in Halston jeans or parachute silk trousers and men in fashion-tailored baggy trousers and high-cut leather boots, or men in Halstons and parachute silk and women in boots—it was a colorful assembly.

A television set in one corner competed with the crashing of the stereo and bursts of laughter, and off-color jokes mingled with scraps of high-tech conversation and witty repartee. A monitor was fixed on the track and every now and again a crowd would gather to watch until they became bored and wandered away in search of fresh amusement. Place names like Biarritz and Cannes were scattered liberally through the conversation. Men in greasy coveralls mixed easily with the factory officials in three-piece suits and the film people in designer shirts and the members of the press in rumpled jeans.

Two or three times during the afternoon Corey came in, his hair plastered to his head and his face white with the effects of heat and stress and bathed in rivers of sweat. Someone had told Beth that the temperatures inside the car could approach one hundred fifty degrees. Corey would bark out orders and answer questions and drink a gallon of Gatorade, then return to the track. Beth stayed out of his way.

A man with a shoulder-length braid asked Beth to go to bed with him. Just like that. She refused politely and about that time she decided she really needed some air.

It was near sunset, and the warm, humid air was a shock after the artificially cooled interior of the trailer.

Almost as many people had gathered in the pit area

as there were inside the trailer, and Beth was in luck—
Corey was there. He was surrounded by people, reporters, mechanics, and design engineers sometimes
six deep, but she started toward him anyway. He was
spraying himself with the open end of a hose, gulping
the water and shaking out his hair while he gave terse
replies to the questions that were put to him and
snapped strident commands that sent men scurrying.
She caught something about "suspension" and "float"
and a turbo system that was kicking in "half a damn
second too late" and on second thought she decided
this might not be the best time to approach him. She
made herself scarce until he climbed back into the car
and refastened his helmet, shouting to Nick that he was
going to open her up one more time and had anyone
done anything about the oil leak he had discovered last
time out?

The roar of exhaust tainted the warm evening air and
her nostrils burned with the odor of high-octane fuel
and buzzing machinery as she wandered into the pit
area, where the men who were not busy arguing among
themselves or working in the machine shop had gathered at the rail to watch Corey fly around the track.
Beth tried not to watch. She had caught glimpses of the
hairpin turns and sharp S-curves on the monitor before
and every time the car had blurred into one of those
curves her heart had stopped. She decided to look for
Jerry instead.

Some of the men leered at her and made comments
she tried not to hear. She held her head up and tried to
look nonchalant and failed. She abandoned her search
for Jerry. She had never wanted anything more in her
life than to simply go home.

A sudden shout from behind her—"Oh, my God,
he's lost it!"—made her whirl. There was a high
screeching in the air above the sudden roar of confusion about her, grinding metal or crying tires, she was

pushed and shoved and sworn at and nearly knocked off her feet and then she was squashed up against the rail with a hot body pressed against her back side and there was no way she could turn away from what they were forcing her to see.

It all happened in a matter of perhaps five seconds; the speed was incredible. The car was fishtailing wildly all over the track, two wheels bounced off the embankment and it was literally airborne, flying like a rocket across the track and heading straight toward them. The crowd began to draw back and there were sounds of alarm, but more than that sounds of amazement and excitement, as though it were all a carnival show being produced especially for their entertainment. A screech of tires wailed against the asphalt as the vehicle landed with an awful crash, did a one-hundred-eighty-degree turn, and plowed into the infield without seeming to lose an ounce of speed. There it spun again, smoking and tearing up a mountain of turf, bounced, flipped twice, and landed with an ear-splitting crash with its wheels spinning in the air—all in the time it takes to draw a breath that could not make a scream.

Just like on television, the fire crew was there in seconds, covering the vehicle with foam, dragging a body out of the wreckage. Beth was gripping the rail in a white-knuckled paralysis and her head was roaring and it seemed the gray-green twilight around her receded into a foggy, badly made silent film, skipping into slow motion and blurring about the edges. Then Corey was on his feet, stripping off his helmet and flinging it to the ground and swearing profusely, and someone said close to her ear, "Oh, good lord, someone grab her quick. She's going to faint."

But Beth was not the type of woman who fainted. She was the type of woman who smiled politely as she refused all offers of assistance, made her way calmly through the crowd telling herself with each step in a firm rational voice, *I am not going to cry. I am not going to cry.*

She coolly brushed off Stretch's advances when she entered the trailer, then locked herself in the bathroom and burst into tears.

Terror, shock, and anger got all mixed up inside her and she beat her fists against the sink and sobbed out loud, not worrying that anyone would hear her because the music was so loud it vibrated the very door on its hinges. She did not know who she was angriest with— Corey for scaring her, or those crazy people outside who partied on as though nothing at all had happened, or herself for being so scared...or maybe Corey for climbing so blithely out of a wreck that would have killed another man or maybe herself for even caring. *Are you mad at him because he's not dead? Are you mad at yourself for crying about it?* She didn't know. She only knew that she did not belong here in this madhouse filled with crazy people who laughed at death and joked about tragedy and were disappointed when the matador didn't draw blood, and she wanted very, very badly to go home.

After five minutes she determinedly stopped, blew her nose on a wad of toilet paper, and splashed water on her face. Then she went back outside. The occupants of the trailer had momentarily moved their party to the infield, and Corey was in the middle of them. Someone popped the cork on a bottle of champagne and suds flew everywhere as Corey, with a shout, snatched it up. He had apparently completely recovered from the episode, which Beth was convinced had taken ten years off her life. He chugged half the bottle amidst whoops and shouts of encouragement, poured the remainder over his head, and christened the dead vehicle with the empty bottle. Then he saw her.

Beth wandered away from the edge of the crowd,

keeping her back toward the still-steaming wreckage, and sat on the grass, folding her legs under her. Corey dropped down beside her. She did not look at him.

He said in a moment, "Are you okay?" There was concern in his voice. "Somebody told me you were sick."

She looked up at him with a bright smile. No way. There was no way in the world she would ever let him know. She would not be the woman in the pits who was worrying about him, making him look over his shoulder and refuse to take chances. Not this lady. She said, "Sick of all the noise and smoke, maybe. I'm in a lot better shape than you look right now, anyway."

He looked at her soberly. "You've been crying."

She laughed. "Heck, no, cowboy! I was just as impressed as I could be. You were terrific!"

His smile was a little slow in coming. "Like I said," he returned nonchalantly, "it's easier than turning cartwheels on your front lawn." He leaned forward and brushed a kiss across her nose, and even with that light touch she could feel the adrenaline that still had him charged up like a jet engine ready to take off. "Welcome to my world," he said and lifted an eyebrow dryly as he glanced around. "Such as it is."

He smelled pungently of gasoline, champagne, and sweat, and he laughed when she wrinkled her nose in distaste. "I know, I know. I'm going to peel out of these clothes in a minute and see if I've got any skin left, but before I do—want a taste?"

Without giving her a chance to respond, he brushed his cheek across her lips and, before she had a chance to think what she was doing, her tongue slipped out to caress it. Her reaction surprised her—which only goes to show you what sheer terror can do to otherwise perfectly stable mental processes—and so did the taste. Salty champagne on a smooth and scratchy surface. Interesting.

His eyes glowed under heavy lids. "Umm," he murmured. "You wouldn't believe what fantasies just started racing through my head."

His hand still held the back of her neck and he leaned toward her again, but she stiffened her spine, moved her face away a fraction, and inquired as casually as she could, "You're not hurt?"

He made a small grimace and his fingers trailed across her shoulder before sliding down her arm and finally coming to rest on her hand. "A little bruised in places that are not polite to mention. The car made it through all right, though." His eyes wandered back to the crowd toasting the valiant and temporarily decommissioned vehicle. "A little paint and body work and she'll be as good as new."

"Is it part of the act to flip it over a few times just for good measure? Sort of a grand finale?"

He feigned surprise with dramatically lifted eyebrows. "Didn't you know? That's the only way you can get out of one of those things. The eject seat doesn't work when the wheels are on the ground." He grinned and pulled her to her feet. "Come on, I've got to hit the showers before I start offending myself. You can watch."

"Thanks, but I've had about all the spectator sports I can take for one day." She paused and looked around the busy infield. "Where's Jerry?"

He laughed. "Somebody's got to clean up this mess. My work may be finished for the day, but his is just beginning. He'll be so ragged by the time my crew finishes with him he won't even be able to lift a cigarette, much less light it." He winked at her. "You'd be surprised how much total exhaustion can improve a boy's manners too. Bet you don't have the urge to wash his mouth out with soap once tonight."

Beth might have hoped, dimly, that they could go home now. No such luck. Corey was still too wound up, he needed a place to expend the excess energy and to come down by stages, and Beth began to understand that that was the purpose of the entire party. She could not bring herself to complain.

He left her alone in the chaos for only about ten minutes while he showered and changed into white denims and pale blue silk shirt. From the moment he returned he did not let her out of his sight. Constantly he was touching her—his arm around her shoulders or her waist or his hand on her arm or knee or wrapped around hers, even when he was pulling another woman onto his lap or stretching across a sofa to kiss an "old friend" on the lips. The women did not bother Beth; everyone loved Corey and it was all in the spirit of fun. But his protective, highly proprietorial attentiveness was a little embarrassing for Beth. He took the teasing good-naturedly, but Beth did not like being made a spectacle of. The night wore on and on as he downed one Scotch after another, laughing and joking and flirting and, gradually, relaxing a little. Beth's tension only mounted as the hour grew later. At one point she accepted an invitation to dance, but her partner insisted upon putting his hands in her back pockets and kept weaving his ankle between her legs to caress her calf. Corey rescued her immediately with some cheerfully threatening remark to the man and an arm clamped tightly around Beth's shoulders. Beth knew that Corey sensed how uncomfortable and out of place she felt and she could not help being grateful for that sensitivity and for his attempt to reassure her. But his protective instincts were just a little late in coming. All Beth wanted to do was to go home.

It was after midnight when her silent wish was finally granted. Corey found another pilot for the return trip; Beth suspected that it was because by now his blood composition was roughly two parts Scotch to one part hemoglobin he did not trust himself at the controls.

Beth silently conceded the wisdom of that decision. She knew she would not survive another flight in the copilot's seat.

As it was, Jerry occupied that position and Beth and Corey took the backseats. He held her hand on his knee and stroked her fingers, and it was a wonderfully silent, oddly relaxing journey through the night. Jerry fell asleep in the car on the way home from the airport, and Beth and Corey shared an amused look when Corey had to help him to bed.

"All tucked in and sleeping like a baby," Corey announced upon his return. "What did I tell you?"

"Fatherhood suits you," she replied, and then simply stood there, smiling at him. She did not know why she was smiling. She should have been furious with him. He had been the cause of her having spent one of the most miserable days of her life and she should have been glad to see the last of him. But she said, "Would you like some coffee?"

"That would be great. I have to catch a four-o'clock flight to Washington and I'll need something to keep me awake until then."

"Washington? What's in Washington?"

He followed her into the kitchen. "The President."

She turned, her eyes wide. "You're kidding!"

"Nope. At least, that's what I heard." Then he grinned. "Also a lot of other things, among which Capitol Hill is at the bottom of my list. I have some business there."

She turned to make the coffee, and he perched on the same stool he had vacated this morning. What was she doing making coffee for him when all she really wanted to do was go to bed and forget this horrible day? Why was she encouraging him to stay when she knew perfectly well the less she saw of him, the better? And why did she keep cutting her eyes toward him when she was sure he would not notice, seeming to be drawn against her will to the way the soft blue shirt clung to his chest and turned his eyes to turquoise? She glimpsed an unexpected twinkle in those eyes and she jerked her gaze away from the taut outline of thigh muscles against white denim, her cheeks tingling. Whatever else could be said about the man, he did have gorgeous legs.

The coffee was perking and she turned to the cabinet to take out cups. She could have left it and gone back into the living room but she heard him rise behind her and she needed to stay busy. She took out sugar and cream, not remembering whether he used either, and then she felt the warm touch of his hands on her shoulders. She gasped and a drop of cream splattered on the counter as she set the pitcher down, a rush of blood tingling to every part of her body at the simple touch of his hands.

"Princess, you're as tight as a steel spring. Relax."

Relax? A hysterical urge to laugh gripped her as his fingers began a firm massaging motion against the back of her neck and the span of her shoulders. How could she relax when her heart had started pumping twice its rate and she felt as though she were in the first stages of a bad fever? Instead she stiffened herself against what his fingers were doing to her aching muscles, swallowed hard, and said conversationally, "You drink too much, don't you?"

"Umm." His voice was soothing and absent, his fingers in ultimate control of the tight cords of her neck. "It's in my heritage."

"Oh, yes." Her voice was becoming tight, a little high. "The famous California winemakers." She was pretty sure she had discovered a new aphrodisiac whose market potential was nearly unlimited. Take one softly lit kitchen, one open window with the scent of roses on the night air, add a smidgen of aromatic coffee and ten masterful fingers and knead until done.... *Oh, Corey*, she thought a little desperately, *why am I letting you do this to me? Don't do this to me....*

Her head was beginning to sway with the deep gathering motions of his hands on her back, vertebrae began to loosen and muscles melted into his fingers. *Get hold of yourself, Bethy, you're starting to sink....* His hands dropped down to her waist and she folded her arms across her chest in self-defense. It was difficult to breathe, and when his hand slipped with easy adeptness beneath the back of her T-shirt, it was impossible.

"Don't freeze on me, princess," he murmured, and his hand moved with firm, smooth motions up the length of her back. "It's all right." She was torn between obeying his command—which, incidentally, also coincided with the instincts of her own body—and trusting her rapidly failing reason. One arm rested loosely around her waist and she tightened her fingers over his wrist as though to pull it away. But she found she was actually attempting to urge him closer as the other hand moved so soothingly along her back, sure warm motions electrifying bare flesh in a steady repetitive motion. The kitchen seemed brighter, almost pulsing in tune with her heart as every sense pushed steadily upward toward new peaks of awareness. Unconsciously she began to lean into the motion, wanting to feel more of him against her, wishing he would turn her into his arms and press his warmth into every part of her body, wanting him to touch her, needing him to touch her so badly it hurt.

"Better," he whispered against her neck, and she thought, parting her lips for breath, *Better. Oh, yes....*

He dropped one long warm kiss upon the side of her neck just where the collarbone dipped, and another on the peak of her shoulder beside the thin strap of her T-shirt. Her breath was light and rapid and the pressure of her heart within her chest seemed to push against her breasts, making them heavy and aching. His hand moved around to her front and she stopped breathing. Corey's lips touched her temple, his breath fanned against her lashes. His fingers moved lightly over her stomach, brushing and caressing bare flesh, a soft up and down motion over her ribs that startled such a rush of anticipation to her chest that she actually felt dizzy. This couldn't be happening to her. She shouldn't let him move her this way. She shouldn't be thinking the things she was thinking or wanting the things she was wanting.

"Uncross your arms, princess," he said. His voice was husky and his breath hot against her ear. The sound of it made her legs weaken and a soft flooding sensation begin in the pit of her stomach and spread downward. Beth's arms fell slowly and helplessly to her sides.

His hands moved upward and flesh throbbed where he touched. Her suspended breath floated outward as the curve of her breasts pressed into the flat of his palms, wonderful sensation, dizzy pleasure, mindless and satisfying. His fingers danced over her fullness, tightening around her throbbing nipples and caressing with a gentle circular motion. Beth breathed his name as she sank back against him, her head against the silky hardness of his shoulder, her buttocks cradled by his pelvis and his strong thighs pressing into hers. Corey's fingers tightened at the curve and made soft drawing motions from the nipples, pulling her outward, sharpening the point of desire to an unbearable ache. She whispered again, barely above a breath, "Corey..."

He turned her slowly with a gentle pressure on her ribs. His eyes reflected the bright blue of his shirt and the vibrancy of desire, yet they were soft, urging her with tenderness. "What is it, Elizabeth?" he whispered. "What do you want?"

Her voice caught in her throat and fluttered there as he bent his head and she felt the soft warmth of his

tongue upon her breast. *I want...* Lips clasped around
the nipple and his tongue was a soft abrasive there.
"What?" he whispered, breath cooling the moisture
on her breast and trailing softly across her chest to work
the same madness on her right breast. She sagged
against the support of his arms around her and her
hands gripped his waist, fingernails digging into his
leather belt. She closed her eyes and what was rising in
her throat felt like a sob. *I want... you. I want...*

His lips traveled upward along the point of her sternum, to the hollow of her throat, across her chin. His
voice was husky. "Tell me."

I want... She bit her lip as his hand moved to warm
her breast where his lips had left it aching and tingling.
I want you to make love to me.... And then his mouth
was upon hers and with a small muffled cry her arms
were traveling up his back as she pressed herself into
him, feeling him against her, opening herself to receive
him. His hand left her breast and moved to her back to
draw her closer as his tongue explored the inside of her
mouth with urgency she reciprocated. Her nipples
pressed into the softness of his shirt and responded to
the heat that throbbed against them. Her arms tightened around him so desperately the muscles ached and
the emotions that assailed her were a tangle of ecstasy
and despair. She did not know why. She did not know
how he could do this to her or how she could let him.
Maybe it had something to do with the brief nightmar-
ish moment when the sound of grinding metal had still
echoed in the air and the sight of lifeless wreckage had
been printed indelibly on her mind. She only knew that
she wanted to hold him, wanted to feel him alive and
strong and sure, that something hurt deep inside her
and he could make it go away and she wanted him. But
for all the wrong reasons. She wondered if there would
ever be a right reason for wanting Corey.

Beth's arms began to tremble with holding him so

tightly. Her legs ached with straining against him and her lips were bruised and throbbing as his own lips began to travel over her face, downward to her chin, across her jawline, nibbling at her ear, upward to her temple where he tasted a tear. His lips moved very slowly then to kiss her forehead, and his fingers brushed across her cheek, gathering another tear.

There was confusion and tenderness in his eyes as Corey looked down at her. He inquired softly, "Am I moving too fast again?"

Unsteady hands pulled the material of her shirt down over her breasts and Beth turned her face away, trying to breathe deeply without sobbing. The aching he had left inside her made her ashamed and angry, hurt and confused. In less than five minutes he had twisted everything inside her into a mass of knots and tangles and there was nothing she could do about it.

She tried to move away, but he held her arms. "I want to make love to you, Elizabeth," he said quietly.

She responded shakily, "That's not the best-kept secret of the century," and this time he let her go. She could feel his eyes upon her as she crossed to the counter and began the clumsy job of pouring the coffee. She struggled with alternating rage and despair and chewed her lip until it throbbed with the effort to keep from sobbing. Her throat ached and her nostrils burned from the effort of drawing in air and there was an awful sick feeling in the pit of her stomach. Her head ached with the concentrated effort not to look at him. Her biggest fear was that when she turned around he would not be there, and she knew if that happened she wouldn't be able to fight it anymore. She would sit down on the floor and cover her face and burst into sobs for no good reason.

How could he do this to her? She didn't know. Hadn't she read somewhere that fear has the same physiological effect on the body as sexual arousal?

Maybe she was crying now for the same reason she had cried this afternoon, whatever that was. She didn't know. She only knew that he had swept her up and whipped her about and nothing was the way it should be anymore. A month ago he was just another name in the news and now....

"I don't even know how you take your coffee!" she said out loud, and the light comment had somehow become laced with despair as she stared helplessly at the cup.

"Black," he said, watching her carefully.

She turned, bracing herself against the counter with her fingers digging into the aluminum edging, her palms flat and straining. "What do you. want from me?" she pleaded, hardly above a whisper.

He looked at her soberly, and his hand came forward to lightly brush a wisp of her hair. "Just a chance."

Oh, no. She turned quickly and sloshed cream into her own cup. Oh, no. He wasn't going to do this to her. Not with those soft-sad eyes and the mesmerist's touch and the heartbreaking little smile. Not the man with the private plane and death-defying stunts and hundred-dollar silk shirt. *Not with this lady, you don't.*

She swallowed hard, squared her shoulders, and even found a tight smile as she turned to hand him his cup. Something changed in his expression as he took it from her, a narrowing of the eyes and a tightening of the lips. Something glittered in those eyes—anger, sexual frustration, disappointment, she could not be sure. But his face was hard as he invited casually, "So. Tell me about him."

She blinked and took a sip of her coffee. Too hot. Too much cream. "Who?"

A muscle in his cheek flexed. "Steve."

She dropped her eyes, then lifted them again bravely. He would not cow her. He had done enough to her for one evening. "We grew up together," she answered him evenly. "We've been together forever. We've never wanted anyone else but each other. We have everything in common. He's kind and gentle and level-headed and secure. We're going to have a good life together. He's the finest man I've ever known. He—"

"Enough," snapped Corey and turned away. "I didn't ask for a damn eulogy." The muscles of his shoulders strained against his shirt as he lifted the cup to his lips; she saw the other hand tighten into a fist.

"It wasn't a eulogy. And you did ask! You—"

"I know what I said." He sat the cup down on the table, hard. A brown puddle formed on the tablecloth. There was an unpleasant little smile lurking at the corners of his lips as he turned. "So, you and young Doctor Kildare are going to build a cottage by the sea and live happily ever after, all comfy and cozy raising kids and tea roses until you're old and gray. Is that it?"

She was trembling as she tightened her hand around the cup. Finally she had to use both hands. "I'm sure that seems very dull to you! I mean, what is life without jetting from one world capital to the other with a trail of glamorous women kissing your hand and licking your boots! Oh, and let's not forget those *mad* pot parties in Malibu and the *divine* Med cruises!" Her voice rose with sarcastic mimicry. "And my *dear* how gauche to walk away from a table leaving anything less than a fifty-dollar tip or to appear in broad daylight in a polyester suit! Heaven forbid!"

His eyes glittered dangerously and the ugly little smile still lurked. "Remind me to put you at the top of the guest list for my next Malibu pot party," he said smoothly. "And you're more than welcome to count my tip the next time we go out to dinner. You've got a hell of a nerve, lady."

"*I've* got—" She broke off, choked with emotions too numerous to catalog and too violent to express. She felt the tears stinging again, and she swiftly turned and poured her coffee into the sink. "Just go away," she said tightly. "Go away and leave me alone."

It was only a moment before he said quietly, "I think I will." And he left without another word through the back door, closing it firmly behind him.

Chapter Eight

Four days later Beth was lying in the cramped space beneath her car draining the oil. That remedy was very much like prescribing an aspirin for terminal carcinoma, but it was the only thing besides filling the gas tank Beth knew how to do. In fact, the reason Beth rarely drove her car was because it rarely ran, and that was a situation that showed no immediate likelihood of improvement.

She reached blindly for the drain plug and her hand plopped into the bucket of slimy oil. She bit back one of Jerry's favorite expletives and said instead, "Ugh!" She wiped her hand on the front of her T-shirt and turned her head to look for the plug. Her eyes rested on a pair of exquisitely styled western-cut boots, and a familiar voice drawled, "Want a job, fella?"

She crawled out of the dark space, her eyes traveling upward to a khaki-covered calf, over the shape of a male thigh and hip, touching the hem of a safari shirt. Corey Fletcher knelt beside her, grinning as he brought from behind his back a large, dripping chocolate-dipped ice cream cone.

She wiped a greasy hand across her forehead, looking at him warily. "What's this?"

"A peace offering."

She accepted it slowly, trying to deny to herself the fact that her heart had once again lurched into the familiar double-time and that funny crawling sensation had begun in her stomach that seemed to afflict her constantly when he was around. She said hesitantly, "Chocolate dip."

His eyes twinkled as he sat on the driveway beside her. "I thought you could use some excitement. Go on, live a little."

She concentrated on licking the drips away from the napkin-covered cone so that she did not have to look at him. Her mind was racing frantically and she wasn't certain whether it was from excitement or relief or distress. He had come back. Why had he come back?

He nodded toward her car. "What's the problem?"

She bit off a waxy square of chocolate and licked the smooth ice cream from inside. "How much time have you got? What I really need is a new car."

"Happy to oblige, ma'am. How about that one?"

She followed his gaze to the shiny gold Ferrari parked at the curb, and then her eyes flew back to him in alarm. It would be just like one of his crazy, arrogant stunts to present her with the keys to a gold Ferrari. Then she saw the laughter in his eyes and she tried quickly to hide her expression.

"Don't worry," he assured her. "I've got better sense—and taste—than that. Besides, it's not mine to give. It's rented."

Again her eyes flew up in surprise. "Where does one rent a Ferrari?"

"In Washington," he replied, just as though it were the most natural thing in the world to cruise down from D.C. in a gold Ferrari dripping ice cream all over the velvet upholstery. She had missed him. In just four days she had missed him. She must be going crazy.

"Ah, yes," she said nonchalantly. "Washington." She finished the chocolate cover and began working on the soft interior. "What did you do there?"

"Went to parties mostly. Met some people. Shall I name-drop?"

"Don't bother. I'll catch the gossip column in the Sunday paper."

He took out his handkerchief and wiped away the oil stain on her forehead. For just a moment her breath stopped and her throat constricted on the cool liquid. Then he took his hand away and inquired thoughtfully, "One question, if I may. Why is the sweet flower of southern womanhood engaged in such menial labor when you have a certified mechanic living on the premises?"

"Jerry?" She bit into the cone, determinedly slowing the race of her pulse. "He'd rather cut off two fingers on each hand than do anything that remotely resembles a favor to me. Besides, working on this junk heap is just that—too much like work."

He glanced around the yard. "Where is he anyway?"

"He left about an hour ago."

"Aha," he said thoughtfully. "That means we have the entire house to ourselves."

Her throat constricted and her wide eyes met his. Was it anxiety or anticipation that tightened her stomach? She did not say anything.

He smiled slowly and a lazy light crept into his eyes as he brought one forefinger up to catch a drip of ice cream that had landed on her chin. "Forgive me, princess," he said softly. "Ice cream has that effect on me. It's been that way ever since—" His hand slipped around her neck; his face came slowly forward.

She couldn't help herself. Her arms went around his neck and her lips parted under his, letting him taste the cool sweetness that rapidly warmed beneath his leisurely, deliberate exploration. She sat on the front drive in the bright afternoon sun with a gold Ferrari in the background and traffic moving slowly up and down the street and she let him kiss her, she let herself respond to him. Let herself? She couldn't stop herself. He was addictive, and it was insane but she was glad, so glad he had come back. It was insane but happiness soared as pleasure blurred the day into golden edges and he made her forget everything but the gentle tasting motions of his mouth upon hers and the light warmth of his hand against her waist. Ice cream smeared in his hair and dripped on his shoulder and when he moved away there were oil stains all along the front of his tailored khaki shirt.

She was flustered as she looked from the rivulet of ice cream running down her arm—the cone was crushed—to the curious passersby behind them, and then to the mess she had made of his shirt. His eyes twinkled tolerantly as he caught her distress. "Not to worry," he said, "it's only money." He wiped her arm with his handkerchief, then caught her hands and pulled her to her feet. He took the mangled cone from her and announced, "Go inside and get cleaned up. We have three hours of daylight left and we're going to the beach."

Corey had had the foresight to wear swimming trunks under his slacks, and in a shirt borrowed from Jerry's closet—"He owes me," he had grinned as he pulled it on over his bare chest—they walked hand in hand along the shore. It was useless to ask what he was doing here, to wonder why he had come back. It seemed she had spent the past month asking herself that question and had she yet gotten a satisfactory answer? Every time he left she was convinced it was for the last time, but he always came back. She could spend the rest of her life wondering why. It was an exercise in futility. At last she sighed, dug her toes into the sand, and said in exasperation, "All right, I give up. Why did you come back?"

"I had a sudden craving for ice cream," he responded immediately.

"Are you never serious?" she demanded, close to

the breaking point with frustration and suspense. Nothing about this man was solid, real, or predictable. He was as ephemeral as the sea spray, as changeable as the tide, and he was driving her close to the point of insanity trying to figure him out.

"What's the point?" he answered her question. "You know better than to believe anything I say anyway."

Oh, yes. That she did know. At least she knew that.

She looked up at him defiantly. "You just don't know when to give up, do you?"

His eyes caught the sparkle of the setting sun and reflected a wicked mirth. "Do you know who you're talking to?"

She let the cool foam swirl around her ankles as the corners of her mouth turned down in dry resignation. This was the man who had driven last year's winning vehicle across the Indianapolis 500 finish line on two flat tires and a smoking engine. She supposed one could say Corey Fletcher was a man who did not know when to give up.

"I'll tell you what, though," he volunteered suddenly. He took her arms and pulled her a few steps up the beach, forcing her down onto the sand and sitting across from her with his legs crossed and his elbows upon his bare knees in a very studious attitude. "You want to talk serious; we'll talk serious. What shall it be? Politics? Religion? Quantum truths?"

The setting sun had turned the day to silver all around them. The sea was a mobile sheet of aquamarine and crystalline chips, the shore a glittering carpet of broken mirrors. His eyes were so clear they had no color at all, slightly narrowed against the glare of the sun in a golden face as transparent as windows. The wind parted his hair in four different places at once, creating a fascinating cloud of color around his face. His open shirt billowed and flapped gently with the breeze and the sun glistened on the light hairs of his legs. She was suddenly moved by an almost irresistible urge to run her fingers along the tight muscles of those legs, and she jerked her eyes away quickly. She said skeptically, "I don't think you're capable of talking seriously. I think if you can't taste, touch, see, hear, or smell it you ignore it. Ideas and emotions are just a waste of time to you."

"If that's a polite way of asking whether I ever use my head for anything other than growing hair," he retorted, "the answer is yes. Frequently. Try me. Ask me a serious question."

She shrugged and picked up a broken shell, absently beginning to dig a hole in the sand. "Will you give me a serious answer?"

"My word of honor."

She glanced at him cynically. "For all the good that does."

"Play fair," he warned mildly.

Beth looked at him, straightened her shoulders, and decided she had nothing to lose. "All right," she challenged him, "tell me why a superstar jet-setter with the world at his feet wants to waste his weekends on a sixteen-year-old juvenile delinquent and a small-town druggist with about as much sophistication as a turnip?"

He regarded her mildly. "I thought you were going to ask me something hard. You've already answered that question: I don't have the world at my feet. How can I, when I'm still getting doors slammed in my face and being ordered out of charming rose-covered houses every day of the week?"

"Ah, yes," she said softly, glancing at him through slanted eyes. "You told me you're not used to being turned down."

"Cheap shot, princess," he said, and under his steady gaze she turned back to digging her hole.

There was only the sound of the tide and the feel of his eyes upon her as the light faded in slow, lingering starbursts and rainbows. Virginia Beach sunsets were a lot like Corey Fletcher—flamboyant show-offs, playing an audience for all it was worth. Beth said in a moment, rather grudgingly, "Anyway, I suppose I should thank you for the interest you've taken in Jerry. That must be a sign you've got some character, at least."

"And I've waited my whole life for a chance to prove my character," Corey returned somewhat dryly. "As for Jerry..." He shrugged. "We're kindred spirits. It's no strain on me to 'take an interest' in him, so please don't nominate me for canonization yet. Wait until I do something really noble."

"Like giving up racing?" She did not know why she said that.

"Like risking my life to rescue a blind puppy from a burning building. Something that would really impress you."

She dropped her eyes and concentrated on digging her hole. The mound of sand grew and she struck water, but still she did not look up. Sitting with him like this, she could not help remembering the last day they had spent at the beach, when he had held her at the top of the lighthouse and they had looked out over the sea, telling tales and sharing fantasies—only another side of the multidimensional puzzle that was his character. What you see is not always what you get. It wasn't fair.

Beth could feel his eyes upon her and it was making her nervous. She had never known him to be silent for so long. Was this his way of proving to her that he was capable of being serious? At last she ventured a glance at him. "What are you thinking about?"

The subtle light that had grown in his eyes surprised her. If she had known that he had been looking at her all this time with that expression she would have been very nervous indeed. "Your legs," he replied softly, and his fingers lightly brushed her smooth calf. She jumped. "And how they would look on either side of me." He smiled, very faintly, his eyes searching hers. "You wanted the truth."

The muscles of her throat tightened and elongated as she tried to swallow. Her heart began to trip as his fingers tightened very slightly on her knee. She held her digging shell suspended in midair and she looked at him without blinking. And then, gradually, as his soft bright multicolored eyes flickered over hers his expression began to fade. The tenderness and question was replaced with a tightening of the muscles of his face, a downward curving of his lips, and his eyes reflected what was as close to bitterness as she had ever known from him. He removed his hand. "Princess," he said dryly, "if you had any idea what a power thrill it gives me to be able to put that look of sheer terror on your face, you wouldn't have to ask me why I keep coming back. It's a real rush."

And then, as swiftly as it had come, the expression was gone. He grabbed both hands and pulled her to her feet. "You know what I have a craving for now?" His lips quirked wryly. "Besides the obvious, that is. Cotton candy and carnival corn dogs. Let's go to the park."

"You're flirting with food poisoning," she warned him dourly, her heart just now beginning to resume its normal pace.

"I've said it before, and I'll say it again—"

"Live dangerously," she echoed him simultaneously, and suddenly they were both laughing.

He forced her to eat one greasy corn dog, threatening her with a paper cup of Coke held over her head until she swallowed every bite. They shared a cone of cotton candy and when Corey, without regard for his status or hesitation for thought, enthusiastically dragged her on to the bumper car ride she laughed until she thought her sides would split. High above the circus-colored lights with the dark of the night above them and the dark of the sea below them, he kissed her in the swaying chair of the Ferris wheel. She snuggled happily into the warmth of his arms and let the blurring whirl of lights and crazy carnival music absorb her and float her away on the salty night air. What did it matter why he had come back, why he was here? What did it really matter? *Just relax and enjoy it. After all, you only live once.*

They ate more cotton candy, and when the pink fluffy stuff got smeared on her nose Corey licked it off. They shared a bag of popcorn and a quart of Coke and held hands as they wandered through the jovial brighter-than-life confusion of the park. She lost three dollars and fifty cents to him at Pac-Man. Being with Corey in such a setting was perfect, for it was where he belonged, all glitter and make-believe, high thrills and canned sound.. And for the first time she was able to relax and enjoy his world.

He led her with an arm around her shoulders toward the carousel, but she hung back. "Kid's stuff," she said.

His eyes danced with the reflection of rotating colored lights against the night sky as he wiped a piece of chocolate from her chin with his finger. "Yes, Miss Sophistication."

She said, "When I was about six I saw this horror movie." She glanced at him, and noticed how young and innocent he looked in the shadows of the night against the panorama of colors and laughter and jostling activity. More illusion. "You know how filmmakers love to use amusement parks as background for horror stories. Well, it was late at night, you see, after the park had closed, and these two kids sneaked under the gate to have some fun. It was all still and silent, not a creature stirring, all the rides frozen in a sort of grotesque midair dance, just waiting for daylight to bring them to life again...."

Around them barkers competed for attention with the clashing wails of multiple calliope tunes and the squeals of thrill and fear, but for a moment it receded against the spell of her tale. Corey fixed his attention upon her, letting his hand slip from her shoulders to trail down her back, resting lightly at her waist. Her voice was quiet and half-musing as she stood watching the gaily colored horses move around in their lilting up-and-down dance.

"Well, these two smart aleck kids go sneaking around the park, half-scared to death, you know, but not about to admit it to each other. Then they find a switch and the park bursts into life—I mean lights, music, Ferris wheel turning, roller coaster rattling, the whole works. And it's just the two of them in the dead of night with all this sound and color, and they have the whole place to themselves. They're on the merry-go-round, laughing and going up and down and trying to catch the brass ring and everything is fine at first. They're having the time of their lives. And then the music starts to speed. You realize the carousel is going faster, then a little faster, and faster and faster until the whole thing is just one big blur and the kids are screaming and the horse's eyes are gleaming and their teeth look like fangs and you think the whole thing is just going to take right off and sail through the air. I've never felt quite the same way about carousels after that."

He was silent, his hand warm and light on her waist as she stood there, looking in wonder at the pretty children's ride and listening to the gay, inviting music, and marveling over how skillfully it had been distorted. Then she said softly, hardly aware that she was thinking aloud, "Sometimes it's that way with you. You've come into my life and put me on a merry-go-round, and at first it's just a harmless little ride. Then it starts going faster and faster and spinning out of control and it scares me to death because I don't know where it's going to end."

She became suddenly aware of the intensity of his gaze, and she was embarrassed. She had not meant to say that, to reveal so much of herself to him in a childhood memory and a private correlative. She glanced at him shyly and briefly, shrugging her shoulders a little in self-deprecation, and then looked quickly away.

Corey said suddenly, and so quietly she could not be certain for a moment whether she had heard it at all, "I think I love you."

And just as her eyes flew to his, whatever emotion had ruled his face the moment before vanished. "Come on," he said abruptly, grabbing her hand. "The only way to beat a childhood fear is to face it in the cold light of day. We're going to ride the carousel."

Two hours later Beth placed on the lamp table the brass ring Corey had captured for her and the budding rose he had snapped off the leaning fence and placed in her hair just before they came inside. "You look sleepy." He smiled.

Her eyes watered and her lips tightened with a grimace of a smile as she suppressed a yawn. "That's because I am. You sure know how to show a girl a good time, Fletcher."

"It cost me a bundle, but it was worth it." He took her shoulders and looked down at her indulgently. "Give me a kiss good night then, and I'll let you get some sleep."

A mischievous spark danced in her slanted eyes as she moved forward to brush his cheek with a kiss. But he moved too fast for her. He turned his head and her lips were instead upon his, parting under his gentle urging, drawing his breath into her lungs. His fingers grazed lightly over her back and her hips and sought the sensitive flesh beneath her arms as she wound them around his neck. She gasped and tried to move her face away as those fingers brushed delicately over the curves where her breasts began. She tried to lower her arms but she had to tighten them around his neck for balance as she felt herself being moved and gently lowered. He was sitting on the sofa and she was on his lap and not once had he broken the contact of their mouths. His fingers kneaded the inch or so of bare flesh where her short T-shirt did not quite meet the waistband of her shorts, but sought no further. She wanted him to go further. He was turning the liquid in her veins to gold dust and her heart choked out a powerful rhythm whose only need was to be touched by him—everywhere, and for a long, long time.

He rubbed his cheek against her face, slowly, in a gently abrasive circular motion and his breath against her ear was like a hot-cold chill. She cupped her hands at his neck, her eyes closed against the unwilling discoveries her fingers were making in the silky threads of his hair and the smooth hot flesh of his throat. A low sound formed in his throat and vibrated against the pad of her fingers as his tongue tickled her cheek daintily. "Elizabeth," he whispered. His breath was slow and even, but she felt the strain within him that kept it that way. It felt so good like that, the strong muscles of his thighs against her buttocks and his fingers warm and sure where they touched her bare waist. His rough face against the hot flush of hers, suspending her breath as fingertips teased the inside of her shirt toward the back. Too good. She knew she was in danger. Each time it was harder to listen to that warning alarm and each time she had less and less desire to listen to it.

"Elizabeth..." He was losing the fight to keep his breathing steady. "This is..." His mouth covered hers. *So good. Just let this feeling last....*

A lazy voice drawled behind them, "You guys want

to give me a quarter to go to the movies or something?"

Beth jerked away and only Corey's steadying hands kept her from tumbling to the floor. He guided her with as much dignity as possible under the circumstances to sit beside him, and he turned to greet the intruder. His face was flushed faintly and his eyes looked strange, but his voice was perfectly normal as he said, "Good evening, Jerry."

Beth tried to imitate his casual demeanor but she couldn't. She wanted to crawl under the couch. It was with great difficulty that she kept herself from tugging at the hem of her shirt and covering her knees with her hands. Her face was on fire.

Jerry leaned against the doorframe, regarding them through half-closed eyes and a nasty grin. He had been drinking. "Suit yourself," he shrugged. "I gotta warn you, though, her bedroom walls are awfully thin. You wouldn't believe how excited a guy can get just lying there listening, you know what I mean?"

Beth felt her color begin to slowly drain. Corey's face hardened. "Well, I tell you what, Jerry," he suggested, "why don't you go on back there and start listening? You'd be surprised how quick you fall asleep. Better than counting sheep, I'll bet."

He gave a short little snort of laughter. His eyes glittered. "What, and miss all the fun out here? This could be a real educational experience, man. Tell me something, Fletcher, can you make her squeal? Can you?"

Corey stood slowly. His eyes were like chips of ice. "I think," he said smoothly, "you and I need to have a few words in private. Outside."

Jerry straightened up, tensing himself for the conflict he had been trying to provoke since the moment he had walked into the room. There was an almost avaricious excitement on his face. "Oh, yeah? What if I don't want to?"

"Then," replied Corey politely, "I'll save us both a lot of trouble and shove your teeth right down your throat."

"I'd like to see you try, you little..." And Jerry called him a name so foul that Beth blanched, then went scarlet with horror and shock.

Corey took one swift look at Beth's face and closed the distance between himself and Jerry in two strides. In the same motion he caught Jerry by the arm and slammed him back against the wall with such force that his head bounced and a picture crashed to the floor. Beth choked out a cry of protest and leaped to her feet, but Corey did not turn. While Jerry was still staring at him and blinking dazedly, Corey jerked at his arm with one smooth motion and propelled him toward the door.

"Move it, kid," he snapped. And when Jerry turned, fighting mad, Corey caught him by the collar with one hand and almost sent him sprawling. "If you need any help finding the door," he ground out, eyes glittering dangerously, "the point of my boot will be more than happy to show you the way. Move!"

One final powerful shove, and the front door slammed behind them.

Twenty minutes later Corey returned—alone. Beth whirled, her heart in her throat. "Oh, Corey," she gasped, "you didn't hit him?"

A corner of his mouth twisted upward in a dry smile as he dropped Jerry's keys on the table. "Not necessary. All I had to do was let him know I knew more dirty words than he did and it was smooth sailing from there on. Give those back to him in the morning if you think he deserves them."

She stared at the car keys, and he assured her, "Just a precautionary measure. You've got to think like a sixteen-year-old to know what to expect. He'll cool down in an hour or two; meanwhile, no sense letting him loose on the road."

She drew her eyes slowly from the keys on the table to his face. "What," she asked in mounting trepidation, "did you do to him?"

He grinned and took her shoulders. "Just a long overdue father–son chat, princess. It would have bored you."

She looked at him soberly. "I doubt that. Corey—" She hesitated. "Do you think—do you think he's jealous of you?"

He nuzzled her cheek. "No, I think he rather likes me. Otherwise, he would have planted a bomb under the hood of my car long ago."

She laughed nervously and tried to step away. "Oh, Corey!"

He drew her firmly back into the circle of his arms. "Don't tell me about the Jerry Fieldses of this world, princess. I used to be one, remember?"

But just as she looked up with a question on her lips, he moved away slightly, a sigh feathering across her face as his eyes closed briefly and regretfully. "Elizabeth," he said softly, "this is not working out."

Sudden alarm tightened in her chest as he said that, she did not know why. It sounded very much like a prelude to goodbye, and that was what she wanted... wasn't it?

His smile was sad and reluctant as he added, "We can't go on like this. I don't mind a little competition, but we've got to have some time alone together." He touched two fingers lightly to her cheek. "The thing is, there's not much I can do about it right now. If I call you, will you try to make some time for me?"

She looked at him. Her throat was dry when she tried to swallow. "I...no. I can't. You know that I— No."

He smiled again and very gently bent to kiss the corner of her eye. "I'll call you," he promised.

For the next three weeks Beth diligently avoided answering the phone. Corey called every day and talked to Jerry. Twice during that period he was in town, but he picked Jerry up while she was working and they did not get home until after she was asleep. It was odd that he did not persist. He could have very easily called her at work, but he always called Jerry at home while she was at the store. She thought he might have gotten the hint that she did not want to talk to him when, after the first eight or ten times that he made his calls during the evening, she let the phone ring until Jerry answered it and then went to the bathroom so that Jerry would not have to lie when he said she was unavailable. She knew she was being childish and she had no excuse for it; still, it was very unlike Corey not to insist. He could have easily taken a few moments to stop by the store when he was in town, just to say hello, but he didn't. It was all very strange. But stranger still was the transformation that gradually began in Jerry, making Beth marvel at the miracles that could be wrought via long distance.

She came home not a week after Corey had last left her to find her little Volkswagen all washed and waxed and sparkling like a jewel in the afternoon sun. She had to look twice, thinking at first some stranger had parked his car in her driveway. And Jerry offered casually, "Fletcher said you needed some engine work. I gave it a good going-over, cleaned her up a little for you. What you really need to do is take her out on the freeway and blow some of the dust out of the carburetor."

She had to forcefully close her mouth. "How—how much do I owe you?"

He shrugged. "The parts store is sending you the bill."

Not long after that Jerry asked her rather grudgingly if her offer of a job was still open. It seemed there was some part for his car he wanted to buy, and Corey had promised to help him install it when next he was in town. Beth gave him a job helping out in the mornings stocking shelves and after she closed up cleaning and sweeping. She did not question the divine workings of good fortune.

The day after Jerry's first paycheck Beth came home to two boxed chicken dinners on the dining room table. Jerry offered only, "Thought you might be tired after working all day." Beth sat down and they shared the meal in silence, and she began to think of her modest little home as possible competition for Lourdes. Surely no greater miracles had been worked there than the ones that were happening right here before her very eyes.

Everything was perfect, almost too good to be true, until Steve came down for the weekend. Beth knew something was wrong the moment he walked in the door. No, it wasn't something wrong exactly...it was just something different. Perhaps he looked different. No, the smile was the same, the familiar offhand greeting—"How goes it, kiddo?"—the gentle brown eyes; the broad shoulders and fair complexion; the strong, competent hands. He was the same. Maybe she was different.

The thought panicked her. What was it he had said— "Don't start making comparisons"? Yes, it frightened her to realize what a small part of her life Steve had been these past months, when there never before had been anything they could not share and confide. He was almost a stranger to her. It was panic that made her rush into his arms and kiss him with an unaccustomed passion, and she felt like an adulteress. It was shame that made her back away before he could even begin to overcome his surprise with an appropriate response, because there was nothing there. She had been trying to prove something to herself, or to him, and had failed.

Steve looked down at her with a very odd expression, puzzled and reticent, and Beth was miserable with confusion and self-loathing and not a small amount of shock. Steve was a male with a perfectly normal sex drive and he was not completely immune to the passion she had just exploded upon him. But he was a gentle man, sensitive to her wishes and patient with her needs, never complaining when she pulled back. For the first time in the two years of their "serious" relationship Beth thought she understood why she had always pulled back and he had never complained. The magic simply wasn't there between them.

Beth hated those reflections and the creeping doubts that were beginning to nag at her. She tried to shake them away but they clung. And as she stood there with his hands lightly caressing her elbows, lost in her embarrassment and confusion, the telephone rang. She was glad to give him a small apologetic smile and go to answer it.

"Is this the home of the world's last nickle ice cream cone?"

"Corey!" she gasped the name out loud before she thought. She glanced at Steve just in time to see a small frown crease his brow before he turned away, and that only increased her confusion. "What—what do you want? Jerry isn't here."

"I know that. It's ten o'clock on a Friday night. I called to talk to you."

She glanced again nervously at Steve but his back was to her. He was looking out the window, holding back a drapery with one hand, apparently absorbed in the view of the darkened street. "But—but why? What do you want?"

"There's a rose garden outside my hotel room," he said. "Princess, you've never seen so many roses. Red and yellow and white, pink and orange and a whole spectrum of colors in between. They smell like you."

She turned away from Steve, trailing the cord behind

her, bending her head to cradle the phone. "That's nice," she said lamely.

He laughed lowly. "Something tells me I caught you at a bad time."

"Well...yes, as a matter of fact—"

"How's Jerry doing, anyway?"

"Corey," she said, for this was something she had been wanting to tell him for a long time, "it's unbelievable. How in the world did you do it?"

"I'd love to tell you over dinner on the French Riviera. Shall we say sevenish?"

She reminded him dryly, "It's after ten."

"I meant tomorrow, my dear little linear-thinking princess." But as she drew a breath he conceded with a chuckle, "Spare me the lecture, but save me part of the weekend anyway. I'll be on your doorstep about three o'clock tomorrow afternoon."

"Corey—"

"Sharp."

"I won't be here. I—"

"Sorry, princess, I didn't quite catch that. Must be a bad connection."

"I said I won't be here. I have to—"

"I'm afraid you'll have to tell me tomorrow, love, we're losing our line. See you then."

Damn him, she thought tightly as she replaced the receiver. He even had the telephone company selectively piping in static over parts of the conversation he chose not to hear. She turned hesitantly to Steve.

His smile was vague and there was a lurking sadness far in the back of his eyes as he extended his hand to her. She knew every expression that had ever crossed his face, but she had never seen this one before. She only understood enough of it to be frightened.

"Come over here, Beth, and sit down," he said. "I want to talk to you for a while."

They sat on the sofa and he held her hand lightly

between his smooth cool ones. But once there she waited for him to speak and he said nothing. The dread in the pit of her stomach grew. He kept looking around the room as though for inspiration, but never once did his eyes light on her. At last he gave a small, nervous laugh. "Funny. I had this all planned out and now I can't seem to remember how it begins."

Slowly she withdrew her hand, swallowing hard. "It doesn't sound like something I much want to hear anyway. Maybe I'll just pass."

He looked at her. "Basically," he said, "I guess I just wanted to tell you that I won't be coming down, or calling you, for a while."

The dread eased as her worst fears began to unfold. Still she searched his face anxiously. "But why?" It was almost a whisper.

His gaze wandered to the now-silent telephone and rested there meaningfully. "I just think you need the space."

She tried to defend herself vainly, knowing that what she was trying so desperately to hold on to had already slipped through her fingers. "Steve, don't be silly. That phone call—it was nothing. I told you about Corey, how he's been so good for Jerry and taken such an interest in him."

"A man doesn't call a woman at ten o'clock at night from France because he's interested in her nephew," he informed her.

She blinked. "France?" He had called her from *France*? "What was he doing there?"

Steve shrugged. "Some race he was driving this week," he answered vaguely. "Don't you read the papers?"

She had made a conscientious effort to avoid the papers this last month for precisely this reason. She hadn't known he was racing; she didn't want to know. Even thinking about it now, after the fact, made her mouth a little dry. "But," she floundered, "he said he would be here tomorrow."

He smiled at her patiently. "Do you see what I mean?"

She tried one more time to desperately get a grip on the situation. She couldn't believe this was happening. She took a breath, wet her lips, and began calmly, "Steve, this isn't a bit like you. I don't know what you've been hearing...." But she knew very well what he had been hearing. His mother had lost no time in rushing to the store to inquire who that famous person was who had driven Beth home from church—Robert Redford? Paul Newman?—and neither had any of Steve's other numerous friends and relatives in town. A girl was not exactly invisible sporting around town in a gold Ferrari, and neither was she immune to curious eyes poking around hedges and peering over mailboxes when she sat on her front lawn wrapped in the arms of a superstar.

But worse than that, how many of her conversations with Steve over the past month had begun, "Corey says..." or "Corey does..."? She had never thought about it. Steve knew exactly how often Corey had been here, how much time they spent together. The only thing he didn't know was what they had done while they were together. Or did he? She looked up at him helplessly.

His smile was affectionate, understanding, and a little sad. He said, "Honey, I've known you since you licked the icing off my sixth birthday cake. Give me a little credit for knowing what's going on inside your head, huh?" He dropped his eyes briefly. "It wasn't easy for me to admit at first. I thought he was just kidding. But I'm not going to compete with a man like that."

"Compete!" she gasped. "You don't have to—"

He silenced her with one finger laid firmly across her

lips. His eyes were very serious. "I asked you to give me some credit. Bethy, I know you better than I know myself. I know something has changed about you. I was just afraid to admit to myself what it was. I could hear it in your voice, see it in your eyes every time we met. I don't blame you for being infatuated with the guy, if infatuation is all it is. And I know I can't keep you if you don't want to stay."

"But I do want to stay!" She felt tears burn her eyes and she was being swept away by a tidal wave of her own making, spinning out of control.

He shook his head slowly, firmly. "No, just listen to me. You need to go with this. Maybe I can see what you can't, Bethy, but I think you're in love with him."

"No! I—"

"All right," he said quietly, firmly. "We won't get into that. But, Beth, you know as well as I do that this just isn't working for us. You can't say you don't know that."

She dropped her eyes slowly, and she could no longer deny what she had been trying to avoid for... she did not know how long. Maybe since a chilly spring night on a deserted pier while the ocean pounded in her ears and something new sprang to sudden life inside her. She understood now why Steve never complained when she pulled back. She understood why his kisses never turned her to fire. She said very low, without looking at him, "You don't love me." And she realized for the first time that they had never said those words to each other: "I love you." It was always just assumed. And all the time a central ingredient was missing from the lovely, quiet, secure relationship they had built together. She had not noticed its absence because she had never known what it was.

Steve placed his hands on either side of her shoulders, and slowly she lifted her face to look at him. "I do love you," he said quietly. "I love you so much that when you've worked this thing through and gotten Corey Fletcher out of your system I'll be here, waiting. But"—he bent slowly and placed a gentle kiss upon her forehead—"you've got to work it through. Alone."

When he was gone she sat where he had left her and one slow, sluggish tear rolled down her cheek. She did not know whether she was crying for what she had lost or what she had never had. She only knew that he had finally said the words, and it was too late.

What had happened to her? How could this have happened to her? She had her life all planned out; everything was going according to an orderly, concise, preset pattern. She expected and sought no surprises in her life. All she had ever wanted was the status quo. And now all of a sudden nothing was the way it should have been anymore, everything was torn apart. She hadn't asked for this.

She lay awake muffling sobs in her pillow so that Jerry wouldn't hear, alternately clenching her fists against her eyes and beating them on the mattress in wide swings of misery and anger. Steve loved her. He had said so. Good, calm, quiet Steve, who understood her so well and was all she had ever wanted from life. Steve, who always knew where she had left her skate key, who bandaged scraped knees, and knew how to make her smile...who cared for her enough to wait. Who knew her well enough to know he must.

And Corey Fletcher. A shooting star, a glittering firebird who had cut a scorching path across her life and left only devastation in his wake. A fantasy, an illusion, a summer storm with much sound and color and little substance. "I think I love you." What was that supposed to mean? Corey Fletcher, who lived each moment to the fullest, constantly enriching his life with props and settings. This was the man who could let his imagination roam free in conjuring shipwrecks and pirates on a calm sea, who enthusiastically let himself be caught up in imaginary tales about lost sailors and lonely ladies, adding to the script whatever the moment required. Corey Fletcher, who lived in the world of high thrills and make-believe.... Nothing. It meant nothing.

And yet this one man had taken twenty-eight years of security and stability and predictability and with a flick of his wrist had left it in rubble. He had burst into her life on a trail of sparks and white lights and pulled the very foundation of her world out from under her. She hadn't asked for it. She hadn't wanted it. *It wasn't fair.*

Her father came by at noon, took one look at her pale face and red-rimmed eyes, and asked her what was wrong. She told him.

He listened silently to her tale of despair, which began in bitterness, moved to sorrow, and finally ended in a sort of floundering confusion. The incredible thing, she kept repeating as though to convince herself, was that she was guilty of nothing. She hadn't even seen Corey Fletcher in three weeks, and even then.... That was when she blundered into confusion, her cheeks tingling and her voice tight. They both knew that Steve was not the type of man to leap to conclusions for no reason or to see imaginary shadows behind every door. This was not a scene from a soap opera and jealousy was not in his nature. It wasn't a lover's spat to be resolved in a day or two. They both knew that Steve was right.

Her father was silent for a long time after she had finished. Then he said soberly, "Steven is a fine man, and I want you to know this is not going to change our professional relationship. I'll admit I always thought the two of you were perfect for each other, and I can't say I'm glad to hear this has happened. But, Bethy"—he lifted her chin gently with his finger, and there was a softening of his features that confused her—"Steven never put that sparkle in your eyes. He knows it as well as I do."

She stared at him incredulously for a long moment. When at last she could speak it was only to cry, "That's not a sparkle—it's a glitter of rage! It's all Corey Fletcher's fault! He comes whizzing through town like he owns the place, making a spectacle of me and upsetting my life and he's even got you on his side!"

Her father only smiled and left her alone. Perhaps it was then that she really began to believe it. She could waste time and emotional energy with anger and blame-casting but it wouldn't change the facts. Steve was gone. The one sure, solid, and dependable thing in her life had evaporated as though it had never been and there was nothing she could do to bring it back. Somehow she didn't belong in his world anymore. Perhaps she hadn't for a long time now. She didn't know. She only knew that Steve was right, and she knew it with a sadness and a fear like none she had ever known. She had to work this through on her own.

At three o'clock she turned to deliver a prescription to Mrs. Fuller, and Corey Fletcher was leaning against the counter. "Hi there," he smiled lazily. "Remember me?"

Chapter Nine

He was wearing a pale blue turtleneck sweater and a soft crinkly leather jacket—ridiculous garb for this weather. His hair was lightly tousled and his eyes picked up the blue of his sweater. Where had all the anger gone, the resentment, the grief? She had never realized before what a long time three weeks could be, and seeing him now was just like the first time when he had sauntered into her shop after having been run down by her car. She looked at him for perhaps five seconds of slow wonder and tingling pleasure, and then she became aware of Mrs. Fuller's excited fluttering and Ellie's curious stares, and she jerked her eyes away.

She rang up the purchase quickly, presented the package to her customer—who showed an obvious reluctance to leave—and then she turned back to him. She wanted to snap at him. She wanted to flounce out of the shop and slam the door behind her. She wanted to let him know exactly how furious and hurt she was and how he had caused her suffering without even trying. This was the man who had effortlessly wrecked her entire life and all she could say to him was a curious "Did you really fly in all the way from France?"

"And I have the jet lag to prove it." He took her arm and pulled her gently around the counter. "Come on, I'll drive you home."

"That must be why you're dressed so funny."

"The very height of fashion on the Champs-Élysées. I've got your car outside, I hope you don't mind. I didn't have time to rent one."

She was standing right before him now, in her white knee-length working smock and her peach calf-length jersey skirt with a stain on the hem—she had dropped a bottle of gentian violet that morning, knelt to pick up the pieces and ruined the skirt forever. His fingers were light and warm on her arm and his eyes were gazing down at her with a sort of drowsy confidence, and suddenly she recovered herself. "Sorry," she said stiffly, pulling her arm away. "I don't close up until seven."

She went back behind the counter and he stood there for a moment longer. Her heart actually lurched as he turned and walked away, and then it speeded crazily with relief and curiosity as he went, not for the door, but for the cosmetics counter where Ellie was halfheartedly replenishing stock. He leaned with beautiful grace with one elbow on the shelf as he spoke to her, the tight fit of his trousers outlining the shape of a casually posed leg and the jacket falling away from the sweep of his slim waist and firm chest. His voice was soft and pleasant, once interrupted by Ellie's giggle and the companionable roll of his chuckle. Beth strained her ears for a hint of their conversation as she busily began to total up the receipts, but she could catch nothing. Her cheeks began to burn as he strolled casually back to her and she refused to look up.

"There you see," he said calmly, "all taken care of. Your relief will be here in"—he glanced at the clock over her head; he still was not wearing a watch—"exactly ten minutes. Jerry and Ellie are perfectly capable of minding the rest of the business and I've asked your father to stop by to check on any problems." His eyes fixed her with a mild challenge. "Any more excuses?"

She stared at him. He had certainly gone to a lot of

trouble to see that she took a few hours off, but wasn't that his style? Issuing directives, giving commands, making the world spin on the tip of his finger. "You think of everything, don't you?"

"I try to." His fingers brushed against her shoulders as he slipped her smock off. "Shall we go?"

She hesitated before her little car, which waited patiently at the curb, still shiny and looking very self-satisfied since Jerry's latest efforts with a polishing cloth. "How did you get out here then," she inquired dubiously, "if you don't have a car?"

"Jerry."

Why did she suddenly feel the whole world was plotting against her? "You didn't have to bother," she said somewhat irritably as he opened the door for her. "We could have walked."

He gave her a suddenly amused look and walked to the other side of the car.

Of course she should have known he had no intention of merely driving her home. She kept her mouth determinedly shut during the short drive to the marina and made no reply when he offered only, "It's too nice a day to stay inside."

She tried to be angry with him as he went inside, presumably to charter a boat. She looked down at her rope sandals, stained skirt, and flowered cotton blouse and reflected that she was hardly dressed for boating— but would that make any difference to him? She walked along the dock, determinedly ignoring him as he came back out with the proprietor, looking the other way as the two of them checked out the boat and made preparations for departure. Her car was still sitting in the parking lot. She could drive off and leave him here. She walked slowly back to the boat where Corey was standing inside, preparing to cast off.

It was a medium-size outboard with bucket seats, a storage compartment, and wind deflector. The name painted in blue letters on the gleaming white hull was *Elizabeth*.

"Nice touch," she commented dryly.

He grinned up at her as he held her forearms to help her on board. "I thought so."

He was right about one thing: The day was too nice to spend inside. The sea was calm and glistening and the day was bright. Against an electric-blue sky transparent scraps of cloud clung like spun sugar. Corey's eyes were narrowed bits of sparkling cobalt in a sun-crinkled face and wind whipped his hair about gaily. One brown hand rested lightly on the throttle and his face was turned away from her, whether in concentration upon navigation or in pure sensual worship of the sun upon his skin she could not tell. Sea spray beaded on his leather jacket and dampened the front of Beth's blouse, tickling her bare arms. Her skirt caught the wind and billowed playfully about the seat as warm air rushed between her knees. She wished she could recapture just one small portion of the rage and resentment she had felt for him last night.

When he began to slow the motor and approach a small island, she thought she just might be able to find a new perspective on anger. But all she really felt was a slight uneasiness, a nervousness that was actually more like anticipation.

The outboard hummed in neutral as he expertly guided the boat to a small dock. The island was not quite as small as it had seemed from a distance but, putting her admittedly sketchy seafaring abilities to work she estimated it was less than a square mile in land mass. The presence of a dock was curious. "Is this a private island?" she shouted to him.

He killed the engine. Utter, unearthly silence was the only background for the slapping of the waves and the cracking of the rope as he tied the boat off with two deft movements. "Umm-hmm. Utterly uninhabited."

His eyes flashed mirth at her. "Except for us, of course."

She climbed carefully over the bow and used his hands for balance as she stepped onto the shore. Then she exclaimed, "There's a house up there!"

From a narrow strip of sandy beach protected from erosion by an elevation of sandbags a grassy bank rose sharply upward. The wind ruffled the tangled ropes of grass and through the parting Beth could just make out the shape of a beach cottage. "So there is," Corey conceded mildly, and she glanced at him sharply as he leaned over the boat to take something from the storage compartment.

It did not take a particular gift of perception to notice that Corey had been nursing an amusing secret since he had first called for her at the shop, but perhaps Beth had simply chosen to ignore the signs. He commented ruefully, "Now comes the hard part." She did not know why she should be astonished when he pulled from the boat two articles: a brown leather duffel bag and her own flowered canvas suitcase.

Very smooth, Beth thought, and she was proud of the way she kept her emotions under control. Their eyes met for a long moment and nothing at all registered on her face. Behind the conversationally polite pause there might have been a hint of curiosity or even wariness in Corey's eyes but Beth ignored it. She said in a voice totally devoid of expression, "At least you didn't take me to a motel." And she did not blink or shift her gaze away once.

"I've got class," he agreed mildly and touched her arm to lead her up the hill.

She moved her arm away. "I hope you also have a good memory for the way back home," she replied in the same carefully controlled tone, "because that's exactly where we're going. Now." She turned back to the boat.

"In the first place," replied Corey behind her, "this house happens to belong to some friends of mine, a very stable married couple in their fifties who would be utterly outraged at your suggestion that they would lend out their house for illicit assignations. In the second place," he told her with a steady, very nearly intimidating gaze, "you should wait until you're asked before you start jumping into bed with the first man you meet on a deserted island. This also happens to be where I've been staying the last few weekends I was in town. Other men bring their dates home for a drink and it's perfectly socially acceptable; why can't I?"

"Other men," she spat back viciously, "don't usually have a suitcase in each hand. Take me home!"

"Oh, that," he replied, ignoring her request and glancing instead at the canvas suitcase in his hand. "Jerry packed for you. I hope he didn't forget anything."

Jerry again! They *were* plotting against her. She stood there for a moment, seething, and when he made no move to help her on board she turned to clamber over the bow without assistance.

He retorted mildly behind her, "I hope you have a good memory." And he turned to walk up the hill.

For perhaps thirty seconds she stared at him, her vision turning red at the edges with pure, unadulterated fury. On top of everything else the last thing she had needed this weekend was to be the victim of another one of Corey Fletcher's high-handed stunts. He had already managed to turn her emotions to confetti with an entire ocean separating them and with no effort at all on his part. This was entirely too much.

He was waiting for her at the top of the hill. The sea breeze lifted his hair and ruffled it gently. His eyes were as opaque and unreadable as a still forest pool. "Look," he said simply, "I'm tired. I've flown back and forth between three continents this week and all things taken into account I haven't had any sleep in thirty-six hours. I know your first inclination is to claw my eyes out but I'm asking you as one human being to another to just hold that thought for a little while. There's something I want to show you first."

For the first time she sensed a carefully restrained anger just beneath the surface of his own words, and she was both confused and outraged. What had he expected her to do then, leap joyfully into his arms and smother him with mad passionate kisses at the prospect of spending a weekend alone with him? But she found herself following him across the short stretch of grassy turf and up the steps of the stilt-supported cottage without another word, too enraged, confused, or perhaps simply disappointed to speak.

She caught a glimpse of a small cozily furnished room with two picture windows looking out over the ocean and a compact kitchen to the right, but Corey did not pause there. She followed him down a short stretch of hallway and watched as he opened the door to a bedroom and dumped her suitcase inside. "One," he said, and opened the door to another room across the hall. "Two."

She stood on the threshold of the second bedroom as he placed his suitcase in a closet and stripped off his jacket. Her mind was turning and raging in confusion. "I want to go home," she said.

"Well, I'll tell you what, princess," he replied equitably, "right now I'm in no mood to argue with you. But I am also in no mood to make the trip to the mainland and back again with dark coming on. In fact"—he pulled the sweater over his head and tossed it onto a chair; she blinked in astonishment but said nothing, she did not even move—"the only thing I am in the mood for is bed." Her eyes were drawn irresistibly to the patterns of light and shadow that played on his bare torso from the open shutters of the window, and suddenly he grinned disarmingly. His hands went unfalteringly to the catch of his trousers. "Staying for the floor show?" he invited.

Beth turned and stalked out of the room, missing his wince as she slammed the door behind her. She made it to the front room and then she stopped, pacing back and forth in tight, angry circles, her mind in a turmoil. Half of her expected him to follow her. The other half knew perfectly well that he was just arrogant enough to bring her all the way out here and then leave her to fend for herself while he went to sleep. And all the while most of her was turning and spinning in a cyclone of confusion.

There was a long white envelope on the floor beside the door, and after a moment she went to pick it up. It was a Mailgram adressed to Corey. For just a moment she paused, half turning toward the bedroom, and then placed the envelope down on the table by the door. Let him take care of his own business and urgent messages. The last thing he would get out of her tonight was cooperation.

She stood at the window, her eyes narrowed and her arms crossed, one finger tapping a tightly controlled rhythm against her elbow. Of course there was the boat still docked in the cove. She knew how to operate an outboard. She wasn't much on navigation, but there was always the coast guard. How far out could they be, anyway? It would serve him right. Of all the arrogant, underhanded tricks!

Fuming was exhausting work, and it was warm in the cottage. It took time for the fine edge of her anger to wear itself down, but at length she went into her own bedroom to change her rumpled work clothes for something cooler. She found a pair of shorts and a halter on top and closed the suitcase. Then she turned back. At first her search was curious, then hastily haphazard, finally exasperated. Shorts, skinny rib-knit midriffs and strapless halters, the entire contents of her underwear drawer, every cosmetic, perfume, and cologne she owned.... She slammed the soft cover of her case shut with a tight breath and glared at it. The rotten kid had not packed her a single nightgown.

She slipped on her sandals and left the house with no particular destination or purpose in mind, simply following the overpowering instinct for action, to do something even if it was utterly futile. She walked along the shoreline, making patterns in the wet sand with a trailing piece of gray driftwood, searching her soul for deficits of character or errors in judgment that had led to being held captive on a deserted island by one of the world's most glamorous men. She looked back over the events of the past month with a sort of detached curiosity, wondering what she had done, where she had gone wrong. She had always been such a simple soul. She had a good life. She liked her life. She hadn't asked for any of this.

Beth walked around the island twice until her legs began to ache and she was short of breath, then she climbed up the embankment overlooking the cove and sat down with her knees drawn up to her chin, looking out over the sea. What was she doing here? This was Elizabeth Greene, born and raised in the same small town in which she had contentedly contemplated spending the rest of her life. She had her family and friends, her business, her daily routine... and Steve. Steve at least had given her the freedom to choose, but Corey Fletcher had kidnapped her, ruthlessly and selfishly, without pausing to consult her opinion.

So there's the boat, stupid. Go.

Was this her choice, then? To become one of those sleek women with their tight jeans and clinging glittery blouses who hung around the racetrack and nibbled on Corey's fingers instead of hors d'oeuvres at all the best parties? One of the flock who trailed him around the world adding color and glamour to the brilliant aurora of his life-style? She didn't know. She only knew that Corey Fletcher had sailed into her life one spring morning not quite three months ago and suddenly nothing made any sense anymore. She didn't know who she was or where she belonged or what she wanted anymore. It wasn't fair.

She doubled her fists and pressed them into her eyes briefly, trying to clear her head with the short burst of physical pain. What was she doing here? All she wanted was her little house and her very ordinary little business, the people of the community she served who liked and respected her, a life filled with small satisfactions and few surprises. Why did it have to happen to her? How could everything have gotten so tangled up with absolutely no effort whatsoever on her part?

The boat bounced and rocked invitingly in the cove. Well?

She leaned her cheek on her upraised knees, looking away from the boat. She knew she wouldn't leave. She didn't know why. She hated what was happening to her but she didn't seem to be able to stop it. One man had stepped into her life three months ago and turned it upside down without even trying, and no, there was nothing fair about it. She didn't know how it had happened, she didn't know how to stop it; it was all spinning out of control. Corey Fletcher had appeared upon the horizon in a burst of sound and color and suddenly nothing was where it should be anymore, suddenly everything was changed, suddenly...love.

A powder puff-pink and green twilight was falling when at last she heard a step behind her, and she supposed it must be near nine o'clock. She had been sitting there most of the afternoon. Soft gray shadows cut angular rivulets through the long ropy grass and the warm breeze tasted of salt. Beth rested her cheek on the other knee to look at him. "Short nap for someone with jet lag," she commented.

Corey gave her a lopsided grin and sank with easy grace to the bank beside her. "I sleep fast too."

He was wearing white shorts and a red short-sleeved shirt that he had not buttoned. In the gentle light his face was blurred into youthful planes and contours, his hair soft and fluffy. His eyes were drowsy and placid with the residue of sleep and a vague, sort of permanent, smile seemed to lurk there. She looked at him for a long time and he let her.

Then he said, turning that sweet, innocent face to look out over the ocean, "I'm glad you didn't leave. There's not much more than a week's supply of food inside and I'd hate to be stranded."

A week? *A week?* But she swallowed back her trepidation and replied casually, "Someone would have sent a rescue ship for you long before then. After all, how long could the world survive without Corey Fletcher?"

He shrugged. "Sometimes I wouldn't mind trying to find out." Then he looked at her. "On a scale of one to ten, how mad are you?"

She thought about it. "Six."

"Better than I expected." He took the fingers of one of her hands and placed them in his palm, stroking them absently with the thumb and forefinger of his other hand. He concentrated his attention on that maneuver with a sober gaze, as though he were discovering and protecting a fragile bird, calming, mesmerizing, worshiping. At last he said without looking at her, "I have a confession to make that will probably send your mad index over the top. Jerry told me about what happened with Steve last night. I realize my timing was a little opportunistic."

Beth peered at him curiously, but his full lashes were still lowered, his face shadowed and revealing nothing. It first occurred to her to wonder how Jerry had known,

but it was a silly reflection. Everyone knew by now.
There was no such thing as a secret in her circle. She
said only, turning to watch the way the dying sun
bounced in prisms of color off the horizon, "Jerry's a
little gossip."

"Jerry's a very loyal spy," corrected Corey mildly.
He turned her hand over and began dainty, tickling
feather-brushes of his forefinger across the lines of her
palm and upward to each finger. Her fingers began to
quiver involuntarily and to curl. She clenched them but
he held her wrist as she started to draw away. "And
never let it be said," he added, turning her hand over
and again resuming his absorbing exploration of the
veins and ridges of the back of her hand, "that I re-
warded loyalty with betrayal. You will kindly direct your
snide comments and dirty looks to myself alone and
leave my worthy assistant out of this."

Her hand seemed to be developing a pulsing, highly
charged life of its own beneath the sensitizing ministrations of his fingers. It was a wonderfully pleasurable
sensation that crept all the way up to her armpit and
melted the stiffness of her neck muscles. She retorted,
trying to fight it, "And never let it be said that Corey
Fletcher is one to refuse to take advantage of an opportunity when it stares him right in the face."

He looked at her, and there was not a flicker of
amusement in his eyes. "You can blame me for a lot of
things, princess," he said soberly, "but the actions of
your illustrious young doctor are not among them.
That's one thing," he added, and she thought she de-
tected the very faintest hint of bitterness in his tone,
"over which I have never had any control."

She dropped her eyes uncomfortably and pulled her
hand away. He did not try to retrieve it. Instead he placed
both hands on his splayed knees and added conversationally, "And just for the record, despite what you may
have heard to the contrary, it's not usually my custom to

cross an ocean in record time just for the purpose of bedding a pretty young thing. There are easier ways."

Beth turned a slow skeptical gaze on him and he went on more seriously, "Look, I know that sometimes I have a tendency to be a little aggressive—"

"A little!" she laughed shortly.

"I have the floor," he reminded her, unperturbed, and she shrugged. "I told you the last time I saw you that I was getting tired of a jet-age relationship," he continued calmly. "I just wanted some time alone together."

"So you took it."

"If you interrupt one more time I'm going to tickle you until you can't breathe," he warned soberly, and she jerked her eyes to the ocean view again. "I figured it was only fair. How could you make an intelligent choice unless you had the full picture?" She turned incredulous eyes on him and opened her mouth for an exclamation, then determinedly snapped it shut again. "All I wanted," he finished simply, "was a little time together, to share a few sunsets with you—"

"A few!" she cried in alarm, and that was it. His fingers were upon her ribs and the more she struggled the more ruthless he became. She muffled squeals and pulled at his hands and tried to squirm away and his eyes danced in pure delight at the torture he was inducing.

"You're going to get sand in your hair," he warned, pulling her back as she tried to slide away from him. "Had enough?"

Tears ran down her cheeks and her sides ached from laughing as she gasped, "Enough! I give up! Just stop. I surrender!"

He couldn't resist one last agonizing course up and down her ribs that made her sob with laughter, and then he obediently dropped his hands. The merriment in his eyes was like a sparkling clear water fountain as he mused, "That easy, huh? Why didn't I think of this before?"

He rested his hands on the sand on either side of her, sitting very close and trapping her with his presence, but not touching her. She was still gasping and wiping her eyes as he brought his forehead slowly to lean on hers, and the laughter died as she looked into his eyes. The boyishness and the sparkle had faded there, and he said softly, "Just one sunset then. It's better than nothing. We'll go back in the morning, okay?"

She whispered, "O-okay." She tried to swallow. She wanted to drop her eyes but she couldn't. Their noses touched and their lips were so close they almost brushed. He did not kiss her. He merely continued to gaze into her eyes with a soft, patient gravity and she returned that gaze, arrested, waiting. His hands were close to her thighs, but he did not touch her. She suddenly had an almost irresistible urge to let her tongue slip out to caress his lips, for their faces were so close it would have been the most natural thing in the world. She had to clench her fists in her lap to keep from succumbing to that urge.

He simply continued to look at her, and it was as though he was patiently, painstakingly examining her, searching her soul layer by layer, gently probing into secret corners and lifting her very essence into the soft caress of his approval. Her breath began to quicken and anticipation curled in her stomach, but he did not move. All he had to do was part his lips and he would be kissing her. A millimeter's distance would bring his fingers into contact with her body. But the only contact remained that of their foreheads and the bare brushing of their noses and he simply sat there, waiting.

What was this, some new form of torture? He was so close she could almost taste him. He was so close her mouth was dry and her stomach hurt. What was it he saw in her eyes that made him wait so patiently, so timelessly, demanding nothing when everything within her was coiled into tension ready to spring forth and demand something . . . anything . . . everything.

He said softly, "Touch me, Elizabeth."

She tensed, her eyes wide and filled with question and anxiety as they were held by his. She wanted to. He knew she wanted to and he would wait, not helping, not urging, not moving. She dropped her eyes. She wanted to move her face away, to break the contact, but instead her hand came up to flutter over the silky flesh of his chest. She ventured a quick, shy look at him and there was a trace of a smile hovering at the corners of his eyes. "There now," he whispered, his warm breath fanning a caress across her lips, "was that so hard?"

"N-no." Pleasure grew from the tips of her fingers as they trailed across his chest, the muscular rise of his breast and the flat brown nipple, the hardness of his sternum and across its width to the point where a heart beat hard beneath the pressure of her palm. She felt him tense and his eyes dropped closed, his face moving even closer to hers. His own hands remained forcefully still. She could feel the straining of the muscles in his arm as her fingers traced its course and it delighted her.

His tongue swept across the corner of her mouth and her own lips parted breathlessly, tasting the slippery warmth of his tongue as it gently probed and retreated—not a kiss, more of an exploration, a warm moist trail that circled her chin and the tip of her nose and across her cheek. She tasted coarse salty skin and her surprised tongue met his in a sliding lingering dance as it brushed across his lips and upward to the cleft. She felt his warm rapid breath and she wiggled closer, her tongue licking and dancing over his face as his did hers, warm, wet, tingling, tasting ruffled lashes and smooth cheek, quivering eyelids and the curving indentation of his nose.

Her hand drifted downward over his lean waist and the plane of his cotton-covered hip until her fingers at last found the freedom to explore what they had yearned to touch for so long. His soft intake of breath was a hot chill on her wet face as her fingers trailed along the hard curve of his muscled calf, discovered the sensitive hollow of his knee and explored the taut ligaments there. Luxuriating in the shape of him, the tense muscles, the furry covering of hair. Moving upward across the breadth of sinewy thigh, feeling the faint flush of his face against hers and the quickening of his breath. Weakening with the pleasure that swelled from the powerful expanse of muscle beneath her hand and flowed throughout her body. Her own breath fluttered in her throat as her fingers moved ever upward, feathering inside the hem of his shorts, discovering the heat there, and lingering against the indentation of thigh and torso.

Beth felt the sudden powerful tensing within him, the careful restraint with which his hand slid up her back and rested hard and hot against the back of her neck. His lips and his tongue were against her ear, hot-cold shivers mingling into the rapidity of his breath and melting inside her, making her weak. She moaned softly and tried to turn her head. Sensitive even to so faint a movement, he lightened the pressure upon the back of her neck. Slowly he drew his face away.

Her hand tightened into a fist and slipped across the few inches of flesh to press into the grass beside him. Her heart was choking her and heat burned on her wet face. The taste of him was still on her tongue, and her lips throbbed for him but what was she doing? This was not the way she had planned it, not at all.

He looked at her for a long moment, his eyes searching hers thoughtfully, assessingly, though not without a hint of urgency, and slowly, a shadow of disappointment and perhaps even the very briefest flicker of anger. His scrutiny frightened and embarrassed her. She suddenly wanted more than anything in the world for him to find what he sought in her face, but apparently he did not. There was only the slightest tightening of his lips to show it, a brief lowering of his eyes, and when he looked at her again he smiled reassuringly. He caught her hands abruptly and pulled her to her feet. "You make a fine appetizer," he said, "but not very nutritionally satisfying. Let's go to the house and get some dinner. I'm starved."

Beth tried to lose her embarrassment as she walked with him around the cottage and through the back door, but his hand clasping hers did not make it any easier. When he filled a large kettle with water and placed it on the stove to heat she commented skeptically, "You're going to cook?"

"The man at the marina assured me lobster was one thing even I could manage." He nodded toward the sink, where a galvanized steel bucket apparently held their dinner. "All you have to do is boil them."

"I thought you were supposed to steam them."

He hesitated, a look of thoughtful perplexity crossing his face. "We may have just run into our first problem."

She went over to the sink and peered into the bucket, then gasped. "Corey, they're alive!"

"They're supposed to be."

"Well . . . I know that." Of course she knew that. She had just never before come face to face with a potential meal swimming about before, looking up at her with large, soulful antennae. "But aren't you supposed to—I mean—" She swallowed hard. "How do you . . . kill them?"

"You don't," he replied easily, standing beside her. "You just throw them into the boiling water and cook them."

Her eyes met his in horror, then slowly traveled back

to the bucket. Unconsciously her hand pressed against her stomach and she said weakly, "Are you sure?"

He looked at the two shellfish merrily swimming around in their confined space and he seemed to lose some of his own confidence. "That's what the man said."

A slow expression of ultimate distaste crossed her face as her gaze was drawn irresistibly back to the bucket. "Mine are usually frozen," she said in a very small voice.

He looked at her, then at the bucket, and some of her own trepidation was reflected in his face. Then he took a breath, squared his shoulders, and decided, "There's no time like the present."

She started to protest, "Don't!" but it didn't matter, for as soon as he had lifted the lobster out of the bucket he dropped it again, muffling a startled exclamation and shaking his finger. "The little monster bit me!"

She stifled a giggle—score one for the lobster—but Corey was not amused. "Now you've done it," he warned the bucket of lobster and took a pair of tongs from the drawer. "This is war."

Beth crossed her arms over her stomach to keep from bursting into guffaws of laughter as he went about the serious business of catching and removing the lobster with the slippery tongs. But when at last the feat was accomplished and he lifted one lobster securely out of the bucket, her laughter died. "Corey," she ventured, that sick look crossing her face again, "when you put them in the water, will they...die instantly or swim for a little while in the boiling water? Do you think they'll scream? What I mean is—will they make any noise, or thrash around?"

He looked at her, long and sober. The lobster squirmed beneath the grip of the tongs, flailing its pincers. Corey looked back at it uncertainly, then at her. "How hungry are you?"

"Not very," she replied in a thin voice.

He looked at the lobster with a mixture of repulsion and reluctance, then dropped it back into the bucket. "Me, neither."

She followed him as he gravely lifted the bucket and carried it down to the beach, where he tipped it into the tide. "Live long and prosper, little guys," he said, and they stood for a moment to bid a fond farewell to their dinner. Then they went back to the house and made peanut butter sandwiches.

"I suppose when you're at home you have a chef to do your cooking for you," she commented, licking a glob of grape jelly off her finger.

He laughed. "Hardly. I'm not at home enough to keep one."

"What do you do then?" she inquired curiously.

He shrugged. "When I'm in New York, I eat out. When I'm in L.A. I bum off friends or poison myself with junk food. When I'm in Montana I eat a lot of peanut butter." He grinned at her. "I'd marry you in a heartbeat if you could cook."

Stupidly, she felt the tingle of a blush. Stupidly, there was something like a small dart of pain just beneath her heart. She retorted lightly, "Sorry, cowboy, wrong fella. Shall I do the dishes, or will you?"

"Please, allow me." He crumpled up the paper napkins they had used for plates and tossed them into the trashcan. "Would you like an after-dinner drink?"

"What have you got?"

He went over to the bar that divided the small kitchen from the living area and opened a glass cabinet beneath it. "Crème de menthe, Cointreau, some Southern Comfort, even some wine, if you prefer.

"I'd prefer"—she looked at him thoughtfully—"a milkshake."

He returned her gaze for just a moment, nonplussed, and then rose and went over to the refrigerator. He took out milk, eggs, and, from the freezer, a carton of ice cream. "No well-stocked kitchen is complete without it," he informed her when she lifted an eyebrow. "Go into the living room and sit down. Leave the bartending to an expert."

The uncurtained windows were dark mirrors of floating lamps and disembodied furnishings through which her own reflection appeared with startling clarity. So here she was, alone in a secluded beach cottage with Corey Fletcher and night was wrapping its blanket around them and there was nothing she could do about it if she wanted to. She thrust her fingers into the low pockets of her shorts and walked the room aimlessly. The background sound of the blender was homey and comforting. Pretty soon he would come in and how would they spend the rest of the night? No problem. They might talk for a little while, then she would say good night, take a shower, and go to bed.

No, she wouldn't....

He came in with a tall glass of frothy white liquid for her and an open can of beer for himself. She feigned surprise as she accepted the glass. "You drink domestic beer from a can? How plebeian!"

He gestured her to the sofa. "It's an acquired taste."

She wandered over to the sofa and sat down with one leg tucked beneath her. "You don't have a television," she noticed.

"No telephone either," he pointed out and glanced at her as he sipped from the can. "Which is something I would have thought you would have discovered before now."

She knew he was referring to her determination to flee this afternoon and she avoided his eyes, fighting back a tingling blush. *Guess you weren't so determined after all, huh, Bethy? Any fool would have looked for a telephone.*

"You've got some mail," she remembered just in

time to break what was definitely beginning to be a lapse in the conversation.

"Yeah, I noticed."

"It looks important."

"Probably is."

In his eyes was the same thoughtful, patient look that had been there this afternoon, and the way he kept watching her made her very nervous. As though he was waiting for something. Again. She did not know what it was, and she wanted desperately to know.

She took a quick sip of her milkshake and made an immediate face. "Ugh! What did you put in this?"

"Cointreau." He grinned. "Interesting taste, isn't it?"

She wrinkled her nose and set the glass on the table. "Another lesson in living dangerously? I can't say much for your culinary abilities Fletcher, and if you're trying to get me drunk it won't work."

"Pity." His hand came out to delicately play with the slender strap of her halter and an amused remembrance lurked in his eyes. "You're awfully cute when you're drunk."

She swallowed hard against the rising heat generated by the simple brush of his fingers against her shoulder. "I was never drunk," she said.

"I know. Just overmedicated."

She couldn't prevent her eyes from following the movement of his hand as he absently lowered the strap, baring the curve of her shoulder to his sensitive massaging fingers. She couldn't prevent the fluttering of her heart or the dryness of her mouth. And then he stopped.

He placed his beer on the table and turned back to her, his hand resting again on her shoulder in a companionable gesture, completely asexual. "Well, princess," he said conversationally, answering her secret thoughts, "we actually have quite a few options. We could sit up all night talking or playing gin rummy—there's a deck of cards around here somewhere—which is fine with me, except we would both be dead tired tomorrow and I hate to waste a weekend that way. Or we can say good night now and go to our separate bedrooms and close the doors. Or"—his smile was faint and almost teasing—"we can go to a single bedroom and close the door. Which will it be?"

She looked at him gravely. *Don't play with me, Corey,* she thought. *I'm tired of playing and I think I love you too—only I think it's for real and it scares me to death.*

The half-playful light in his eyes faded slowly as he looked at her, and he brushed his forefinger very lightly across her cheek. "What can I do, Elizabeth?" he inquired softly. "What can I do to get that frightened look off your face?"

But he knew. He knew it as well as she did, and he slowly bent to kiss her on the lips. She caught a trembling breath as his lips left hers, but he only moved his head to kiss the shoulder his hand uncovered. He placed a gentle, deliberate kiss upon her throat and a pulse leaped to life beneath his lips. His hand rested upon the curve of her bare waist and the springs of the sofa rustled faintly as he shifted his weight closer to her. His lips just brushed across her ear. "Don't let me frighten you, Elizabeth," he whispered. "Tell me when I frighten you."

And his face rested against her neck, his hand upon her waist, no other parts of their bodies touching. His hair was as soft as a whisper against her cheek, his skin warm and smooth in the curve of her neck. He smelled of sunshine and beer. He placed one warm kiss on the edge of her jaw and warmth spread through her in slow undulating waves. She knew he would stop if she asked him. She knew she was not going to ask him.

Her hand moved uncertainly to his chest, playing

over bare flesh. Her fingers touched a spattering of pale
brown freckles near his neck, brushed across the uneven collarbone, feathered over a surgical scar near his
shoulder. She felt the quick catch of his breath as her
hand slipped inside his shirt and underneath his arm,
grazing against a slightly damp mat of cornsilk hair before finding and exploring the tight stretch of muscles
across his back. Her heart was thundering but she did
not stop. When he lifted his face to look at her there
was a light of urgency beneath the gentle question, but
in her eyes he found only a hazy passion, a mindless
contentment. His broad hand slipped behind her back
and tugged at the bow that tied her halter. One by one,
he loosened the ties at her shoulder and the garment
fell away.

He looked at her, and the sweet wonder of pleasure
that flushed in his face sent her into a drowsy state
of ecstasy, sheer timeless happiness. Warm hands
cupped and pressed and syrupy pleasure flowed heavily
through her veins. The deliberate pinpointing of his
thumbs weighted down her legs and slowed the lan-
guorous movements of her hands along his back. His
silky head bent beneath hers and the warm, precise
sucking motions drew a gasp from her, tightening electric wires in her abdomen and sending hot quivering
currents to the tips of her fingers and her face. He
straightened up and gathered her to him, the moisture
his mouth had left on her breasts molding her to the
hardness of his chest, and the shock of his flesh against
hers was such a dizzying pleasure that her head spun
and reason drained in slow puddles from her arms and
her legs, leaving them limp and malleable. His heart
reverberated against her chest and she could feel the
slight dampness of his face against the burning of her
own. He whispered, "Elizabeth..." And she turned
her face, seeking his lips.

The strong support of his hand upon her back

brought her down upon the couch, forcing her arms to travel downward as he lay upon his side next to her, cradling her head against his shoulder. His eyes reflected wonder and dazed pleasure as he placed a kiss upon the corner of her lips and moved to her ear. Her concentrated awareness darted breathlessly from the heated sensory magic he created there to the wonder of the hard lines of his thigh beneath her own fingers to the firm, exploring, massaging motions of his hand upon her chest and her waist. He found and released the button of her shorts and all time stopped in a brilliant daze of awareness as his hand slipped beneath two layers of fabric, warm and sure against the tautness of her lower abdomen, then began to melt into a delicious rush of sensation as his hand moved lower, fingers seeking and finding her most vulnerable areas and drawing a breathless, urgent, electric response. Her breath fluttered against his neck and he whispered her name. Her answer was hardly a word at all, barely a broken syllable, "Yes..."

At some point the last barriers of clothing were discarded and his naked thighs were brushing against hers, the heat of his slightly raised body melting into hers. For a moment Corey looked down at her, his hands cradling her face, and there was gravity beneath the fiery network of colors in his eyes, careful wonder softening the planes of his face. A hot, trembling hand touched the corner of his eye, brushed across a strand of his hair, delicately traced the curve of his lips. Then his hands left her face and traveled down her back, his weight eased as firm fingers cupped her buttocks and lifted her upward. Her breath died with the slow easy merging of his body into hers, her eyes dropping closed and her mind whirling outward somewhere into the nether regions of the star-studded night. His tongue entered her mouth with the same slow sureness, the carefully restrained wonder, with which he was guiding the union of their bodies and she wrapped her arms around his neck, lifting herself to him, receiving him with all her heart, all her soul.

Gentle floating rhythms drew her soul outward from its taut center to its finest threads, spinning delicate circles of carousel lights on the fabric of the night. A waterfall of kisses rained on her face and lips and hair, and half-murmured love words—his and hers—were a lilting background tune. Wondrously they discovered together the land where fragments of souls drifted like dandelion seeds on the spring breeze, touching and dancing, mixing and mating, becoming entangled in the hazy network of reality so that no one was quite sure which belonged to whom. Seeking the centrifugal center in the ever-faster rotating haze of color and light, bits of each became enmeshed with one another, so that parts of her were forever woven into him and parts of him meshed into her as it spun faster and faster, dizzily, wonderfully, gloriously out of control. Spinning into space, a high dot of intense brilliance and color exploded into a shower of sparks and bathed the planet in its phosphorescent radiance before drifting slowly back to earth.

For some time she was suspended in that drifting glow, sinking gently back into a sense of time and place. Bathed in radiance and honeyed heat, heavy with the languor of overcharged senses, she lay snug in the cocoon of his arms and legs, the mingling of their breaths the umbilical cord that linked her to reality on a thin stream of silver and gold.

Corey stirred, and it was the movement that locked reality firmly but gently into place. But he only reached for his shirt and drew it over her perspiration-sheened body for protection against the room temperature, which, against the lingering flush of her skin, felt chilled. He hooked one leg over her knees and she snuggled against him contentedly, smiling

going to do her now, and it was pointless to borrow trouble from the future. She had enough of it right here in this bed with her. She smiled at him. "Not really. I'm just tired, and a little sore in unfamiliar places."

That seemed to reassure him. His eyes danced as he bent to kiss her nose. "Me too." He rested his arms on either side of her head and added, "I know tradition dictates I should bring you breakfast in bed, but I'm afraid I'd lose you forever if I did that. I did manage coffee, though. Shall I bring you a cup?"

Once again her eyes skated across his uncomfortably. "I'd really rather take a shower first." *And get dressed,* she added silently, *and sit at the breakfast table and pretend that this is just like any other ordinary day of my life.*

His fingers exerted a mild pressure on her cheek, bringing her face back to him. His eyes were very serious. "Elizabeth," he said softly, "I want to tell you that—" And he paused. A very faint smile haunted the corners of his lips as he shook his head slightly. "Never mind," he finished simply. "You wouldn't believe me anyway." He kissed her cheek and sat up. "I'll leave you to shower in private. Toast and coffee when you're ready."

She took her second cup of coffee into the living room and paused by the table where an unopened envelope still waited. Throughout one and a half pieces of dry toast she had felt Corey's eyes upon her, silently, caressingly, and all it had taken was the brush of his eyes to mesmerize battered emotions and stroke throbbing senses to new life. She really had to get hold of herself. She had no idea what she was letting herself in for. Or maybe she did.

She fingered the envelope uncertainly, needing distraction. She wondered what he would say if she reminded him of his promise to return home today. She wondered if she would remind him. She was very much afraid she would not. "Shouldn't you read this? It's been here at least two days now, and Mailgrams are usually pretty urgent."

Behind her he shrugged and rested his hands on each side of her hips, brushing a kiss across the back of her neck. She shivered and coffee sloshed in her cup. "You can open it if you like," he invited.

She was not usually the type who enjoyed reading other people's mail, but it was better than standing there letting him turn her into a dripping puddle of sensual nerve endings. She put her coffee on the table and opened the envelope.

She glanced over the single piece of paper and wished she hadn't. She cleared her throat uncomfortably and handed it to him, but he ignored her. "Read it," he invited, nibbling at her neck. She hesitated for just the amount of time it took to pretend she didn't care, and she read out loud, perfectly tonelessly, "'Sorry, stud. Trouble in Indy. Get your butt up here on the double. No excuses unless D.O.A. in E.R.'" And the hardest part. "It's signed 'Chris.'"

He took the paper from her and let it float to the floor. "Chris is my sister," he explained calmly.

Beth disguised the sudden relief that flowed through her with irritation, and tried to step away. "I know that."

He held her firm with the pressure of his hands on her hips and the touch of his lips on her shoulder. "She's the only one who knows how to reach me down here."

She was trying very hard not to melt. He was not making it easy. "It sounded pretty important." Her head swayed to the side against the gentle pressure of his teeth on her neck.

"Sure did. Someone's mad as hell at me."

"Aren't you—" Every nerve ending flamed to fire as his hand came around her waist and undid the top button of her shorts. "Don't you think you should at least answer it?"

His fingers worked the second button. "I guess I'd better. They might fire me."

The whole weight of her body sagged against him as the third button was opened. It was hard to breathe. "Are you going to leave?"

"In a minute," he murmured against her neck. The fourth and final button fell free. "There's something I have to do first."

Three days later, they left.

Chapter Ten

The day after he left her, a bouquet of white gardenias and red carnations arrived from Corey. The scent was heavenly, and the card read, "I woke up this morning with you on my mind." The next day brought a vase of tiger lilies and bright blue asters interspersed with baby's breath and black-eyed Susans. The unlikely combination was, to say the least, original and in fact stunning. The card said, "Today too." The third card accompanied a brilliant arrangement of birds-of-paradise and said, "This is getting to be a habit." The latest double bouquet of yellow roses filled her shop with its heady scent, for she was running out of room at home. The card was tucked into the pocket of her work smock and she took it out at intervals to look at it. "If I try to show you all the colors and textures and scents I experienced when we made love, I'll run out of flowers long before I do ideas."

He had not called her.

Beth knew he was busy. She knew why he was busy and that knowledge was something she spent her days diligently trying to shove to one side. According to the sportscasters he had arrived in Indianapolis twelve hours before he was to run the time trials amidst rumors of problems with his car. Whether or not those rumors were founded she did not know. She did not want to know. She did not watch the trials, but Jerry explained to her that he had run a pretty good time—obviously, Jerry thought he could have done better and somehow Beth got the impression that Jerry was laying the blame for Corey's comparatively mediocre performance solely at her door—and had drawn a fair position for the race. Again, Jerry could not resist adding with a cynical look at the room full of flowers, it could have been better. Beth tried to ignore him. She didn't listen to the news and she didn't read the papers and she tried valiantly to forget the fact that in two days Corey would be driving one of the most arduous and dangerous races in the world. She was torn between terror that he would call her and ask her to join him and fear that he would not, and she didn't know which was worse. She only knew that she was caught up in his tailspin, the infectious world of danger, glamor, and high thrills—uncontrollably this time, completely now—and there was nothing she could do about it. She did not belong there but a part of her would always be there, living on the edge with her heart in her throat and a nightmare as a constant companion. Was this what the rest of her life would be like?

It was after closing and she stayed as Jerry did his routine cleaning and sweeping up, trying to reconcile her drug count. It seemed she had lived the entire past week with sweaty palms and butterflies in her stomach, unable to concentrate, vacillating between ecstasy and despair. There ought to be a cure for this, she thought wearily as she rubbed her eyes and blinked away the dancing spots. Acute involvement, terminal heartbreak.... She got up and went to the narcotics cabinet to recheck her count. It was definitely off.

Five minutes later she turned thoughtfully away from the cabinet, absently tapping her pen against her ledger. Some color had faded from her face and her brows drew together grimly. There was no mistake. Last night's drug count was dutifully and accurately

logged. She had done it herself. She had had the shop
to herself today and dispensed no narcotics. Some time
between leaving Jerry alone in the store last night and
returning to do her drug count today....

Despite a rather antiquated security system and her
proximity to the beach, Beth's store had only been bur-
glarized three times. Those three times had been during the summer two years ago when a row of beach
cottages a few blocks away had been occupied by a
group of long-haired refugees from a commune, and
the only items taken were oral contraceptives and peni-
cillin. Beth had laughed with the police about preventa-
tive medicine and the incidents stopped at the end of
the summer. Actually her shop was not at all a prime
target for professionals because of its location in a resi-
dential district with nosy neighbors and spot-lit lawns.
Beth had never worried too much about security. Her
drug cabinet contained only one old-fashioned lock,
easily jimmied. She could not prevent her eyes from
wandering to Jerry's figure as he indolently pushed a
broom across the floor and trailed cigarette ashes behind him. She wondered what the street value of
Quaalude was these days.

There was a real and concrete reason for the clammi-
ness of her palms and the coldness in the pit of her
stomach as Beth walked slowly back to the counter. She
placed the ledger on the counter and turned deliberately. She said without further preliminaries, "Jerry,
the narcotics cabinet has been tampered with. Drugs
are missing."

Jerry glanced up without much interest, grinding out
the cigarette on the sole of his shoe. "Oh, yeah? I told
you you should fix that broken window in the back.
What'd they get?"

She fixed him with an unwavering gaze. "Don't you
know, Jerry?" she asked softly.

"Hell, no, I got no business back there. Why should

I—'' But she knew from the moment he spoke that she had been wrong, she could not believe she had even thought it, and a miserable shame flooded her, which twisted in craven self-knowledge and despite. Jerry looked at her in the slow dawning of understanding, which turned inexorably into disgust and a hatred so raw and pure it would have been ugly in the face of a sixty-year-old hardened criminal. In the eyes of a six-teen year old boy it was both heartbreaking and terrify-ing.

She began quickly, "Jerry, I—"

"You bitch," he said slowly. There was no violence in his tone, only a simple statement of fact. That was perhaps what was the most frightening of all. She watched helplessly as emotions of loathing and disillu-sionment filled his face and a summer of nurturing, believing, working, and hoping faded to a pile of fine ashes at her feet. He let the broom clatter to the floor and he repeated very quietly, "You damn bitch."

She tried to speak once more but the final look he gave her quelled the sound in her throat. Behind con-tempt and the hard anger in his eyes was a raw agony that spoke more eloquently than any words could have done of exactly what she had done for him. He turned and jerked open the door with a loud and anticlimactic clanging of the bell; five seconds later his car roared to life and tires screamed on the asphalt.

In a heavy fog of pain and fear she called the police and reported the burglary. She gave them what infor-mation she could as they made their routine investiga-tion but did not mention Jerry. How could she have been so stupid, so thoughtless, so quick to condemn? She tried to justify herself through the enormous up-heaval her life had been in the past few weeks, the emotional strain and the whirlwind of confusion, but it rang hollow. There was no justification. Once she had accused Corey of destroying the boy's faith in humanity, and ruining his life; what she had done was far worse.

Throughout the night Beth sat up and paced, half looking for his return, half knowing he wouldn't. She had betrayed him, and betrayal from her was the last thing he had expected. He had learned to be tough, whether from necessity or exposure; he had grown used to being hurt and striking out first. In her house this summer his shell had begun to soften a little. Through Corey's skillful guidance he had matured, started to look outside himself and to trust and rely on others. Not two weeks ago he had even dropped a casual word about returning to school. In all the weeks he had worked for her he had never been late or in any way shirked his responsibilities, she had even sensed a secret pride in his job despite his tendency to be slovenly when he was being watched. He saved his money diligently and spent wisely. He was growing up. And in one fell blow she had destroyed all of that, all that Corey had worked for and she had hoped so hard for. How could she have done it?

By four o'clock she was in tears. She was terrified of what might become of him, of where he might go or what he might do. She was miserable with the consequences of her own failure. She wanted someone's hand to hold, someone strong to take charge and tell her everything was going to be all right. But Corey was in Indianapolis preparing himself for a duel against death and he would hate her if he knew what she had done. He couldn't hate her any more than she hated herself.

At nine o'clock the police reported they had apprehended two suspects who had been seen by witnesses lurking about the back of the shop the night before last. They still had the drugs on them, and they had apparently gotten in through the broken window. At ten o'clock Beth began to realize she was going to have to call her sister. She could not even get up the courage to call her father. She should report Jerry missing to the police. She did not go to work but stayed in the house, pacing tightly back and forth and bringing her white, strained face to the window hoping against hope that he might return. At one o'clock in the afternoon, Corey called.

"I hope you haven't done anything foolish," he said. "Jerry's with me."

"Oh, God." The breath was drawn from her body with that single whisper and so was her strength. She sank to a chair and through pulsating waves of relief managed, "Is he all right?"

"Still mad, but wearing down." His voice was low, as though he was afraid of being overheard. "Listen, I've booked you on the next flight out. I don't want to leave him alone, so I'll have a car meet you at the airport."

"Yes," she said dazedly. "I'll be there."

"Are you okay?"

"Y-yes." Her voice was faint, and she strengthened it. "Corey, thank you."

He laughed softly. "Hey, no strain. That kid doesn't know it, but he gives more than he takes. After all, he's getting me you, isn't he?"

It was early in the evening when the car pulled up in front of Corey's hotel. He opened the door in a pale yellow velour shirt and low-slung jeans, bare feet, and silky soft hair. For a moment she just looked at him, drinking him in like a restorative potion after a long bout with fever, and then she stepped wordlessly into his arms.

It had taken only a glimpse of her strained and stricken face to cause immediate sympathy to cross Corey's, and he held her tenderly, comfortingly. "Poor baby," he murmured, stroking her hair. "You must have been through hell."

She held him and let him absorb her anxiety, her

guilt, her fear. All the strain of the past twenty-four hours drained into the softness of his shirt and the hardness of his chest and subtly evolved into a new emotion—desire, plain and simple. She wanted him, wanted the surity of his arms about her and his flesh against hers, she wanted the fleeting permanence of his body inside hers, she wanted to hold him tightly and fiercely and never let him go. The need was so clear and real that it seemed to be only an extension of the suffering she had experienced this past day—no, the entire past week. She wanted him, she wanted to hold on to him tightly and pretend for a time that she need never let him go, and the strength of her desire was so powerful it shook her. She had to step away.

His hands slipped from around her and down her arms where they linked with hers. He smiled down at her gently, reassuringly. She had to drop her eyes and pause for a moment to steady her voice, and then she asked, "Where is he?"

"Sacked out in the room across the hall, dead to the world. The crazy kid drove straight through and then it took him the rest of the afternoon to wind down." A trace of anxiety crossed his expression as he peered at her. "I called you as soon as I could."

Her hands trailed away from his as she turned and stepped away. "Oh, Corey," she said tiredly. "I was such an idiot. How could I have been so stupid?"

His smile was both mildly teasing and encouraging. "I told Jerry it was just hormones."

She glanced at him, noticed the way the color of his shirt sparked golden lights in his eyes and the way his hair fell like a halo around his head, the sensuous fullness of his lashes and the coarse skin covering his throat. Hormones. Yes. She clasped her hands together and it was more in an effort to subdue the sudden yearning quivering that had begun in the pit of her stomach than to express anxiety, which, now that Jerry had been safely found, was almost nil. "I knew I was wrong as soon as I said it," she went on tightly. "I don't know why I said it. How he must hate me." She tilted her head back in abject despair. "Why is it people are always ready to leap to the worst conclusion? I thought I was above that! He was just beginning to trust me and everything you've done for him is just ruined. How could I *do* such a thing?"

He was silent for just a moment. Then he said mildly, "If you're finished with the sackcloth and ashes I'd like to point out that, while an apology is definitely due, there's hardly any reason to throw yourself off a twenty-story building over this thing. I think Jerry's already halfway there as far as forgiving you goes, and he can't help but realize he got the better end of this deal. After all, how many sixteen-year-old kids get to work on a pit crew at the Indianapolis 500?"

She turned, quickly trying to subdue the alarm that sprang to her face. Even the mention of the race could do that to her. "Pit crew?"

"Well, not work, actually," Corey admitted, coming over to her. "Mostly he'll just be hanging around trying not to get in anybody's way. I was going to ask him to come up anyway, but I wasn't sure how you would feel about it. I knew you wouldn't come."

"But I did," she said in a very small voice. She was here, no doubt about it, whether through a twist of fate or a teen-ager's manipulations she was in the one place she had wanted desperately to avoid ever being—and the one place it seemed her destiny to forever be. By his side, dueling terror and grasping for rainbows, trying to hold a shower of sparks in her hand—and watching helplessly as with each heartbeat the very essence of all she needed and wanted and treasured slipped like mercury through her fingers. She did not belong here in the eye of Corey Fletcher's hurricane, she wanted no part of his glittering thrill-filled world, but here she was and there was nothing she could do about it.

"So you did," he said softly. His hand fell upon her

shoulder and fluttered like a whisper across the back of her neck, sensitizing every nerve and fiber of her body. "I think maybe I was wrong. I got the better part of this deal."

He turned her gently in his arms and for just a moment she looked at him, the gentle starlit eyes, the small scar parting his eyebrow, the golden face, the two freckles on the textured skin of his neck just above the collarbone, the sweetly curving lips. Then she was kissing him with a sudden depth of need that surprised an impassioned response from him, winding her arms around his neck and pressing herself close to him, trying to melt into him and make him a part of every cell and fiber so that she would never have to let him go. When he lifted his face a little there was dazed delight beneath the heavy glow of passion in his eyes and a flush of pleasure and desire sheened his face. She whispered, her hand unsteady against the warmth of his neck, "Let's go to bed. Make love to me, Corey."

Without hesitation, his hand found the zipper of her dress and he bent to carry her the few steps to the bed. He laid her down gently and knelt over her to remove her clothes, but her own fingers worked impatiently to assist him and then to divest him of his own clothing. He tried to slow her movements with long, deliberate kisses and soothing words but the urgency was building and the yearning was too painful and she whispered raggedly, "Please, Corey."

"No. Hush." He dropped dewy kisses over her face and linked his fingers loosely through hers, stilling her roaming hands. And even though his own breath was harsh and his heart hammering so potently she could almost see its pulse against his chest he insisted, "Wait. I don't want to hurt you. Elizabeth, love, what is it? What—"

She moaned, "No..." and turned her head into the pillow, pulling at his hands. But he made her wait until the fire was an inferno and their final coming together was a sweet, sharp explosion of intense needs and rocketing desires. For a moment the present merged with the future and her grip upon it was tight but all too soon it was over and she was left holding only memories. She could pull him to her again but as soon as his body withdrew from hers her fragile hold on promises would begin to slip. She could hold him and love him and try with all her might to pretend that what they shared was forever, that somehow, some way, they would be able to carve a place in the world where they belonged. But that was all it was. Pretending.

Corey slept with his arm around her waist and one leg thrown loosely over hers, boyish and innocent in the place where his dreams had taken him. Physical satisfaction could not fill the gnawing emptiness deep within her soul and Beth could not sleep. She slipped quietly out of bed and went over to the window.

She sat with her knees drawn up to her chin and looked out over an unfamiliar network of bright lights and neon signs, and the distant rush of road sounds was like an echo from the future. This was Corey's world, strange hotel rooms and harsh landscapes, always changing, never the same. This was the moment-by-moment world and the men and women who lived here cut a thin path across the razor's edge of reality, stepping carefully between what was and what might yet be. To try to hold on to anything in this spinning, shifting nimbus was to dance with dreams. Even now all that remained of the love he had given her was the warmth that lingered on her body and the tight yearning that coiled in her soul, and tomorrow loomed ahead like the memory of a nightmare.

Corey left the bed and knelt beside her. "Okay, pretty princess," he said softly. "Let's talk."

Beth turned her face to look at him. In the misty gray

darkness his eyes were soft and steady, his hair rumpled, and his face heartbreakingly young. He had pulled on a robe and she was suddenly reminded of her nakedness. She lowered her legs and tried to smile at him. "About what?"

"Whatever's upsetting you. Whatever is making you feel so bad."

Beth wanted to reassure him but her throat was too tight to speak. Tears burned the back of her eyes.

"Is it Jerry?" Corey insisted quietly. "Are you still beating yourself against a rock over that?"

She shook her head. "No," she managed. "No, that's okay. I'll find some way to make it up to him. I'm just glad he had you to go to. I'm glad he's all right."

Corey was silent for a moment. His eyes never left her. "Then it must be me. Something I've done."

Beth shook her head again, almost violently. "No, it's not. It's...nothing, Corey, really."

Even as he smiled his eyes searched her face anxiously, vainly trying to part the shadows that separated them. "Then tell me why you're sitting all alone stark naked in the dark. What are you doing?"

Beth looked at him, long and gravely. Her chin was pointed bravely and did not quiver. She answered, "Just"—her voice almost broke on a whisper—"trying not to love you quite so desperately."

The slow light that filled his eyes was the sea breeze that parted the fog, the touch of his hand upon the back of her neck a warm welcome home. "Darling," he said, "you can love me as desperately as you like." A soft rustle of movement and sighs as he gathered her into his arms. "And know that it is returned."

Then don't race tomorrow, Beth wanted to say with a sudden bleak urgency. *If I must love you then do this one thing for me.*

But Corey's lips were upon her fingers, her throat,

her eyelids, sweet soothing motions lulling her savage fears into a semblance of quiescence. "Come to bed, princess," he was whispering. "Let me make you feel good."

And, for the space of one more night, it lasted.

The next day was a collage of impressions that was burned indelibly on Beth's mind, whirling and spinning in nonstop activity and overlaid with brushstrokes of sharp definition. There was the hostility in Jerry's eyes and the courage imparted to Beth through Corey's arm around her shoulders as she made a fumbling apology; the disdain that curled Jerry's lips as he inquired, "Well, did you catch your thief?"; and the strange sense of surprised relief that flooded Beth that he had actually spoken to her at all. The brassy hot day contrasted the granite fist of dread that closed around Beth's stomach as they made their way to the country's most famous racetrack, secured passes for the pit area, and lost Corey in a swarm of reporters. The mangled sounds of an excited, bloodthirsty crowd and the thick smell of gasoline and rubber mingled incongruously with the smells of a backyard barbecue that came from the campers on the edge of the infield. The confusion, the noise, the shifting, sucking sea of colorful humanity...the heat. The awful heat.

Beth met Corey's sister. She had once again been entrusted to the dubious protection of Stretch Marinara and it was he who dragged her over to the group of laughing, smoking, and drinking sophisticates. Christine Fletcher was a svelte woman with butchered blond hair that could not be more than half an inch long at its greatest thickness, dark red lipstick, and emerald-green eyes that twinkled just like her brother's. She wore loose-fitting cerise cotton trousers and a gauze blouse that just shadowed the nipples of her small breasts, and in stiletto heels she was perhaps an inch taller than

Corey. She wore heavy gold and silver rings fashioned into various shapes—a snake, a tiger, a lover's knot—on every finger; she held a Manhattan in one hand and a cigarillo in the other. She greeted Beth with a dancing smile.

"So *you're* the one! My beloved brother did his best to kill the messenger when I sent him that mailgram down in Virginia and I swore I was going to dog him like a shadow until I met this paragon. Tell me, what kind of spell have you cast over him? I wouldn't mind borrowing a little of your potion myself; it would make him a lot easier to handle!"

"You and half the other women in the world," replied Stretch, digging his fingers into Beth's waist. "I'm just wondering when this one's going to realize she's got a tiger by the tail."

Beth realized she was staring, and recognition of the fact registered in cynical amusement on the other women's face. "I—I'm sorry," she stumbled, flushing. "It's just that I've never met anyone whose phone has been tapped by the FBI before."

Christine Fletcher burst into a full-bodied, delightfully approving laugh. "I like you, honey," she said, and rescued her from Stretch's embrace with an arm entwined companionably with hers. "You know," she confided, leading her through the crowd toward the little man who was darting about with glasses of mixed drinks on a tray, "when my little brother first told me about you I felt really sorry for you. I practically begged Corey to let me meet you—which is not something I normally do—but he wanted to keep you all hidden away like some kind of hothouse flower that would wither in the real world. I think if I had met you back then I would have done my Christian duty and told you to set your sights on meeker game, because I speak for a hundred broken hearts when I say no one can love you better or forget you faster than Corey Fletcher.

But"—a thoughtful look of amused perplexity crossed her thin model's face as she exchanged her empty glass for a full one—"I'm not sure that's true anymore. I almost think I should say 'Women of the world salute you'." And she raised her glass to her, behind twinkling eyes. "You've shot one more Flying Ace right out of the sky."

Then there was the time when Corey himself parted the crowd, a streak of color and electric sparks, carrying his helmet under his arm and fending off jostling well-wishers and cracking jokes. The crowd was too thick for intimacy or even a private word, but across the shifting bodies and bobbing heads Corey's eye caught hers. He started to move toward her on that bright, air-lifted step, but someone was pulling him the other way. He simply paused for a second and grinned, "Catch you later, princess," winked at her, and was gone.

And suddenly the flashback of that moment seemed to be frozen like a snapshot forever on the face of time. Corey in a bright electric arc of color and vitality, his sweet grin, the quick wink, and laid upon it was the shadow of a darker time, a foggy pier, a desperate whisper, "Let's not ever say good-bye." It echoed endlessly through the corridors of her mind, reverberating and gathering strength with a low scream that formed desperately in her throat, *No....* She wanted to run after him, to hold him, to beg him not to go, and the urge was so great that for a moment the scene around her actually blurred into a cold sweat with its impact. But she didn't move. She didn't speak. There was nothing she could do. It was too late.

Gentlemen, start your engines.

Beth pressed close to the rail as the monstrous blur of noise and color tore around the track. It was not a desire, but a compulsion. People drifted past her, occasionally Stretch or Christine would come over to her, but Beth hardly saw them. Her eyes were fixed almost unblinkingly on car number forty-two, her body strained into a tight paralysis of waiting, of knowing, of dreading and hoping. She couldn't move away. An hour passed and no one could make her move away.

"I know how you feel, honey." Christine spoke into her ear, almost shouting to make herself heard over the background roar of thunderous engines. "I hate these damn things, I don't know why I came." A cynical spark touched her eye as she looked out over the track. "It's so hard to know what to wear to the gladiator fights, isn't it?" And she slipped her arm around Beth's waist. "Come on, sweetie, let's get out of this awful heat before you pass out. We can go up to the press tower."

Beth, half turning, knew it before it happened. She was not surprised at the slow roar of horror and excitement that spread like a cresting wave from the stands nor at the sudden white shock on Christine's face or the flurry of streaking, madly uncontrolled activity around her. It all faded away as in slow motion she turned and saw the car—number forty-two—careen off the track and into the wall, scraping a trail of sparks and sulphuric smoke before it bounced and flipped and crashed with a horrific sound that split the earth beneath her feet and drew her slowly downward. She did not move, she did not scream. She simply watched as one split second later Corey's car burst into flames and the roaring yellow-white fireball stretched toward the sky, bathing the earth in its phosphorescent glow.

Chapter Eleven

The surgeon was not hopeful. By the time Corey's body had been dragged from the flaming wreckage too much blood had been lost, circulation had been cut off to vital areas and oxygen deprivation had taken its toll. Besides the burns and fractures, his chest had been crushed. His left lung was punctured and his spleen was ruptured. He was developing cardiac tamponade. He was in surgery for ten hours and he arrested twice on the table. Not one of the eight surgeons and specialists on his case believed he would make it to the recovery room.

It was a foggy dream where events blurred into one another without the restrictions of time or space, a murky fog of composite memory. Beth sat in the small waiting room beneath the sharp haze of Christine's cigarillo smoke and Stretch's taut pacing back and forth and Nick's endless nervous recounting of other hospitals, other injuries, other times worse than this and she waited it through. When Christine ran out of cigarillos she smoked Jerry's cigarettes one after the other and when Nick said for perhaps the fiftieth time, "Hell, he's seen worse than this! He's gonna pull through," she snapped at him to shut up. Jerry sat beside her, silent, white-faced with shock and the agony of grief that was as deeply buried as her own. It was a horrible thing to keep such suffering locked inside. It was like a dam wanting to burst with no outlet.

Corey's parents came. She had a dim impression of a tall woman with strain tightening the lines of her well made-up face and fear in her eyes, a grim man who spoke little but exuded a quiet strength simply by his presence. She thought she talked to them but did not remember what was said. Christine went down the hall every hour for another pack of cigarettes and Nick's bluster began to die. They waited.

A doctor came in and told them Corey was being moved to intensive care. His condition was guarded. Christine burst into tears and mother and daughter comforted each other. The men shared cautious, uncertain looks of relief and hope. Beth thought, Alive. *For now, alive.* Emotion stirred deep within her but she only added another brick to the dam. Guarded, but alive. She felt Jerry touch her arm, and she looked at him. Then she was holding him and he was clinging to her, a little boy whose tears wet her neck and who was trying so hard to be strong. She stroked his hair and felt his silent shuddering and comforted him the best she could. She could not help thinking about all the gifts Corey had brought into her life. But she did not cry.

Corey was in intensive care for fourteen days. Only immediate family was allowed to visit for five minutes four times a day, but Beth went to the hospital and watched him through the open venetian blinds on the separating window. She saw his shrunken body and the catheters and cannulas, which were his only fragile hold on life, and a little of her died each day. Christine insisted that Beth and Jerry share her hotel suite with her during the vigil, and she was constantly attempting to persuade Beth to eat or sleep or to get some fresh air. Beth tried vaguely and listlessly to please her. Christine requested that Beth see a doctor. Beth refused. Beth's father called and offered to come up. She refused.

When Corey's condition was stable enough to allow him to be moved to a private room, Christine returned from a brief visit with a burden of worry lifted from her shoulders. She reported that he was much improved, but that he was so shot up with morphine it was useless to try to talk to him. He had asked for Beth. Beth scheduled a visit for the next day and requested from the nurse that she be allowed to see him before his next scheduled injection.

When she walked into the room she caught a brief glimpse of the exquisite agony that was carved into his face before he noticed her and forcefully controlled the suffering with sharp lines and small harsh breaths. He tried to smile. He was thin, colorless, weak. A gauze bandage stained with yellow Furacin covered the burns on one arm, an IV tube trailed from the other. His hair was dull and his eyes overbright. "Hey, princess," he drawled with only a faint imitation of his old grin, "don't look so stricken. Nothing important was damaged—just arms and legs and stuff like that there."

She came slowly over to the bed. The effort to smile gradually faded into the crevices and furrows of a pain-ravaged face, and his effort to hold on to courage was visible as he looked into her eyes. "Take it easy," he said softly. "No big deal. I'm used to it."

"I know you are, Corey." She bent and touched his hair lightly, then moved her jerky hand away and placed an unmarked envelope on the bed beside him. She managed just before turning. "I—I'm sorry." And she left the room before she could see the expression in his eyes.

Then she cried.

Those were not the last tears Beth had shed in the past four months, but it was getting better. She sat beneath the yellow glow of her living room lamp and turned over a rain-splattered envelope and told herself it was only the gloomy day and the clicking of a December rain against the darkened windowpane that made her want to succumb to self-pity now.

The letter she had left with Corey so cravenly had read:

You already know why I couldn't say this to you in person. And because you'll probably start thinking a lot of dumb things after you've read this I want to make sure you understand that it's not because of the accident, because I blame you for it or even myself—yes, I know you would think that. It's just that you gave me a choice, Corey, in your own arrogant, overbearing, wonderful way you gave me a choice and I choose the quiet life, small thrills and little disappointments, ordinary people, and a routine that's so dull sometimes you could scream, but it's what I know and what I love. I can't help it. I wasn't cut out for the fast lane.

I know that doing this to you now is cruel and unforgivable, and walking out on you while you're helpless in a hospital bed is, I agree, about the dirtiest trick I've ever heard of. I hope you hate me for it, at least as much as I hate myself.

If you call me I'll change my number and if you come to see me I'll move and if you write me I'll return your letters. Please don't. I don't think I could bear to hurt you any more.

She came back to Virginia Beach and tried to pick up the pieces of her shattered life, and it wasn't as hard as she had expected. She had her friends and her family to support her and she drank in all the love and encouragement she could get.

At first Beth had felt confused and guilty about Steve, but in his quiet, steady way he made her see there was no need for it. The love he felt for her was the love of a brother for a sister; he had told her soon after her return home that, though he would always be there for her if she needed him, to try to deepen their relationship with marriage would have been disastrous. Steve realized that now—perhaps he had even suspected it all along—and so did Beth, thanks to Corey. Steve remained in Boston to finish his residency, but he called her regularly and nothing had changed about their friendship. Beth knew that when he came home to join her father's practice there would be no awkwardness, and if one day Steve brought a wife to his imaginary house on the hill Beth would love her in the same way she did Steve—as a member of the family.

Things had changed, but not all of it was bad. Beth was surviving.

As soon as Corey got out of the hospital, the letters began to arrive. There was one every day for the past four months, all diligently marked "Return to sender" and placed in the mailbox unopened. Every day for four months, unopened, unread, coldly returned. That was approximately one hundred twenty letters. At first agony had torn Beth every time she saw the spidery black scrawl and she had cried a lot in those first weeks. Sometimes the temptation to open them was so great it hurt. But gradually pain began to turn to tenderness, frustration to amusement. As persistent as ever, Corey Fletcher had not changed a bit.

The latest of these letters she had retrieved from the mailbox only moments ago. It was puckered with rain and still cold from the outside temperatures, and as she looked at it a slow, soft smile touched her face. On the outside of the envelope was written: "The U.S. Postal Service loves you...and so do I."

The telephone rang and Beth went to answer it, once again successfully resisting the urge to open the envelope just once. It was Jerry, and she greeted him happily.

Jerry called her once a week now to report upon his progress in school and the goings-on in Phoenix, and their conversations were easy and natural. Beth wondered if he had any idea how much it meant to her that he called of his own volition, promptly and regularly, and wanted to share his life with her. He was maturing into quite a young man.

"So," she inquired, sinking into the easy chair to pull off her dripping galoshes. "How did you do on midterms?"

"Not too bad. World Lit is still driving me up a wall, but Dad thinks he might be able to get me into MIT if I keep up my average."

There was an unmistakable note of pride in his voice and Beth exulted for him. "Hey, that's great! Are you still going to be speaking to us common folk when you're a rich and famous engineer?"

He laughed. "Give me a break, Auntie."

She rubbed her cold and aching feet and sat back in the chair. "How're your folks?"

"In Aspen, on a second honeymoon or some such garbage."

"Leaving you alone for Christmas?" She knew the feeling. Her own father had left this morning for a Caribbean cruise and would not return until the twenty-sixth. She had bravely cheered him on his way even when he hesitated, for she would not for the world let him know how much she did not want to be alone this Christmas.

"Heck, no, they've gotten too mushy lately for something like that. They're coming back Christmas Eve."

"Must be nice to have the house all to yourself. Throwing any wild parties?"

"Well, I don't exactly have the house to myself. No

wild parties. As a matter of fact I don't even have the house. I'm in Montana." There was just the slightest pause. "With Corey."

Of course she knew Corey still kept in touch with Jerry. His name came up in conversation now and again, and she always quickly changed the subject. She did not want to admit to Jerry, or to herself, how hungry she was for news of him, any news, even the sound of his name. "Oh," she said as casually as she could. "I thought he always spent Christmas with his family in California."

"Not this year."

Her eyes drifted back without conscious control to the letter on the table, the familiar handwriting, the Montana postmark. It was not the first time that she wondered what she would do when the letters stopped coming. How she would feel when she opened the mailbox one day and it was empty? She tried not to think about it.

One did not hear much about Corey Fletcher these days. Until his recovery was complete there had been progress reports sporadically on the sports spots of evening news broadcasts. A single sentence in a television-personalities column reported that he had postponed filming on his television movie indefinitely, no reason given. She gleaned from scraps of Jerry's conversation that his health was fully restored—he was, indeed, indestructible. She received occasional letters from Christine, which were not accusatory or pressuring, merely expressing concern and inviting confidence. It was a confidence Beth did not feel free to give, and of the details of Corey's personal life she knew nothing.

"Listen." Jerry's voice broke into a reverie that was beginning to turn painful. There was a rather odd, restrained tone behind his words and her senses sharpened to discern the reason for it. "I'm supposed to tell

you that there's a ticket waiting for you at the airport."
Now he spoke in a rush, as though anxious to get it out
before she hung up. She had no intention of hanging
up. "Flight Forty-seven leaving at eight fifty-three."
She found herself glancing at the clock. It was seven
fifteen. She found herself jotting down the flight number; she did not know why.

Jerry took a short breath, his tone changed. "Aunt
Beth—" Again her listening quickened. But he finished
only, "Nothing. That's all."

"Jerry, I—" Her heart was thundering.

"Listen, I gotta go. Chow's on." His voice was bright
again. "See you later, huh?" And he added just before
he hung up, "It's going to be a white Christmas out
here."

She stared at the phone for a long time after she
had hung up, her heart racing and fluttering and surprising a tingling flush of excitement and uncertainty
to her face. What could be said about a man who, having been deserted by a woman while virtually on his
death bed, wrote her one hundred twenty letters and,
even though each of them was returned unopened,
had the gall to leave a ticket for her at the airport and
the arrogance to assume she would use it? That he
was a man who simply didn't know when to give up.
That was all.

Would she want him any other way?

Slowly she reached for the envelope on the table.
She looked at it for another moment, and her pulse rate
was beginning to approach a dangerous level. Then
with a deft movement of her fingernail she tore it open.

Having a Christmas party and need someone to do
background vocals on "We Three Men." Thought
of you immediately.

I don't think I can stand another season without
you.

Come to me, love. Please.

Corey.

Her hand began to shake in rhythm with the pumping of her heart. She placed the single sheet of paper on the table and smoothed it out firmly, staring at it.

Live dangerously.

It was almost seven thirty. She couldn't possibly pack and be at the airport in time for her flight. Montana? Who wanted to go to Montana in the middle of the winter? She had a business to run, she couldn't just up and fly to Montana, of all places, on a moment's notice. What was he, crazy or something?

Probably.

She was changed and packed in fifteen minutes. Just before she left she called Ellie and told her she wouldn't be in Monday and she didn't know when she would be back. Ellie was as flabbergasted as Beth felt. She didn't leave a note for the milkman or stop the paper or turn off the pilot light. She just left.

Rain was coming down in sheets and the drive to the airport took forever. She arrived in just enough time to claim her ticket and check in and then she realized in horror that she had left her purse in the car. She made a mad dash through the rain and discovered she had also left her headlights on. And locked her keys inside. *That's what happens when conservative middle-class people make mad, reckless decisions on the spur of the moment.*

She stood shivering and dripping in the icy rain and watched her battery slowly die while a saintly security man patiently jimmied the lock on her car. She wanted to pay him for his trouble when the door finally sprang open, but he refused. It was just as well. Checking the contents of her purse, she discovered she had only one dollar and forty-seven cents; hardly enough to be decently called mad money. She thanked him profusely in lieu of anything better and hurried back inside the building—only to discover that her flight had left five minutes ago.

She could not believe it. Surely this was a first for any airline in the country. In the midst of a storm and the Christmas rush the last flight for Montana for thirty-six hours had departed on time. Vainly she pleaded with airport officials who did their best to arrange a connecting flight, but to no avail. Everything was booked up. The Christmas rush.

She suddenly thought of Corey waiting on the other side of the country at some airport, searching each face, not knowing whether she would come at all and hoping...and when she did not show up, thinking what? She could not let him think that. She had to reach him.

It was impossible to forget the return address that had been scrawled across the top of one hundred twenty letters, but still it was without much hope that she dialed long distance information. "Sorry, we have no listing for a Fletcher at that address." Of course, superstars did not have published numbers. She went again to check on possible cancellations on connecting flights.

At eleven o'clock it became apparent to one of even her rapidly diminishing mental capacity that she could either sit here at the airport until sometime Monday morning or go home and try to find some way to get word to Corey. Go home? How?

She began to pump coins into the pay phone in search of a service station with an available road truck. It was the rain. All the trucks were out, but if she would try again in a couple of hours.... Finally she went and stood in the rain with the hood up, shivering and sneezing, until some man with jumper cables took pity on her. After half an hour it became apparent that it would take more than a jolt of electricity to bring her car back to life. Since Jerry had left she had more or less let her car go downhill, and it had obviously now hit rock bottom.

Wearily she went back inside the building, and wincing at the time revealed by the airport clock, she dialed Ellie's number. She explained the situation to her sleepy friend twice, and then the only reply was "Which airport?" It was after midnight when Ellie finally came to rescue her.

Ellie offered to drive her home, but Ellie's house was closest to the airport and Beth still had to do something about her car. She went home with Ellie and spent a sleepless night thinking about Corey waiting for her.

She had her car towed in the next morning, soliciting a faithful promise that it would be returned by six o'clock. In clothes borrowed from Ellie, which were three sizes too big for her, she padded around the house all day restlessly watching the sky alternately ooze drizzle and pour icy rain, and she tried to think of some way to reach Corey. She racked her brain for everyone she knew who might be able to get in touch with him. She even called California, but the families of superstars did not have listed numbers either. On an inspiration she asked for the number of Magnum Enterprises, but it was Sunday. All offices were closed. The same was true for Verdi Vineyards. In desperation she finally called her sister's house hoping against certainty that someone might be there who knew how to get in touch with Jerry. Of course no one was.

Weary, dispirited, and totally frustrated with herself, she sat curled up on Ellie's sofa and tried not to cry. And she had always thought Corey was unpredictable, irresponsible, and inconsistent. What must he think of her now? And deep down there was the terrible fear that he would never ask her again.

It was five o'clock in the afternoon before Ellie came

up with the brilliant suggestion of sending him a telegram. Beth simply stared at her, kicking herself for not
having thought of it before. Without wasting another
moment, she dispatched an apologetic telegram to the
Montana address and was so relieved she didn't even
scream at the mechanic when he called to tell her it
would be nine o'clock before they would be finished
with her car.

Actually it was closer to ten, and Beth drove home
through sheets of winter rain feeling weary, drained
and very depressed. The telegram should have arrived
by now. Would he forgive her? She thought back on
the wording and realized it had been very cold. One
does not like to broadcast secrets of the heart to West-
ern Union—or at least Beth didn't. Would he be able to
read between the lines? Would he call her?

She turned onto her street with relief and homesick-
ness seeping through every muscle of her body, and
then she slowed the car incredulously. A cold knot of
fear tightened around her stomach and her throat went
dry as she stopped the car before her shop. Every light
inside the little building blazed and even from the curb
she could see that the front door stood halfway open.
Someone was inside.

A quick memory of last summer's burglary flashed
through her head and she knew she should call the police. The house next door was dark and by the time
she got to her own house they would probably be
gone. Anyway, why would any half-sensible burglar
commit a crime beneath the glare of every light in the
building and leave the front door open at eleven
o'clock at night for all the world to see? Perhaps her
father had returned unexpectedly, or her assistant had
come over for something he had forgotten. She knew
she shouldn't have, but she crept silently up the rain-
soaked walk and slipped through the front door.

"Jerry!" She sank weakly against the wall, her hand

at her throat to still the pulse of surprise and relief, but her own astonishment was nothing compared to the dark shock that dilated her nephew's eyes as he whirled to see her.

And nothing could have prepared her for the sight of Corey Fletcher, walking through the curtain of the back room at just that moment.

Chapter Twelve

Wet jeans clung to his calves and there were huge water splotches on the shoulders of his tan sheepskin-lined jacket. His hair was rain-darkened and clung lankly to his forehead. But it was his eyes—pure black with shock and seeming to take up half his face, the lids swollen and red as though, as though he had been crying. And his face looked pinched and frozen, its color the purest white she had ever seen on a living being. He stared at her, unblinking, unmoving, for a long long time, and just as she found the breath to whisper, "Cor—" He flew at her.

"You little idiot!" His fingers dug into her shoulders with a grip that would surely break the bones and he shook her. His eyes were blazing pure unadulterated rage, galloping out of control as her head snapped back and forth beneath the force of his wild shaking. His voice roared in her ears. "What the hell happened to you? Where have you been? What—"

He was hurting her and she cried out. Tears of outrage and despair and confusion stung her eyes. His voice faded out but his murderous gaze bored into her brain and slow nausea bunched in her stomach because the fire in his savage eyes looked very much like hatred. Her head began to spin as he shook her like a rag doll and pretty soon she couldn't see anything anymore.

It was Jerry who recovered himself first and rushed to them, pulling at Corey's arm and trying to break his grip. "Come on, man, you're gonna snap her neck! Ease up!"

Corey stopped shaking her but his fingers still bruised the bones of her shoulder. She stared at him through a breathless mist of tears and then he released her so abruptly that her head hit the wall and she saw stars.

When her head cleared, Corey had walked a few steps away from her, his back to her and one fist doubled tightly against grimly closed lips. The sound of his harsh breathing ticked off the unearthly silence within the shop. Suddenly she thought of the desperate, miserable twenty-four hours that had just passed and she wanted to cry. She had tried, hadn't she? She *had* tried! Suddenly four months of pent-up yearning and desperation swept her and she almost did cry.

Then Jerry's flat, stunned voice drifted across to her and she forgot all about crying. "We thought you were dead," he said.

She turned slowly widening eyes on him and Corey's clipped, hoarse voice broke in on her. "You picked up your damn ticket!" He turned, tense as an animal ready to spring and there was such raw, savage pain on his face that she shrank back even as her heart broke at that moment into two ragged pieces. "Why did you pick up your ticket?" His voice almost broke. "Your luggage was on the flight." He turned away again abruptly and stood stiff-necked and straight staring at the window, his fists slowly clenching and unclenching against his thighs.

"Man, that flight went down over the Rockies," Jerry explained to her softly, and a sudden lurching horror severed the nerve endings between her brain and her vocal cords. She simply stared at him, dimly registering the shock and disbelief and remembered anxiety on his face as every word he spoke sent new waves of watery sickness through her. "I mean, your name was on the passenger list. They even found your luggage. The boarding list was all screwed up and we spent all night— We couldn't reach Grandpa and the only thing we could think to do was to come out here."

How does it feel to be resurrected from the grave? What's it like to know that the flight you missed by five minutes has crashed into frozen mountains absent one passenger? For Beth it was the slow rising of bile to her throat and ice water seeping through her veins, a dim faraway pounding that might have been her heart and Jerry's voice becoming only a thin whine far in the background.

She blinked hard to try to clear her vision and Jerry's voice focused, rushed now and almost incoherent with the normal near hysteria of a teen-ager who has just had a close experience with tragedy and death. "So we came here because I still have a key to the shop, you know, and thought we'd try to find Ellie's number and try to reach somebody—my folks weren't at their hotel where they're supposed to be." Suddenly Beth thought of what they must have gone through during the night. The fear, the anxiety, the awful certainty. Shock redoubled in on shock, theirs and hers, and she felt herself sway. Jerry's voice was weak, "Oh, Lord," then sharper, "Fletcher!"

Corey caught her just before her legs gave way, easing her to sit on the floor, his cold hand against the back of her neck forcing her head between her knees. She thought of how he must have felt, knowing that he had sent her the ticket, what he must have experienced when he heard the plane had gone down, how, even now as she thought how close she had come...how except for a freak twist of fate...how she was supposed to be dead but she wasn't. She started to cry, silently and helplessly, into her knees.

"Oh, Elizabeth." Corey's voice was hoarse, the motions his fingers made against the back of her neck were meant to be soothing but they were rough, unco-ordinated. "Oh, baby. Why didn't you let us know? Why didn't you—"

She lifted a white and tear-streaked face to him and suddenly all the emotions inside her got tangled up in anger and she cried, "What do you think I've been try-ing to do for the past twenty-four hours! Did you ever think of getting a published number, Fletcher? I spent so much time on long-distance information the opera-tor got to know me by my first name, but no, the great Corey Fletcher is not to be reached at any cost!"

"Hey, lady, come on. The guy's been really freaked." But Beth did not need Jerry's slightly stunned voice to remind her how inappropriate her accusations were. She saw it in the confusion that crossed Corey's eyes, but even the confusion was better than the ragged agony that had last been there.

She said weakly, "I sent you a telegram." But by the time that telegram had arrived they were already franti-cally checking passenger lists and on their way to Vir-ginia Beach. The sickness started to creep over her again.

"Come here." Corey said softly. Sitting on the floor he drew her into the support of his knees in one sure motion and their lips met at once in the sudden gasping wonder of having cheated death—not once, but twice. Feeling one another real and solid as their bodies pressed together, the pumping of hearts, the streaming of breaths, the movement of life. His arms crushed her and hers choked him and their mouths bruised one another's as cold faces rapidly grew warm, drinking in the wonder of it, the truth of it, the overwhelming joy of it.

Corey's breath was hot and uneven against her neck and she felt a tremor in the muscles of his arms. She clung to him, her open mouth pressed in wonder to the curve of his jaw as she tried to catch a breath that threatened to turn into a sob. Behind them Jerry's voice sounded a little uncomfortable. "Come on, you guys, give me a break. I mean, I'm glad you're alive and everything, but this is beginning to look like an X-rated movie."

Corey looked down at her. He was smiling, but his eyes were still bright and incredibly large with hardly believed joy and residual distress. He ran his hands up and down her arms once, bracingly. "For heaven's sake, let's go home and get dried off," he said, and the smile deepened, "before we all catch our deaths of cold."

Whether out of a subtle sense of propriety or because he was really tired—Beth realized that neither of the men had slept in almost two days—Jerry went immediately to bed in his old room. Corey was the wettest and most uncomfortable, so he showered first, and when Beth came from the bathroom belting a long terry robe about her Corey was sitting cross-legged on her bed, a blanket wrapped about himself toga-style. He had brought no luggage.

"Very sexy." She smiled.

He grinned and sat up straight, looping his fingers through the sash of her robe. "You should see what's underneath."

"Corey," she protested as he pulled her close with a gentle tugging on the sash. Even the sight of him had made her heart race, his touch and the increasing nearness of him set off a slowly spiraling dizziness of anticipation that weakened every muscle of her body. She still couldn't believe it was true. No one had a right to be as happy as she was at this moment, as lucky or content. But she felt compelled to object, although a little breathlessly, "Jerry—he's right in the next room."

His eyes danced sparks as he fastened his hands on her hips, his knees pressing into her thighs. "You're not really afraid we're going to corrupt his morals, are you?"

Her lips tightened on a reproving smile and her fingertips tingled to touch him. "No, I guess not." Her hand touched his shoulder, releasing the loose fold that held the blanket over his chest, but then too many sensory demands overwhelmed her at once— the need to run her fingers over every inch of his body, to assure herself he was really there, to hold him and feel him melting in to her and try to make herself believe it was really happening after all this time, to feel his mouth on hers and his breath flowing like new life into her body. And she could do nothing but look at him, her eyes rapidly and hungrily scanning every part of him. The tousled cornsilk hair, the thickly shaded glowing eyes, the little scar on his eyebrow, and the new pink burn scars on his arm, the darker, more angular ones on his chest and abdomen; hurting for him, aching for him, yearning for him and needing him so badly.

Immediately reading the changing expressions on her face, he guided her around him to sit on the bed. "Someday we're going to talk about it," he said firmly, "but not tonight. I'm still too shaky to do a very good job of listening or communicating." His smile was rather vague, and his eyes were probing deep into her, lightening and darkening with the same effort to subdue turmoil she was undergoing—to assure himself that it was real and she was really there. "I will do one thing for you, though," he added in a slightly lighter tone, his eyes never relenting in their intense search of hers. "You're wondering how I like being on the receiving end, and I'll tell you, princess: Not much."

She was perplexed. "What—"

He laid two fingers lightly against the pulse in her

throat, and it leaped to fluttering life beneath his warm touch. His eyes were somber. "You scared the hell out of me, lady," he said quietly. "I thought I knew what fear was. I faced it every time I strapped on a helmet or counted down the seconds before I pulled a ripcord or went through a stunt no one else had tried before." And when her eyes widened in disbelief he assured her grimly, "Yes, I was afraid. Only a complete idiot wouldn't have been. But none of that—not any of it— bore even a remote resemblance to what I went through last night. I don't know." Briefly his eyes left hers and a breath fluttered across her cheek. "Maybe I was too stupid, or too selfish, to know what you were suffering every time you watched me drive, and the accident—" He looked at her. "I thought I knew, Elizabeth. I really thought I understood what it must have done to you. But last night I realized I had never had even the faintest idea." His fingers spread slowly over her throat, caressing her collarbone and exploring the ridges, and the distress in his eyes faded and then soft- ened to pleasure as he felt her melting response to his touch and basked in the sensation of her skin beneath his fingers. "But that's one thing neither one of us has to worry about anymore, as you would know if you had bothered to read even one of my letters. I'm through with racing. Even before the accident I toyed with the idea, and afterward I could read the writing on the wall." He smiled. "After last night I'm beginning to have second thoughts about flying too."

"Corey, I—"

"Now, wait." His fingers floated down the open path of skin revealed by the parting vee of her robe and his eyes followed. He could not have missed the sudden quickening of the rise and fall of her chest. "Before you protest that you're the cause of my giving up a brilliant career, let me tell you that you're absolutely right." Again there was a soft sigh, but because his eyes were lowered in patent absorption on the curve of her breasts his fingers were uncovering, she could not see his expression. "I don't know, maybe old Nickie was right all these years. It does make a difference knowing there's someone waiting for you. It makes a difference when you've suddenly got something real and concrete to want to go to when you leave the track. I didn't really enjoy one race I drove this summer. All of a sudden it seemed like kid's stuff and the thrill was gone." Inch by inch, more pulsing flesh was exposed to his view. "I guess..." Something changed in the tenor of his voice and there was a slight unsteadiness to the fingers that gently brushed the undercurve of her breast. She thought she would have become used to the electric currents his touch could send through her by now, but four months was a long time. She would never become used to it. "I guess since the first time I kissed you, that night on the boardwalk—" His own breath was becoming rapid as his thumb and forefinger gently closed around one nipple. A very faint flush of color was beginning to spread over his face, and hot wires of sensation jumped in her stomach. "It was like I started living for you, and it made all the difference in the world."

He looked at her, his eyes softened with pleasure and glowing with subtle happiness and certainty. His hands slipped downward inside the robe and curved around her bare waist. "I don't know," he said quietly, "whether I ever made this clear to you, but I do love you. I tried to tell you once that loving you was more than making love with you, but I lost my courage. I thought you wouldn't believe me. Do you believe me, Elizabeth?"

"I believe you," she whispered. Heat was bathing her body and a fine mist of perspiration began to gather on her face, all from the feel of his hand, warm and firm, outlining the indentation of her waist. It was hard to think, in fact it was almost impossible, but they had to talk about this thing. She gathered her strength almost desperately and began, "But, Corey—"

"I have the floor," he warned her. Once again his eyes traveled slowly down the length of her body. "I've written this speech down so many times I know it by heart and this time you're not going to send it back to me unopened." Even as chagrin flooded her for her heartless treatment of him Corey banished that emotion with a deft tug at the tie of her robe. He deliberately pushed the two parts of the material aside and for just a moment as he looked at her he seemed to have forgotten what he was going to say. Then his hand began to roam delicately over the curve of her hip and outer thigh and he went on in a voice that was almost steady, "You were no doubt about to say something foolish about my glamorous life-style and the differences between our values. Well, let me tell you, princess, they may not be as different as you think. As for glamour and high living, it's all relative. There's got to be a compromise somewhere. I'm going to spend more time designing, and that's not a profession that's likely to put me much in the public eye, but I've got to tell you acting is my first love—no, second." He smiled at her, suddenly and brilliantly. "I'm going to continue to do films. I'll have pretty leading ladies who will no doubt bore me to death and there will be an occasional set party that you will be expected to attend with me. When I go on location you'll come too, and if all that jetting around from one world capital to the other bothers you, you'll just have to get over it. Because," he informed her firmly, "I am not letting you out of my sight again."

Beth breathed, "Just like that?" It was meant to sound indignant but his head had bent slowly to her breast and she was lucky to make any sound at all. Her hand curved around his shoulder, tightening there, and her head swayed slowly backward as she tried not to gasp.

"Just like that." He lifted his face. He placed a slow hot kiss on the pulse of her throat and she shivered.

"You're asking me to sacrifice a lot, Fletcher." Her voice was squeaky, punctuated with short little breaths and breaking on every third syllable into a whisper.

"I know." His fingers rested featherlight against her cheek, stroking it, turning her head into their pressure. "But I said compromise. You can learn to love my money..." His tongue flickered over the curve of her jaw. "And my crazy sister and my avant-garde friends..." Warm brief nibbles brushed her eyelashes. "And maybe even my watch..." He was becoming a little breathless and his face was hot as it nuzzled hers, his fingers threading through her hair. "And I'll learn to love the Atlantic Ocean. As a matter of fact"—she dropped her lips to his silky clean hair instinctively, tasting it, breathing in his warm, familiar scent in shaky gulps—"I already have. As for letting you sell or otherwise part with the home of the world's last nickle ice cream cone..." Hot breath flooded her ear in the slow maddening motions of moist tongue and lips and she shivered violently, sinking, sinking fast. "I'd kill first. Are you cold?"

"No."

But in a series of fluid movements he unwrapped the blanket and draped it over both of them, laying her down and drawing her into the warm nest. His hands, with more freedom to explore now, began to roam luxuriously, and so did hers. She traced intriguing muscled lines from the crook of his knee upward to his thigh, fingertips tingling with psychic electricity and the sensation of fine abrasive hair against bare nerve endings. Her hand moved adoringly over a taut stretch of abdomen and he caught his breath, her lips parted beneath his and she rose to meet his passion with a soft sound deep in her throat.

His eyes were dark and glowing when he looked at her. She could see the heavy rise and fall of his chest. "Princess..." His voice was ragged, a little raspy. "Seems there was something else I wanted to tell you but I"—he pressed another kiss on her mouth—"can't for the life of me think what it was."

"You talk too much," she murmured, arching her head to seek his lips again. Every time she touched him or he touched her in old ways or new it was like being born again, suddenly plunged into a world alive with light and color. There would never be enough of what they shared together, not ever. And when he looked at her so adoringly, his fingers spreading through her hair and caressing her skull as though to memorize every inch of her, soft glowing wonder filled her, his and hers.

"I remembered," he whispered suddenly, dropping a light kiss upon her chin as his hand moved over her abdomen in slow, circular, painfully tantalizing motions. "Marry me."

She gasped in a rush of voltaic pleasure as his hand moved lower; the fire in his eyes leaped in response to hers. "Was that a request?"

"No."

"I don't know, Fletcher." It was amazing that she was able to actually form patterns of semicoherent speech when it took all of her concentrated energy just to remember to breathe. "I never thought about it."

Deep kisses pressing into her breasts drew the very essence of her outward to meet him. "Think about it," he murmured.

"You drink too much," she objected

"I know."

"You have pierced ears."

His breath fanned jerkily across her face. "You'll get used to them."

"You're crazy."

He separated her thighs with a brush of his fingers. "Marry me."

"You're always"—her gasp of pleasure was low and harsh—"giving me orders."

"You *will* marry me."

Utter silence as he slid into her, arrested breath and motion, spiraling dizziness of delight, starbursts far up in the stratosphere. And then in a long sweet rush as soft and certain as the sea breeze on a still night, "Yessss...."

Corey propped himself up on one elbow to better look at her, his hand lovingly stroking her hip, his eyes alive with light lazy sparks of contentment and wonder. And his lips curved slowly into a teasing smile. "You're not thinking about changing your mind, are you?"

She looked at him soberly, but the affected gravity could not disguise the soft glow of certainty in her eyes nor the radiance in her face. She supposed fifty years from now she would still be looking at him and wondering over him; that over all the people in the world he had chosen her to love. And that of all the people in the world he had come into her life so unexpectedly, so unpredictably, so totally without warning, and had changed it forever. She inquired, "Are you trying to get me to change my mind?"

"No." The teasing slowly faded into sweetness, into adoration, as he drew her fingers to his lips and kissed them one by one. "I just don't want you to make any sudden decisions."

"Sometimes," she sighed and melted into his arms, "those are the best kind."

THE GOLDEN CAGE

The first Harlequin American Romance Premier Edition
by bestselling author ANDREA DAVIDSON

Harlequin American Romance Premier Editions is an exciting new program of longer–384 pages!–romances. By our most popular **Harlequin American Romance** authors, these contemporary love stories have superb plots and true-to-life characters–trademarks of **Harlequin American Romance.**

The Golden Cage, set in modern-day Chicago, is the exciting and passionate romance about the very real dilemma of true love versus materialism, a beautifully written story that vividly portrays the contrast between the life-styles of the run-down West Side and the elegant North Shore.